KNIGHTS OF NYX

WAR ON DARKNESS | THREE

S BOLANOS

CHAOTIC NEUTRAL PRESS LLC

CONTENTS

CHAPTER 1

DENHAM

ALEXI

My hope that Matt would accompany me to the Harvest Festival in my hometown shriveled with each day that went by without so much as a glimpse of him. It officially died as I packed my bag. Perhaps the time away from each other was for the best. Maybe I'd even extend my stay beyond the weekend. I'd completed all of my assignments and had no pending projects. Missing a few days of class wouldn't hurt.

That I was contemplating skipping classes—intentionally—was enough to give me pause. It also reminded me of how I'd unintentionally played hooky with Matt the week prior. When I'd invited him to go with me. For all his enthusiasm about seeing my hometown, he'd vanished faster than water in a desert. Not even the sweet picture of me sleeping made up for the lackluster apology scribbled next to it or the fact that he'd left. What he was apologizing for, anyway? Leaving? Being an ass? Lying about wanting to come?

I nearly ripped the zipper of my bookbag off its track as I slammed it home with a little too much force. A glance at the clock on my nightstand confirmed what I already knew—time was up. He wasn't coming, and no amount of stalling would change that. Tears pricked at the back of my eyes. Would he even tell me we were over or would he keep ghosting me until I got the hint? I willed my eyes to dry as I carried my bag into the living room.

"Good, you're still here," Matt said, appearing out of nowhere. His gaze flicked from me to the stuffed backpack. "You still going home?"

I fought to keep my glimmer of hope at seeing him from flourishing. If he truly wanted to go, he'd have been here this last week. "Um... yeah," I said, hating how raw my voice sounded. Was this it? Had he planned to wait until the last second to break up with me so that he wouldn't have to deal with the fallout? I braced myself for the inevitable, carefully keeping my gaze fixed on the carpet, so he wouldn't see the hurt threatening to swallow me whole.

"Still want me to come?"

My head shot up. "What?"

He took a tentative step closer, that same hint of sheepishness to his features that I'd once found so endearing. "I'd like to go to the Harvest Festival with you. If you'll have me."

"Of course," I said too quickly.

Despite my over eager reply, the biggest grin I'd seen from him in a long time stretched across his face. Then a tide of words flowed out. "When do we leave? Where exactly are is Denham? How are we going to get there? What's a fair like? I've never been to a fair before. How long does it last? Do I need to bring anything? How many people will be there?"

I held up my hands to stem the rush, unable to hold back the laughter at this unexpected energy. "One at a time, please."

His mouth snapped shut with an audible bubble sound while the rest of him appeared to vibrate in place with the force of keeping his questions restrained.

"Okay, one question."

He took a deep inhale that puffed his chest, then let it out in a burst. "What's Denham like and how are we getting there?" He winced. "Oops. That was two."

A laugh burst out of me, bringing forth the tears I'd been fighting before.

Panic flashed across Matt's face as I dropped my bag and doubled over in my fit. "What? Did I say something wrong? I know I should have been here sooner. But I had a thing I had to take care of and—"

I held up a hand once more to stop his babbling. I barely even cared that he said "a thing" instead of whatever he'd actually been doing. He was here. He wanted to come with me. And he was excited. "You didn't say anything wrong. I just... missed you," I said as I straightened and wiped my eyes.

A light pink stained his cheeks. "I-I've missed you too."

My heart soared. He didn't want to break up. I cleared my throat and picked up my bookbag again before the emotion had my crying... again. "Denham is nice, if quiet. Like most small towns, everyone knows everyone. As for how we'll get there, I made a portal."

"Really?"

"Yep. It's on the roof." I neglected to mention that it had taken nearly every day since I'd invited him to make the damn thing and get it to stay open. Much as I'd have liked to keep the portal for future visits home, I wasn't sure it was quite worth all the effort to keep it maintained. Abruptly, I realized we were staring at each other and smiling. "We should get going if we don't want to miss supper. Do you need to pack anything?"

He smirked and reached into the couch. When he pulled his hand out, he held a small duffel bag.

My eyebrows shot up. "How long has that been there?" And did I need to check the rest of the dorm for other "hiding places"?

"I've... uh, been packed for a few days." His smile slipped. "I didn't mean to cut it so close."

I searched his face, but the answers I wanted weren't there. "The important thing is that you made it. Now, let's get out of here before my mom calls to ask where we are."

Matt brightened and slung the duffel across his body. Without warning, he stepped forward and planted a chaste kiss on my lips, then dashed to the door. "What're you waiting for? Let's go, slow poke. I could use a break from this place," he said, though that last bit was more to himself.

My head spun as I situated my bookbag on my shoulders and moved to join him. Who was this person? He bore no resemblance to the Matt I'd had to endure the last couple of months.

Unbridled joy danced in his eyes as he flashed me a wide smile and reached for the door. I flattened my palm on the door to keep it closed and his eyebrows pinched into a V. "What—"

I cradled his jaw, cutting him off with a kiss. It was truly a shame we didn't have more than the lingering press of lips, but if we waited much longer to leave, my mother would start calling. "I love you, Matt," I said, then opened the door. We smiled at each other, neither of us making a move to leave. My heart felt like it might burst as I waited for him to say it back.

"Alex."

"Yeah?" I whispered, anticipation making my voice thin.

Wickedness darkened his crystal blue eyes. "Race you to the top."

He took advantage of my stunned state to turn and bolt. I shadowed to catch up while the door slammed shut, automatically locking, but didn't shadow again. Our feet pounded against the lush carpet that absorbed the sound of our frantic race. We careened around a corner, nearly taking out one of our RAs, pushing and shoving each other to get to the stairwell first. We burst onto the rooftop, laughing and panting for breath. Matt caught my gaze, and we shared another smile. Then he straightened and looked around at the flat—noticeably empty—roof.

"Uh... Where is it?"

I gestured to the side of the maintenance room.

Matt looked from me to the innocuous wall, then a knowing smirk spread across his face. "You cloaked it." The pride in his voice filled my chest with a warm glow. He held out his hand for mine. "Well, what are we waiting for?"

I wrapped my fingers around his and led us through the portal. The cool mist of the barrier brushed over my face until it encompassed my entire body. Then the infinite darkness of the Shadow world gave way to bright sunlight and a crisp autumn afternoon. A light breeze ruffled my hair as we stood at the edge of a forest with nothing but open field between us and Denham. I took in Matt and his expression of awe and knew I'd made the right decision not to put the exit by my house, or even better, in it.

"That's..." He dropped my hand and took a step forward before stopping to look back at me. "That's Denham?"

I walked up beside him and wrapped an arm around his shoulders. "Sure is. And if you look over there." I pointed to our right where you could just make out the Ferris Wheel and some low-lying buildings. "That's the fair."

"It looks as big as the town."

I chuckled and squeezed him close. "Denham is small even compared to Sieben Hügel. But the Harvest Festival Fair is actually for all the surrounding parishes."

"Parishes," Matt repeated like he was tasting the word. Then he wrinkled his nose. "Why does the UK have to have such weird names for everything?"

I snorted. "You mean the right names? You know, since the UK was here before the US."

He rolled his eyes, but leaned into me. We stayed like that for a few minutes, soaking up the sunshine and appreciating the view. Then Matt tilted his head back to look at me with half-lidded eyes and whispered, "I really like it here. Your home is beautiful." He stretched his neck, and I met him halfway for a kiss sweeter than cotton candy.

Seconds from turning to him and deepening the kiss, my phone rang. I groaned and Matt chuckled into my shoulder. "Hello, mother," I said without checking the caller ID.

She sniffed indignantly. "Don't 'mother' me. Have you left the university yet?"

I glanced at Matt, failing to smother his grin. "We're actually at the edge of the forest. Should be there in fifteen to twenty minutes."

"We? Matt came along after all? That's wonderful, sweetie! I can't wait to finally meet this boyfriend of yours."

"He's my friend too, Mom," I countered, cringing at her loud enthusiasm.

Matt leaned toward the phone. "Looking forward to meeting you too, Ms. Roman."

My heart exploded. Or maybe it froze. Whatever it was doing, it definitely wasn't beating anymore. Matt had basically labeled himself as my boyfriend, in public, to another person. Granted, it was my mom, and there wasn't really anyone around to witness it, but it was also the first time he'd acknowledged our relationship extended beyond friendship out loud.

"Lexi. Honey. Are you still there?"

"Huh? Yeah. I'm still here. We'll be there soon." I glanced at Matt, whose lips were twitching in a repressed smile. He knew damn well what he'd done.

"Excellent. I'll make sure the guest room has fresh linens. See you soon. And don't dally!" she admonished before hanging up.

Matt raised an eyebrow. "So, guest room, huh?"

I ducked my head to hide the burn on my cheeks. "My mom has some very strict rules about having boys in my room."

"Almost like she doesn't trust you to keep your hands to yourself."

I looked up in time to catch his cheeky grin. "Well, it might be warranted in this case. I've always had trouble keeping my hands to myself where you're concerned." The blush that stained his cheeks was beyond adorable, but Matt didn't pull away. In fact, he leaned in closer and I wrapped an arm around his waist to keep him there.

"Are we going straight to your house?"

"I thought it'd be nice to show you around the village a little before heading that way." I released my hold on him and resumed holding his hand to make walking smoother.

"Your mom won't be upset?"

Sweet night, Matt's consideration of my mother was melting my heart, but it had been so long since it'd just been the two of us, I wasn't willing to forsake the time. "As long as we're home in plenty of time for dinner, we'll be fine. It doesn't take long to get to my house from town."

"Your house," Matt whispered beneath his breath with an unmistakable twinge of awe.

My heart constricted, and I couldn't help but press my lips against his temple. "Come on, we'll start at the community center. If we're lucky, we'll run into some familiar faces, but I imagine most of them are already helping with the fair."

CHAPTER 2

MRS. ROMAN

MATT

Alex's House. I was standing inside Alex's house. Where he'd grown up. Where he'd made countless memories. And where his mom was currently staring at me like I was an alien. I waved at her, not really knowing what else to do. She positively beamed. Her eyes were like his, albeit with a striking circle of hazel around her irises and a halo of curly blonde ringlets. She was still staring. I was beginning to wonder what Alex had told her about me. He stood there watching me, as if waiting to see what I would do. I wished he would say something.

"Mom, this is Matt. Matt, this is my mom."

"Hi Miss Roman. It's nice to meet you," I said nervously, thinking about the last time we'd spoken. Stealing the phone to talk to some faceless woman hundreds of miles away had seemed hilarious at the time; it was less so now that I was standing in front of the real person.

She waved her hand. "There's no need to stand on such formality. You can call me Yanessa." Well, that wasn't going to happen. "It's so nice to *finally* meet you." She took two steps forward and swept me up in a tight hug.

I looked over her shoulder at Alex in a silent cry for help. What was I supposed to do? I'd never met anyone's mom before. Rather than come to my aid, he smothered his laugh and left me to fend for myself. Eventually, she released me, and I staggered as I tried to regain my balance.

"You do have very nice hair," she said, absently fixing it.

I looked at Alex in confusion, but his laugh appeared to have gone down the wrong way.

"Did you need any help with dinner?" Alex asked once he rediscovered the ability to talk.

"Lexi, my love, I doubt you've learned how to cook in the short time that you've been away."

"Mom."

Miss Roman blatantly ignored his deadpan. "But you and Matt can certainly set the table. I assume you still know where everything is kept?" He barely didn't roll his eyes and motioned for me to follow. When I stepped through into the dining room, Alex was already opening cabinet doors to acquire what we would need.

"She seems nice," I said, accepting the stack of plates he passed me.

"She *is* very nice. Though I fear I'm going to regret most of what she says." He grimaced. "I'll just go ahead and apologize. Things could get...weird."

I chuckled and stepped closer to him. "She's your mom. Pretty sure that comes with the territory."

He released a stuttering sigh when I placed my hands on his arms and leaned forward until our foreheads touched. "Yeah. I just..."

"Just what?" I leaned slightly back to study his face and was more than a little surprised to find it clouded with uncertainty.

"I just really want you to like her."

I snorted. "I'm a little more worried she won't like me, not the other way around."

Despite my self-deprecating statement, Alex's features softened, and he cupped the side of my face. "There's not a doubt in my mind that she's going to love you. Possibly almost as much as I do."

My breath caught, and words failed me. No one had ever made me feel as special as Alex did. I leaned into the caress and let myself get lost in his emerald eyes and the promise of a future I'd never imagined. "Alexi," I whispered as our lips drifted closer.

"Lexi, honey, why don't you go get cleaned up?" Miss Roman called from the kitchen.

We both chuckled. "I'm telling you, that woman has a sixth sense," he said as he stepped back. His hand sliding from my cheek was a painful reminder of just how much I missed his touch. "Don't worry about my mom. She can be embarrassing, at times, but she's been Team Matt the whole time." Alex brushed a kiss across my cooling cheek and flashed me a smile before venturing out of the room into what appeared to be a hallway.

"You're welcome to wash up in the kitchen, Matt."

Startled out of my fuzzy cloud of Alex, I turned to find Miss Roman leaning against the doorway, wiping her hands with a dish towel. "Of course." I scurried past her to the kitchen sink and immediately began washing my hands like I could scrub off every dirty sin from my past... and present.

"Easy, dear. You'll wash the life right out of them." She passed me the same towel she'd been using.

As I dried my hands, I could feel her eyes on me, scrutinizing, weighing. Did she find me wanting? Did she know I was lying to her son? I'd never had the pleasure of experiencing mother's intuition, but if anyone had it, I'd bet Miss Roman did. I awkwardly hung the towel, not sure what to do with myself now. A silence that I was probably supposed to be filling settled between us.

"I hope it's alright that Lexi shared the details of your past with me."

My head jerked up both at the unexpected statement and the overwhelming softness of her voice. "It's fine," I croaked, my throat suddenly tight.

She placed an equally soft hand on my shoulder and held my gaze with eyes that were every bit as intense as Alex's. "I'm truly sorry for your loss. However it came to pass, no child should have to endure what you have."

Great, now my eyes were stinging and swallowing was out of the question. Was this what a mother's love was like?

"Why don't you explore a bit and make yourself at home while I finish up here? And after dinner, we can look at Lexi's baby pictures." She winked and hip-checked me back toward the dining room.

"That would be great. Thanks, Miss Roman, for... everything."

She placed her hands on her hips, her lips twisting into a scowl. "There's no way I'm going to get you to call me anything but Miss Roman, am I?"

I smiled and offered a shrug before doing as she suggested and wandering off. While I'd been in quite a few houses during my stays with foster families, I was no judge of quality. There'd been fancy houses without a scrap of personality and some of the meanest people you'd ever meet, and houses that barely constituted more than a decaying shack with equally cruel foster parents. But Alex's house was different. There was an energy here that wrapped around you like a warm blanket and invited you to stay a while. Rather than art, the walls held photographs, and while nothing looked obviously new, everything was clean and cared for. My eyes stung again as I realized what made Alex's place so different from all the others—this wasn't just a house, it was a home.

Clearing my throat, I made my way into the hall. What was likely the living room caught my attention, but I was more interested in seeing Alex's room. Would it feel the same here as it did in Arminius? Two false stops later, I cracked open the door to a third room and smiled. I flicked on the light and stepped inside.

There wasn't a doubt in my mind that I'd found my destination. Everything about the room screamed Alex, from the historical books piled everywhere to the posters of famous figures from history on the walls. I even saw the bare spot where the poster of the university used to hang. And it did, in fact, feel like his room at the dorm. I glided my fingers over the spines of various books. The most remarkable thing about them being that they were Alex's, though I was sure he would disagree.

"There you are. I was going to give you the grand tour myself, but I see you've gone and done it without me."

I turned as Alex walked in and dropped a hand towel on the end of the bed. "Is it my imagination or are some of these posters *also* in your dorm room?"

He shifted to stand in front of an identical poster of the Roman Colosseum that graced the wall by his window. "I don't know what you're talking about."

My gaze dropped to his lips, and I thought wistfully of our denied kiss. With a significant amount of effort, I brought my focus back to his eyes. To my surprise, he was scrutinizing me much as his mother had done in the kitchen. Before I could question the look, though, he stepped toward the door and slowly closed it. I glanced from him to the now shut, though not locked, door. "What about the rules?" I asked, as he eliminated the distance between us. Each step he took had my heart skipping that much faster.

"What about them?"

The pure ecstasy of Alex's mouth on mine silenced any argument I could have voiced. I broke off long enough to drag in a lungful of air, then returned to devouring his kisses. He slipped his hands around my waist, tugging me flush against him so I had to wiggle my arms free to wrap them around his neck. Our tongues danced together in a perfect balance of give and take that at once grounded me and made me want to fly. I tangled my fingers in his hair, eager for everything he was giving me, yet aching for more.

"Dinner is ready!" Miss Roman called.

I reluctantly released my hold on him, though he refused to do the same. When he leaned down to claim another, even sweeter, kiss, I couldn't help but melt against him. "We should probably get out there before she comes looking for us," I sighed.

"Alexi Roman, I know that's not a closed door, I see!"

Alex groaned and gave my sides a squeeze before letting me go. "I suppose you're right."

As my head cleared, Miss Roman's promise for after dessert had a smile blooming on my face.

"What's that look for?" he asked with a frown.

Excitement continued to bubble in me like candy dropped in soda until it felt like I might explode. "Your mom said we'd look at your baby pics after dinner."

"Oh no we won't!" He spun on his heel and raced for the door.

Rather than compete with his long strides, I shadowed into the hallway where I stuck my tongue out at him before taking off for the dining room. "Miss Roman! Alex says he can't *wait* to share all his baby pictures!" I shouted as I skid into the dining room with Alex hot on my heels.

"He does, does he?" Her eyebrows lifted in twin arcs. "That's quite the interesting hairdo, oh rebellious child of mine."

Alex's hands flew to his hair. His cheeks darkened to a dusky peach as he tried unsuccessfully to smooth it back into submission. I coughed to cover a laugh, and Miss Roman's penetrating gaze swiveled to me.

"Be a dear and grab some napkins from the kitchen."

"Yes, Miss Roman." I quickly bobbed my head and shadowed to the kitchen. By the time I returned, they'd already sat. I took the seat across from Alex. There weren't any dishes to pass around, as Miss Roman had already plated everything. I was about to take another bite when something nudged my foot. Alex gave me a soft smile when I glanced at him.

"You should tell mom about how you figured out that nifty cloaking spell." He looked at his mother. "A third-year level spell."

She, in turn, leaned forward, green eyes alight with curiosity. "That sounds like quite the accomplishment."

"Really?" I frowned. There really wasn't much to it. "I mean, Alex helped."

He shook his head while she scoffed. "Don't sell yourself short, dear. My Lexi has shared some of his struggles and successes with your Shadow courses. You seem like a natural."

What I now realized was Alex's foot bumped mine again before rubbing along my calf. "You should be proud of yourself, Matt. I know I am."

Proud? When was the last I'd been proud of anything I'd done? Despite my doubt, though, warmth spread through my chest at Alex's words.

"Right. Who's ready for pictures?" Miss Roman plucked the stuffed scrapbook from the chair beside her and Alex groaned. All I could do was laugh at how perfectly normal it all felt.

CHAPTER 3

DANIEL

A

Being forced to sleep in my room when only a wall separated me from Matt was torture. It was a wonder I got any sleep at all. But when morning came, I popped up fresh as flowers in spring. To my surprise, Matt was already up and studying the contents of the pantry.

"Would have thought you'd sleep in what with their being no classes or assignments," I said, leaning against the wall behind him.

His shoulders tensed, betraying that I'd startled him, then he he turned around and mimicked my pose. "Sleep and I aren't really on good terms these days."

I fought to keep my expression neutral. Was he still having nightmares? Why wouldn't he talk to me about what was going on with him? Much as I wanted to know, demanding answers while he was cornered was not something I wanted to do. I'd seen how well that had gone last time. "You ready to check out the fair?"

"Did you not want to eat first?"

"Figured we could pick up something on the way." I stretched, shamelessly dragging it out and basking in the feel of Matt's eyes on me. We might be in a rocky place, but he definitely still liked what he saw. "To be honest, I'm not all that hungry." Not for food, anyway.

His gaze flicked back to me when I dropped my arms. "It's important to eat breakfast."

"Oh yeah? That mean you've been eating breakfast?" I challenged, because I knew damn well he wasn't.

He broke eye contact and shuffled his feet. "Where were you wanting to grab something?"

"It's a little out of our way, but there's a decent bakery." I pushed off from the wall and helped myself to a glass of orange juice from the icebox.

"When did you want to go?" Matt asked as I rinsed the glass and set it on the rack to dry.

"Now's good."

He glanced beyond me. "What about your mom?"

"I'll leave her a note. She might join us later, but I doubt it. After years of me dragging her there, you could say she's over it." I smiled at Matt and was pleased to find him smiling back. Once I'd scribbled a quick note, letting her know we'd left, but would return in time for dinner and placed it conspicuously on the counter we made our way to town.

To my chagrin, I'd forgotten that the bakery was a major vendor at the fair. While the shop was open, options were slim. We nibbled on our day-old muffins as we wove through streets that were largely empty even at this hour. By the time we reached the edge of town, I was vibrating with excitement. Then we cleared the last ridge that obstructed our view of the fair.

Matt's sharp intake of breath snatched my attention away from the rows upon rows of stalls, the flashing lights of spinning rides, and the enormous Ferris Wheel presiding over it all. "You okay?"

"Yeah. I..." He trailed off, his eyes wide with wonder. "I've never been to a fair."

"I think it's time we fix that. Don't you?" I squeezed his hand, then let him go. He had just enough time to give me a questioning look before I made a beeline for the fair.

"Hey!" His laughter was all the confirmation I needed that he was following full tilt. He crashed into me just as I passed the first booth and it transported me back in time to that day we'd run in the rain. Everything in the world felt so right with Matt in my arms. He smiled up at me, then seemed to register the voices around us and, most importantly, that we were no longer alone. I didn't fight him when he took a step back and awkwardly ran his hand through his hair.

"So, uh, what do we do first?" he asked, once more sounding uncertain.

"Whatever you want. This event is a pretty big deal and there's no end to the things we could do, but first, I want to make sure you're okay."

His hand dropped, and he turned a suddenly anxious face to me. "Huh? What do you mean? Of course, I'm fine."

I stepped closer and took his hand. Immediately, he tensed up, his gaze flitting around us. "You sure about that?"

"You're not... worried?"

I squeezed his hand. "No." Despite my reassurance, he still looked uncertain, and that was okay. I'd grown up with all the support in the world. My sexuality hadn't even registered on the list of things to be worried about. Now, accidentally fatally wounding a guy while making out because of my demonic strength... *that* had made the list. Matt had already shared he hadn't experienced the best humanity in his formative years. It would take time for him to feel comfortable being openly affectionate with another man, but I had faith he'd get there.

"This place is a lot bigger up close. I wouldn't even know where to start."

"I vote we wander the booths, see if we can find any of the people from DAPS, then we can cap things off with Ferris Wheel."

Matt did a double take, and I barked out a laugh at his twisted expression of confusion. "Did you say 'DAPS'?"

I started off down the nearest row of booths. He fell instep, and I quietly told him all about the Denham Agrarian Poets Society. Sadly, we didn't come across anyone, though that might have been a blessing in disguise. I wasn't entirely sure how Nemo would take seeing *two* Shadow Demons in one place. We did bump into Robbie, but thankfully she'd been in too much of a hurry to give me grief about bringing a guy back from school after her advice to "Mind all them boys".

We spent hours wandering the grounds. To my surprise, Matt wasn't interested in the rides, but the Ferris Wheel was a success. It was worth giving up the other rides to see his face when we stopped at the top. It didn't escape my notice that he continued to be drawn towards the craft and other art-centric booths.

We were walking past a series of gaming booths when something caught my eye. I pulled him up short. Today had been going so well, perhaps I could try my luck with something else. "Do the photo booth with me."

He looked at the curtained box, hesitation written all over his face.

I laced our fingers. "Please, Matt. I don't have a single picture of us. They'll just be for me."

He licked his lips and searched my face. "Just for you?"

"Just for me." I silently willed him to say yes.

"Okay."

I quickly dragged him into the booth, which was thankfully unoccupied before he could change his mind.

"A little small in here, don't you think?" he grumbled, squishing in.

"That's half the fun," I laughed. "Now just watch the camera." I pressed the button to start us off, and it began counting down. The first shot he had a skeptical face. "You're supposed to smile." I jostled him and he laughed. "Okay, a funny one."

"A what?" The camera snapped.

"Try again. Make a face."

He crossed his eyes and stuck his tongue out. We both laughed, and the machine began whirring. So far, so good. Time to really test my luck. I turned to face him and he looked back, a smile still playing around his mouth. Then I leaned forward and kissed him while simultaneously reaching out to push the button again. He hesitated a fraction of a second, then kissed me back. I cupped his face, loving how sweet his lips tasted. When I pulled back to see how many images we had left, it was just in time to get my goofy grin caught on camera for the last slot.

The whirring resumed, and I shoved us out of the cramped space. Once we were both out, I swiped and pocketed the prints before he could realize there were two unique sets. "See, that wasn't so bad."

"Fine, it wasn't torture," he admitted with a laugh. "I'm gonna run to the restroom real fast. Be right back?"

"Sure thing. I'll just be over there." I indicated an open space off to the side of the booths, away from the crowds. He nodded and walked off.

I made my way over to the empty area and waited until he was out of sight to pull out my prizes. As adorable as Matt's clueless expressions and silly face were, my actual interest was in the second set. Had I caught the picture I really wanted? To my amazement, the camera had caught the whole kiss from beginning to end. In the first image he clearly was holding back, but by the second he'd given into the kiss completely. But it was the last image that stole my breath. While I'd been grinning at the camera like a lovesick fool, Matt hadn't turned. I ran my finger over the tiny picture, overwhelmed with the way his soft gaze made me feel. He'd yet to vocalize how he felt about me or us, but a picture was worth a thousand words, and this one held volumes.

The soft brush of lips on the back of my neck tickled as they ventured over the exposed skin above my collar. Today was just full of surprises. First the photo booth and now this. The tickle became unbearable, and I shied away with a giggle. "Matt, what's gotten into you?"

"Who's Matt?" The smoky response sent a ripple of shock through me. I knew that voice.

I spun around, eager to eliminate the unwanted contact. "Daniel." I felt dirty, like I could scrub for hours and still not be clean.

He gave me the same crooked smile that had worked in the past. "Nice to see you too, Alexi. So... who's Matt?"

"None of your damn business," I said emphatically.

"What do we have here? The famous Matt maybe?" he said, his gaze riveting on the strips in my hand. Before I processed the eminent danger, he'd already snatched them away.

"Hey!" I lurched for pictures with an indignant squawk, to no avail. Matt would never forgive me if I didn't get those back.

Daniel feigned looking at them, enjoying keeping me at bay far more than what was on his stolen treasure. "You look good, Lexi. Nice to see you finally gave up those last few pounds."

Mortification heated the skin beneath my collar. "Shut up. Give those back."

"Come and get them," he taunted.

I reached again. Matt would be back any second and I wanted Daniel long gone. It would have been easy enough to shadow rather than try to retrieve them by force, but we weren't exactly on campus. Irritated and fuming, I surged forward in a desperate move, only for Daniel's arm to snake around my waist, effectively impeding my efforts. Now, instead of retrieving the pictures, I was struggling to free myself without causing excessive harm or outing the entire supernatural world in broad daylight. What I wouldn't give to let loose and use demonic strength, but I didn't trust that I wouldn't accidentally tear his arm clean off.

"Alex?" The sound was so small, I almost missed it in my struggle.

This is not happening.

I looked up to see all of happiness I'd worked so hard to cultivate drain from Matt's face. "Matt, it's not what it looks like." The moment the words left my mouth, I knew they were an epic mistake. Daniel turned to see who I was shouting at, finally releasing me.

"*This* is Matt?" he asked incredulously. "A little short for you, don't you think, Lexi?"

Matt's jaw tightened, and a familiar steel entered his sharp blue eyes.

No, no, no. I took advantage of Daniel's distraction and made another swipe to snag the photos. He laughed at my futile attempt, stretching his arm higher. "Give them back, Daniel," I growled, on the verge of shadowing. Consequences be damned.

At the mention of Daniel's name, unfiltered rage flash through Matt's eyes.

A new worry shot through me. I knew full well the violence Matt was capable of, and he didn't have the practice of experience to temper his relatively newfound demonic power.

His focus zeroed in on the two small strips. "Those don't belong to you." His disturbingly calm tone made my skin crawl. While I'd never considered him a danger to me, he was dangerous.

"And what are you going to do about it?" Daniel turned to face Matt, oblivious to his now tenuous hold on life, and tucked the stolen pictures in his front pocket. "Lexi, babe, you can do better than this. But I guess that's the point of a rebound," he snickered. Of all the people to run into today, why did it have to be Daniel?

A muscle twitched in Matt's cheek. "Give them back," he demanded, the calm cracking enough to hint at the promise of retribution.

"Matt," I said, trying to infuse his name with a note of caution. He needed to remember where we were. Had anyone ever talked to him about the importance of blending with the human world? I knew I hadn't.

"That's right, little Matty. Run along. The big boys are talking." Daniel's snide comment rolled over Matt with no visible effect. Then he did probably the dumbest thing he possibly could have—he reached back and grabbed my arm. For a moment, I just stared down at Daniel's hand in shock. "Come on, Alexi. I think it's time we had a proper chat."

"Let go of him." The sheer menace coming off of Matt was enough to make me nervous.

I tried to tug my arm free, but Daniel pulled unexpectedly and I stumbled forward a step.

"Or what?" Daniel challenged, pulling again.

In the blink of an eye, Matt became a creature of pure violence. An aura of darkness hovered around him and I was more than a little surprised not to see the nearby shadows reaching towards us. Daniel made as if he was going to drag me after him. I dug in my heels and he looked back at me, clearly taken aback at my ability to halt his momentum.

"I wouldn't do that if I were you," I offered, in final caution.

"You aren't honestly telling me I should be afraid of your pint-sized rebound?"

I saw Matt's fist clench by his side. Daniel did as well and finally released me. I rubbed my arm and watched in alarm as Daniel advanced on Matt.

"I don't know what you've been smoking at the ridiculous school, Alexi, but I have never, nor will I ever, be intimidated by some scruffy rat half my height."

Searing anger burned in Matt's eyes. If Matt had been a fire demon, Daniel would be a pile of ash right now. Daniel took another step, stopping square in front of him. Arguably, the height difference between the two was laughable, but nothing about Matt's demeanor was funny.

"Matt don't," I pleaded. Too late, I realized saying anything at all was a mistake.

Daniel's mocking laughter poured out into what was feeling disturbingly like an arena. Time stood still as Matt's fist collided with his smug face. Daniel's evil laugh cut off, then he was flat on the ground. He didn't even twitch. Matt squatted down beside him.

"I said, these don't belong to you." He reached forward and calmly reclaimed the pictures, then stood. My knees crashed into the ground by Daniel's face, kicking up clouds of dust. Tentatively, I reached out, stopping shy of actually touching him. I'd never seen Matt really hit anyone before. Knowing he was capable of violence and seeing it firsthand was very different.

"You broke his face," I said numbly, looking up at him. There was still anger simmering in his eyes, only now it didn't seem to be directed at Daniel.

What have I done?

Silently, he turned and walked away, following a path that took him behind a row of stalls. I looked from Daniel to Matt's receding silhouette and back again. Daniel was still breathing, but his nose was definitely broken. I quickly scrambled to my feet and raced after Matt, finally catching up with him several yards into the gloom.

"Hey," I panted, reaching for his hand.

Without warning, he spun around, slamming me into the back of the stall with an audible thud. Before I could panic or attempt to say anything, his mouth was on mine. I could taste the fire that still burned white hot inside of him and felt completely claimed. That was fine by me. I'd made my peace with belonging to Matt a long time ago. I kissed him back fiercely. He needed to know that I was his without reservation. Some part of my mind was in absolute shock—Matt was kissing me in public. Anyone could turn the corner and see. I kissed him deeper, wanting to wrap my arms around him and keep him this close forever. Before I got the chance, he pulled away.

"Try to keep a better eye on these," he said, so close that each word was practically a kiss. His hand slid briefly into my back pocket, then he was several steps away.

"Matt, wait." I thought about apologizing for the whole disaster, but was a little worried that would make it worse, not better. "Give me your hand."

He flexed the hand that he'd used to knock Daniel out cold. For a moment, I didn't think he would. Then he held it out. I gingerly took it into my own, holding it close to see where his knuckles were almost red from the impact. Softly, I rubbed my thumb over them.

"Does it hurt?" I looked up at him through my lashes.

"I don't really feel it anymore," he said, pointedly avoiding my gaze. The way he said that didn't sit right, but pursuing why wasn't likely to help anything. I brushed my lips lightly across the pink skin and he twisted to look at me, surprise evident on his face.

"We should leave," I said, straightening. His shoulders sagged and I could practically see the gears turning; he knew how I felt about him fighting. Before he could jump to too many conclusions, I added, "We'll go back to the house. We'll just be a little early for dinner."

CHAPTER 4

JEALOUSY

M

We walked to Alex's house in strained silence that made my shoulders itch. I didn't know what to say to make it better, though. I could barely make sense of my emotions, let alone put words to them. Easier to shove them down. Forget about them.

"Are you still upset?" Alex whispered as we finished setting the table, no doubt so his mom wouldn't intrude and want details.

I absently rubbed my knuckles. Daniel's face had offered next to no resistance, and it had been difficult to hold back. "Upset about what?" I asked, my voice completely neutral.

He searched me a moment more, but didn't pursue it. I debated speaking up, trying to find the words to express how seeing him in his ex's arms had made me feel. Why had he been with Daniel at all, let alone hanging off of him? As if that wasn't bad enough, he'd let his ex-boyfriend manhandle him. I couldn't reconcile Alex being in an actual *relationship* with someone who treated him like that? And why did that person have to be the direct opposite of me in every way? As much as I didn't want the things his ex had said to bother me, they'd cut to the quick of virtually all of my insecurities.

His mom walked into the dining room, taking the decision out of my hands. "While I certainly wasn't expecting you two back so soon, I can't say I mind the extra pairs of hands."

"Is there anything else I can do to help Miss Roman?" I asked as Alex exited toward the hallway, likely to wash-up before his mom could tell him to. Either that, or he couldn't stand to be in the same room as me. I *had* decked his ex. It wasn't my fault the asshole had a glass jaw.

"Matt, there really is no need to be so formal. I feel like I already know you."

I shuffled my feet, a little concerned at how much she could know. Alex may not see any cause for concern being openly together, but I knew better. We may not be in Nebraska or even at Arminius where I knew about the threat to his safety, but people were people wherever you went, and experience had taught me most of them were bad.

"Snapdragon!" Miss Roman exclaimed, startling me out of my nihilistic spiral. "I forgot all about dessert. I'm going to run down to the corner store real quick and pick up some ice cream. Be back before you know it." She glanced in the direction Alex had disappeared, then left.

I stood there a moment wondering what on earth I was supposed to do now. The *right* thing would be to find Alex and try to make amends. But, then, I'd never been very good at doing the right thing. I wandered through the house, keeping an ear out for him, until I found myself in the den. Pictures covered the mantle, most unsurprisingly of Alex. Alex in a cap and gown. Alex about ten years old. Alex with his mom. One in particular caught my attention. He was leaning against a wall with his hair in his eyes. It looked like he'd been laughing. He really was stunning with those bright green eyes and easy smile. There was a noise down the hallway and I resumed my search. We nearly collided as he came out of what I assumed was the bathroom.

"Oh, hey," he said in surprise, his wet hair dripping in his eyes.

My jumble of emotions crystallized. Had he done the things that we had with Daniel? "Let's go to your room."

"My room?" he echoed uncertainly. He glanced behind me back towards the front of the house, no doubt where he thought his mother still was. "I know making out yesterday kind of contradicts what I said about not having boys in my room, but my mom really is strict about funny business in the house."

"I just want to go to your room, Alex."

His anxiety didn't seem to decrease. "O-okay." He walked the short distance down the hall and I followed a few paces behind. "Yeah, so you pretty much saw everything yesterday. Nothing special. Looks just like my room at the dorm, honestly. So I guess you got me there. It's silly, I kn—" I closed the door closed quietly behind me, but at the look on his face you would have thought the latch clicking was a gunshot.

"Alex, what happened at the fair?" I walked toward him, only stopping when I was definitely too close for comfort.

He swallowed hard before stuttering, "N-nothing happened."

I raised an eyebrow.

"He snuck up behind me while I was looking at the pictures." So there *were* two strips instead of one. "I didn't know. I thought he was you." There was something in that, something he didn't say.

"What do you think I saw?"

His eyes went wide with fear as I confirmed he was defending something I likely hadn't even seen. It took him a few tries to get the words out. While he struggled with the answer, I advanced. He took a step back and ran out of room. The bed squeaked in protest as he fell on it. He attempted to scramble back as I followed, though he didn't get far before I had him laid out beneath me.

"Tell me."

"He kissed my neck, that's all. I swear. The second I realized it wasn't you, I put an end to it," he said, the panic in his voice reflected in his eyes.

I considered him for a moment. That he'd thought it was me, didn't really make what had happened any easier to swallow. "Is it that easy to confuse our kisses?" The question sounded dangerous even to my ears.

"Absolutely not."

"Perhaps you need a reminder."

His eyes flashed black, then green, and his breathing turned shallow. I leaned forward like I was going to kiss him, and he arched up to meet me. I didn't. Instead, I trailed my nose down the long curve of his neck. He shuddered, and I placed a kiss in the hollow. There wasn't nearly enough to work with, though. I slid my hands down and slipped them under his shirt. He gasped at the touch, but didn't stop me from pulling it up. I placed another kiss on his now much more accessible chest. He moaned.

"Matt, wait. There really are rules in this house," he panted. I placed a more aggressive kiss and he let out a gasp. "You really don't care, do you? My mom is just in the other room. If we don't go back soon..." His words faded out as I forced the shirt over his head, causing his arms to go up with it.

"Didn't I say? She went to the store. She's not here," I said, stopping just shy of kissing him.

"W-what store?"

"The corner store."

"You don't even know where that is. She could literally be back any second." He tried to move, but I used the shirt to keep his arms captive, knotting it in my hand and pushing it back into the headboard, then used shadow to keep it there. I was quite proud of my handiwork. Having Alex stretched out before me like this was rather nice, I could see why he was so fond of it. There was a distant sound like that of a door closing. He looked anxiously over at his own closed one. It wasn't locked.

"You're right. I think I hear her now." I shifted to stand and Alex pulled on the bond I'd made. When it didn't immediately give, he looked surprised, then flustered.

"You don't honestly think this can hold me?" he said as he attempted to shadow out of the tie. The spell held though, and he reformed with his arms still stuck above his head. Realization spread across his face. "Matt. Let me go. You can't...she'll..." He struggled with more determination before sagging in defeat. "What do you want from me? Do you want me to apologize? I'm sorry, okay. I'm a complete idiot and I didn't handle any of that very well. Now please undo the spell."

The apology was nice, and I briefly considered it. But if I was being honest, I was still mad. "We wouldn't want your mom to worry about what we've been up to in her absence, would we?" I said, leaning down to look him in the eye. He visibly relaxed. "Best not take too long," I added, then made my way to the door.

"Matt," he hissed, struggling against the spelled shirt. It was useless. The spell would hold with or without me maintaining it. I'd gotten plenty of practice with that while perfecting the barrier to keep him out of my room, or more realistically, me out of his. "Matt."

I opened the door and walked out. Admittedly, I was a little curious about how he was going to get out of that, but was still preoccupied with what had happened at the fair. I found Ms. Roman in the dining room with the table perfectly set and plates served.

"Where's Alexi?" she asked when he didn't materialize behind me.

"He's a little tied up," I said and took a seat.

She frowned and took one as well. "That man is entirely too vain. I don't know what he's so worried about. Well, it would serve him right if his food gets cold. Go ahead and eat, Matt. There's no reason we should have to eat cold food simply because he's dallying."

We were several bites in when he finally joined us. I glanced up to find that he was wearing a different shirt and a scowl. It would seem he *hadn't* figured out how to undo the spell.

"And where have you been?"

The chair screeched as he pulled it up. "I was a little tied up," he grumbled.

His mom glanced from Alex to me, then back at her plate, before letting out a huff. The rest of the meal was awkward, if it was anything. She attempted to fill the strained silence with light-hearted conversation and inquiries about school. Alex stayed sullen through it all, and guilt weighed on me. After dinner, we helped clear the table and nibbled passively at the recently acquired ice cream.

"Alright. It's time for bed. I'm going to assume by the lack of chatter that you two are simply exhausted from your day." She pointedly looked at Alex, who was typically much more talkative. "So, off to bed, the both of you. And Alexi," she called after him, "separate rooms. There are rules in this house." The face he gave her was priceless.

My increasing guilt tempered my desire to laugh. I needed to make this right. I caught up to him just before he got to the hallway. "Alex, wait."

"I told you."

"Rules, yeah, got that, but that's not what I wanted to talk about."

"What is it, Matt?" he sighed, leaning against the wall. The pose was reminiscent of the one I'd seen on the mantle, and for a second I forgot to speak.

I took a deep breath and a step closer so that I was right in front of him. Apologizing really was the worst, but I'd messed up. "I'm sorry," I said, looking up at him. Surprise glinted deep in his emerald eyes. "I shouldn't have embarrassed you like that in front of your mom. That was wrong." I looked down, unsure of what else to say.

He tilted my face back up to look at him. "Thank you for taking the pictures. I'm sorry I almost lost them." I tried to look away, but he held me in place. "He deserved it, you know. I don't know how I ever put up with such a horrid person for so long."

"He is pretty awful," I said, earning me a half smile.

"Not like you at all," he said, stroking the side of my face. Then he leaned forward and gave me a tender kiss that made my lips tingle. "Goodnight, Matt."

"Goodnight, Alex," I whispered back. He shadowed out, presumably to go to his room and leaving me to make my way to bed.

I put on my pajama pants and considered the sleep shirt I'd brought to cover the bruise still healing on my side. In the end, I didn't bother and turned out the lights. As expected, sleep proved elusive as the events of the day played on repeat in my head and the most I accomplished was a semi-wakeful dream state.

Out of the darkness, phantom lips touched mine, and I welcomed them. The sense of Alex was undeniable. There was a noise like the rustling of sheets and a sudden rush of cold air followed by a weight sinking me into the bed. As I felt skin against skin, I realized this wasn't just a good dream. This really was Alex.

I wrapped my arm around his waist and kissed him back. Now that I knew this was real and not another hallucination, it was all too easy to get lost in the world that was Alex. Here we were safe. Here we could be together without putting him in danger. I pulled him closer, deepening the kiss he'd started. Our tongues tangled as I mapped the planes of his back with my hands. Night, I loved Alex. In all my life, I never wanted anything as much as I wanted to drown in his touch and never come up for air.

His hands coasted up my thighs, ghosting over my erection on their way to my stomach. I arched into him, releasing him enough to give him room to explore. He angled his hips to fit between my thighs. We both moaned at the resulting friction. I ground against him as I brought his mouth back to mine for another hungry kiss. Then his hand slipped to my side and I just barely didn't flinch. Once more, I was hyperaware of the mottled black bruise that dominated my left side—the one I'd neglected to hide in the misguided pursuit of comfort. If he touched it any harder, I wouldn't be able to hold back the reflexive cry.

With a force of will, I pulled back, taking my hands off of him so they couldn't betray me. "Alex."

"What?" The sultry heat in his voice threatened to strip my resolve. I wanted to roll us over and press him into the bed, feel him wrap around me, and moan my name as I claimed what was mine.

"What about the rules?"

"*Now* you care about those?" he hissed.

"Alex," I tried again, but he snagged me in a kiss that took all of my focus not to get totally lost in. He gripped my side and nausea rolled through me. Biting back a pained moan, I pulled away once more.

"Shit. You're serious."

"I want your mom to like me," I said as he raised up to look down at me. I didn't have to see his face to know he was doing the sexy smile that always made me forget how to breathe.

"We've been through this. I'm pretty sure my mom loves you." He chuckled huskily before trying to kiss me again.

"Then I'd like to keep it that way."

He made a sound of pure exasperation. "What's the point of fighting if you can't at least have makeup sex?"

I winced. This was not how I wanted to apologize for my behavior earlier. But how could I convince him I wasn't all for makeup sex when all evidence pointed to the contrary?

He shifted. "Fine. Have it your way. I'll go back to my room."

"Wait." I reached up to find his face in the dark. Thankfully moved too far. "Stay. Please." This time, when he leaned back down to kiss me, I let him. It was long and slow and substantially deeper than it should have been. It took me a few moments to find my breath again. "But you have to behave."

He made a choked sound and abruptly his weight settled beside me, mercifully not on the bruise from the hit I'd been too slow to avoid. "You are absolutely incorrigible," he said as he snuggled into my side.

"I know," I responded softly as I rubbed my hand along his back. He gave a huff and relaxed into me.

I had no idea how on earth I was supposed to sleep after getting so worked up. Telling him no physically pained me, but I couldn't risk him asking why I was injured. He wouldn't understand that my returning to the fight club was to keep him safe, that I'd endure every hurt in the world if it meant he wouldn't have to. The sooner I dealt with Thomas, George, and the others, the sooner I could come back to him, could finally stop lying.

I held Alex close and tried to clear my thoughts. Sleeping was going to be hard enough with him there without adding those to the mix. Gradually, I slipped into a deep sleep, my ears filled with Alex's soft breathing and the hint of a snore. And for the first time in months, I didn't have a single nightmare.

When I woke, I knew it was early, but I was determined not to get up until he did. The most he'd moved all night was to drape his arm and leg over me as if they could somehow hold me in place. If only they could.

"Alexi Roman, you better be wearing shorts under there." The sharp voice cut through my fuzzy daze.

My eyes flew open in a panic to see Miss Roman standing in the open doorway, her arms crossed over her chest and scowling. Heat flooded my face, and I silently cursed my hammering heart. Alex stretched beside me beneath the covers, seemingly unconcerned that his mom had caught us in bed together. And *I* was supposed to be the troublemaker?

"Good morning, mom. How'd you find me?"

"It was an easy bet when you weren't in your own bed."

He gave a wicked smile, totally unfazed.

"I mean it about the shorts, Alexi. You know the rules." He sat up, waving away her scolding, and she gave a put-upon sigh.

Eager to be anywhere else than right here, I swung my legs over the side of the bed. It didn't escape her notice that I was wearing pants as I reached out to grab the cotton tee that I was now seriously regretting not wearing.

"At any rate, breakfast is ready," she said before finally leaving. The door intentionally left open in her wake.

I looked back at Alex, who was wearing an exceedingly smug grin, and shook my head. "Are you getting out of bed or what?" He flashed me a devious smile, and it clicked. "You aren't wearing anything under there, are you?"

"Nope," he replied, casually using shadow to close the bedroom door. While the sudden click distracted me, he shadowed out from under the covers to be in front of me. I tried to take a step back, but he caught me first. "What happened to your side?"

"Don't worry about it," I said, trying not to sound anxious. What I wouldn't give to be in the dorm right now. My eyes were undoubtedly black with want.

"I always worry about you," he said, claiming me with a kiss that sent heart curling throughout my body. His hand slid down my backside, and then he forced me hard against him. He was definitely not over last night and there was no stopping my groan. "Still glad you said no?"

"I was never glad." I wanted to steal another kiss, but it seemed wiser to restrain myself. We were already in danger of dissolving into each other and getting into even more trouble.

"I'll meet you in the kitchen," he said, swiping a quick kiss before disappearing into shadow.

I stood there a few more minutes trying to gather myself, then ventured out. My journey slowed as I passed the mantle covered in pictures again.

"That's my favorite one too," Miss Roman said as she reached across and grabbed the picture of Alex laughing. He couldn't be much younger than he was now. "I took it shortly before we found out about the new classes from the Arminius community." She flipped the frame over and started taking it out. "You should have it."

I looked at her in disbelief. "I couldn't."

"Sure you can," she insisted, forcing me to accept the picture. Everything about the image was perfectly Alex. "He really loves you."

"He's said."

She blinked. "He has? Huh, imagine that. Guess he's growing up after all." She shook her head as if clearing something away. "It has been very nice to get to know you, Matthew."

"Mom, I told you not to call him that," Alex bemoaned, suddenly walking past us. It was fascinating to see how he interacted with her. At school he was always so self-confident and assured, but here, here he was just her son. I smiled at his back as he made his way into the kitchen. "Am I the only eating?" he called back.

"Thank you, Miss Roman," I said, pocketing the picture.

"I'm glad for you to have it. Take care of my boy, Matt," she added, brushing my hair back from my face in a way that could only be described as motherly. I'd never had anyone mother me before. Suddenly, sadness welled up inside of me. If something happened to Alex, I wouldn't be the only one devastated.

"I'll do everything I can to keep him safe," I promised, then made my way in the direction where Alex was still bellyaching about our absence.

CHAPTER 5

BETRAYAL

A

I stared at the strip of pictures from the photo booth, much as I had every day since we'd returned from Denham. They were the only proof that the weekend with Matt had happened. Them and the fact that my mom wouldn't stop asking when we were coming back for another visit. I didn't have an answer for that and I certainly wasn't about to tell her he'd all but ghosted me the second we'd rematerialized on the roof of Starling Hall.

Frustrated, I put the pictures back in the dresser drawer where I hoped they'd be safe from Matt should he decide he didn't want me to have them after all. When I walked out of my room, I wasn't even surprised that there wasn't any trace of Matt or his things. I thought back to when I'd learned he was an orphan, how he'd said he'd find another roommate, get all of his things and go. While I was fairly sure he *hadn't* done that...yet, he might as well have for all that I saw of him.

I grabbed a bowl for cereal, then noticed it was the one he usually used. With a sigh, I put it back and grabbed another. This push and pull was killing me. It was as if the closer he got, the farther he would drift afterwards. I glanced around the space and finished my last bite. To think, only a few months ago, this room had been filled with fun and laughter. Now it felt like a tomb. Rather than dwell on the depressing thoughts, I rinsed the dish and grabbed my things. I'd be early to my next class, but it was better than wallowing in misery here. On a whim, I cut through the Witch's College on the chance I might bump into some of my friends from the tutoring group. If memory served, Lina had two classes here and Mariah at least one, despite not being witches themselves.

I'd gotten turned around when I heard a familiar laugh. I immediately oriented towards the sound, my eyebrows furrowing. While there was plenty of overlap between disciplines, Shadow Demons most definitely did *not* have any classes in the Witch's College. And for good reason. Curiosity peaked and more than a little concerned, I followed the laughter to its source. No sooner did I round the corner of a long stretch of hallway, then I ducked back out of sight.

As I'd suspected, Matt was here. Thankfully, he was further down the adjoining corridor and didn't seem to have spotted me. I carefully peered around the corner and tried to make sense of what I was seeing. Matt's stance was about as relaxed as it ever was outside of the dorm, and he wore an enthusiastic smile. Across from him, a startling pretty woman with dirty blonde hair that fell in a perfect sheet to her waist smiled back. Her laughter drifted down the hall, mixed with his deeper chuckle. I couldn't make out what they were saying, but it didn't stop my heart from sinking.

They're just friends. He probably knows her from his Advanced Shadow Spells class. He did say there were witches sitting in.

I pressed against the wall and willed myself to believe it was true.

Face it, it was only a matter of time.

I slammed a hand over my mouth to stifle my squeal of outrage at hearing Daniel's voice intrude on my thoughts.

Seriously, how long did you think it would last? He's not me and you're certainly nothing special, Daniel's diatribe continued, despite me adamantly shaking my head. But there was no silencing him. *Did you think that because he let you fuck him, he'd wake up and decide to be gay?* The mental Daniel that existed solely to torture me snorted. *He's not and he never will be.*

Mocking laughter filled my ears. He was wrong. Matt wouldn't do that to me. He knew Daniel had cheated on me, how he'd gaslighted me.

You're so pathetic. He was simply curious and used you to explore that curiosity. It's all you're good for, anyway.

I squeezed my eyes shut and covered my ears like it could somehow stop the voice coming from inside my head. Not even the pounding of my heart or my stuttering breaths could drown him out.

Fighting it won't change a damn thing. You were an experiment and now he's going back to what he really wants. See for yourself.

Against my better judgment, I snuck another peek at the pair just in time to see Matt take her hand, then snare her in an embrace that nearly knocked her to the floor. My vision went dark, bathing the hall in night as anger washed through me with sickening force. With a snarl, I reigned in the shadows, winking out along with them.

"Where the fuck is it!" I shouted, tearing the dorm kitchen apart. Matt once had a fully stocked liquor cabinet, and I seriously doubted he'd simply poured it all out. He didn't believe in being wasteful. No, it was here somewhere.

The cabinet door nearly burst off its hinges as I ripped it open yet again. I took a step back and considered checking his room, then dismissed the thought. It wouldn't be there. Plus, I doubted I'd be able to step foot in there without ripping the place to shreds. If it was anywhere, it would be hidden in here somewhere.

Think, Alexi, if Matt wanted to hide something, what would he do?

I snapped my fingers as the glaringly obvious answer came to me—he'd put it in the shadow world. Which meant there was a portal hiding in plain sight. I yanked open the freezer and sure enough, there was an unmasked portal staining the side next to a veritable mountain of ice cream. I stuck my hand through it with no concern for what might be on the other side. Judging by how the air felt, I had a serious suspicion my hand was actually floating disembodied above the couch. A quick look confirmed it. Beyond pissed and increasingly frustrated, I slammed the door.

I just wanted to numb the fury and hurt washing through me. But it was like I was stuck in a riptide of heartache, the crashing of waves, the relentless breaking of my heart. That damnable stash had to be here somewhere. I went back to the most likely place to keep liquor bottles—beneath the sink. Except the cabinet doors already hung open, none of the desired spirits were to be found. I got down on the ground and felt around in the barren space, only pausing when my fingers hit something. I carefully extended my arm further under the sink and discovered the smooth glass neck of a bottle..

"Found you." I pulled every bottle out until I was sure there was nothing left, then deposited the obscene assortment on the counter. I mixed a concoction that I hoped would be palatable. It wasn't. I downed the tall glass and tried again. This one was a little better. I polished it off as well and made a few adjustments. Recipe in hand, I made a batch large enough to fill the pitcher and grabbed the almost empty bottle of tequila as well.

As I took a swig straight from the bottle, I tried not to think about the last time this bottle had been out. The anger I'd felt then couldn't hold a candle to the hurt I felt now. Every time I closed my eyes, I saw Matt flash the young woman that dazzling smile—*my smile*. Could hear her giggle as he took her hand. His laugh that had become so rare.

The pain in my chest grew as I remembered how tight he'd held her. When was the last time he had held me like that? Did he ever plan to again? I sank artlessly onto the couch, more interested in drinking myself into oblivion than going to the rest of my classes. Even half a pitcher in my mind still couldn't reconcile my sweet Matt with this heinous betrayal.

How could he? He had to know what this would do to me. Probably never expected to be caught.

I snorted derisively at the likeliness of that. Certainly wouldn't be the first time. I polished off another glass, leaving the liquid to curdle in my already sour stomach. I just couldn't understand. If he was done and moving on, then why string me along? Why go home with me at all? Be sweet? But then, he'd also tried to prevent me from sharing his bed. Perhaps that should have been my clue in a long line of clues I'd willfully overlooked.

I eyed the nearly empty pitcher and debated if I had enough motor control to make another. Then the door opened and in walked Matt. The fact he was here at all was a bit of a shock and not doing anything for my current state. But to have the audacity to smile? Not that he was anymore.

His greeting died as he took in the scene before him. He scanned the kitchen, clearly noting the counter covered in bottles, then his gaze returned to me. "What happened?"

"How could you?" I asked, the words slurring a bit.

"How could I what?"

"You fucking son of Dis. Don't lie to me. I saw you!" Doubt flashed across his face. "That's right. Your secret is out," I said, surging to my feet. The room tilted, and he rushed to steady me. "Don't touch me!" I ripped my arm away from him, effectively spilling what remained of my drink. I felt like I was going to be sick. Actually, I was pretty sure of it.

"I don't know what you're talking about. We need to get you to the bathroom." He reached for me again.

"I told you not to touch me."

"Alex, I'm just trying to help."

I barked a laugh. "Help? You mean like you let me help you?" He looked like I'd slapped him, which actually sounded like a damn good idea, except I couldn't get my arm to cooperate. "She's pretty. No wonder you didn't want my help. You had someone else to lean on." Tears streaked like acid down my face.

"What are you talking about?" His eyebrows pinched together, his forehead crinkling.

"Stop. Lying. To me. I saw you with her. What *else* have you lied about, Matt? Did you ever even quit that stupid bruiser bar? Is that where you met her?" Understanding lit in his eyes, and my stomach heaved.

"That's enough," he declared. "You can yell at me in the bathroom." He gently but firmly grabbed my arm.

"I said..."

"I know what you said, Alex. Now you can either walk or I can drag you. Your choice."

I pulled my arm away, and he had to catch me in order to prevent me from crashing to the ground. My stomach couldn't take this abuse. The world blinked black, and it felt like he touched every fiber of being. I opened my mouth to shout at him and threw up my life instead. Conveniently, it was into the toilet.

"Take it easy," he said soothingly while stroking my back.

I waved my arm behind me to smack the comfort away. It was about as effective as it had been earlier. I heaved again.

"Who is she, Matt?" The question echoed creepily in the porcelain bowl.

"Her name is Misty and yes, I met her at the fight club. I don't know what you think you saw, but nothing is going on."

"Stop lying," I groaned. How much was it possible to hack up before you died?

"I'm not."

"She's into you." Even half a building away, I could tell that.

"I know. That doesn't change that nothing is going on." He pressed a wet cloth on the back of my neck. The cool was welcome except for the part that I was still furious with him.

"But I saw you with her. You were laughing, and you hugged. You looked happy." I couldn't hide the misery in my voice.

"She was helping me with something."

"What?" I asked, finally looking at him. Little shit was barely containing his amusement.

"A birthday present."

"Birthday? Whose?" I asked, the words sounding muffled to my ears, like someone had stuffed my head full of cotton.

He quirked an eyebrow. "Yours. It was supposed to be a surprise."

"Mine?"

"Your birthday is next week, Alex." He flipped the towel over and a fresh wave of cool kissed my skin.

"How do you know that? I haven't..."

"I asked your mom." He brushed the hair out of my eyes. The touch was so tender, it was all I could do not to sigh with relief. "You proud of yourself yet?"

"No," I replied miserably. Quite the contrary, I felt like a total ass.

"Come on, let's get you in bed. I'm pretty sure you're all puked out."

I groaned as he tried to help me to my feet.

"Can you walk?"

"We'll see," I quipped.

He made sure I was steady, then shadowed out, only to reappear a moment later holding a glass of water.

"It's warm," I remarked after taking a sip.

"The cold would just upset your stomach again. I can put a few cubes in if it really bothers you."

I drank some more, trying to clear the foul taste of sick from my mouth. The cool towel made a reappearance as he wiped my face. I hated how good it felt and that he was being so sweet after I'd been such a complete jerk.

"I'm sorry," I whispered, feeling thoroughly ashamed of myself. I'd been so desperate for an explanation for his odd behavior that I'd jumped to the first and worst conclusion.

He paused in his ministrations, looking deep into my eyes. "I would never do that to you, Alex. There are some things you don't forgive."

My heart constricted at his sincerity. I wrapped him in a hug and he carefully squeezed back. I couldn't think of a time I'd ever been so happy to be wrong.

"Alright, alright. To bed with you." He guided me out to the room, keeping a firm arm around my waist to steady me. "She's not really my type anyway," he mused aloud when we approached the bed.

"Really? What is?" I asked as I burrowed under the covers.

"Let's see," he began as he laid next to me, "tall, absurdly small waist, dark hair, green eyes. Something along those lines."

"Are you trying to butter me up?"

"Maybe." He nuzzled my neck. "Is it working?"

"Maybe," I giggled. Despite having lost every liquid I had drank ever, I was definitely still drunk. "Ugh, this is why I don't drink," I moaned, thinking about the headache that would be waiting for me in the morning.

"I don't know. You drinking has led to some pretty interesting things."

I snorted. "And what about now?"

"Got me in bed, didn't it?" he replied, wrapping an arm around me. That was a good point. "Now be quiet and try to get some rest."

"Will you be here when I wake up?"

"No, but I'll stay as long as I can." He placed a small kiss just beneath my ear. It was the last thing I remembered before the world slipped away.

CHAPTER 6

A DAY OFF

M

I slipped into the hall, careful to shut the door behind me so it wouldn't make any noise. Sneaking out while Alex was in the dorm was always so much harder than when he wasn't. Not risking anything to chance, I waited until I was at the end of the hall before stepping into the shadow world. The usual quiet descended along with the all-encompassing dark. I wasn't entirely sure when, but at some point, the shadow realm had stopped scaring me. Not that it wasn't still eerie as hell, but that sense of familiarity, of belonging, had come just like Alex promised.

Alex.

The dark swallowed my sigh. Of all the things for him to accuse me of, I never would have thought it would have been cheating. Sure, I'd been absent, and I *was* keeping things from him, but it was for his own protection. He'd understand that, eventually.

Hopefully.

Sound returned in the form of crickets and the distant babble of students talking animatedly when I stepped out onto the quad. While it would have been easier to materialize *on* Old Fraternity Row, I didn't want to chance leaving a trail Alex could follow. He was far too smart for his own good. The last thing I needed was him showing up unannounced at one of these ridiculous "check-in" meetings with Thomas. Shaking my head, I took off at a brisk pace. Being late wouldn't do me any favors either.

Gradually, the impressive antiquity of Arminius faded into the skeletal remains of a forgotten past. Almost as if the campus was shrinking back from the poisoned grounds of the old row. I still couldn't fathom what could have possibly happened here to have caused such permanent destruction. The place had an ominous air that stuck to it like an unpleasant smell, and it wasn't just because of the damage that had been caused. I shuddered and quickened my pace. Small wonder George and his goons enjoyed coming here.

By the time I reached the crumbled pillars at the end of the row, I had my game face on and my thoughts were as clear as they were going to get. I stepped across the threshold and the spell there tingled faintly across my skin. Once again, I wondered if the others noticed it. Considering they were a bunch of fools on a good day, I'd hazard a no. I'd tried to find a way around it, but the rest of the house was sealed up tight—there was no other way in or out. Again, I doubted that George, Travis, *or* Kyle knew that. But there wasn't a doubt in my mind that it not only alerted Thomas when one of us arrived, but was specific to Shadow Demons. How the others couldn't see the man's obvious detest probably shouldn't have surprised me.

I followed the cleared path past the rubble deeper into the ruined remains of the fraternity house and wondered how much longer I could keep this up. Aside from missing Alex so much, it physically hurt—and now this accusation of seeing someone on the side—my skin crawling anytime I was near George, plus the fight club that was absolutely taking its toll. Yes, all that aside, Thomas made me anxious in a way I couldn't ignore, like when I was living on the street and it felt like eyes were always on me. He was dangerous even if he didn't look it.

"Matty! My man," Travis hollered, slinging an arm over my shoulders. "Where you been?"

I showed my teeth in a forced smile and shrugged him off. "Are you still on about that weekend?"

"You didn't miss your buddies?" Kyle chimed in.

Another forced smile, this one bordering on a snarl. They weren't my "buddies" and never would be. I took a deep breath and focused on the way Alex had held me that night at his mother's house. My smile settled into something more genuine as I slowly let out the breath. "I'll meet up with you guys after my report."

Travis snuck up behind me to squeeze my shoulders. "Just don't take too long. We've got a fight to get to." He released me and trotted along behind Kyle and George to an adjoining room.

"You look pleased with yourself," the disembodied voice of Thomas floated into the room. It could have been coming from the right, but I knew better. That was also a spell. Thomas used a lot of those. Some he seemed to use like breathing, and others... others made my hackles rise. To say I couldn't trust Thomas as far as I could throw him wouldn't do it justice, considering I could throw him quite far, given my demonic strength. "I hope you have some more information for me." This time, the voice came from behind me. I didn't react, nor did I look up to where I knew he still stood on the landing overhead. While this trick hadn't worked on me since that first day, he didn't need to know that.

"Don't I always?"

"You've got a smart mouth for someone spying on your friends."

I hid my flinch. "They aren't my friends."

"Oh? I thought at least one of them was," he said, appearing by the wall of pictures. "Frankly, I would have thought you'd try harder to eliminate him." He touched the edge of Alex's picture.

I quickly checked the urge to tear his hand off and settled for a bored shrug. "He's weird and keeps to himself. I can't help it if there isn't much to work with." I bit the inside of my cheek and decided to roll the dice. "But, uh, something did happen the other day." This gamble would either go a long way toward clearing Alex or completely blow up in my face.

"Do tell." Thomas released the picture and faced me.

Here went nothing. I forced myself to remain casual and hiked a shoulder. "Apparently, he saw a girl with some guy in the Witch's College."

Thomas's eye narrowed, unimpressed. "That doesn't say much, Matthew."

"Considering he was stupid drunk by the time I got to the dorm, it actually says a lot." I stubbornly pushed down my own feelings at having arrived to find him in such a state and moderated my tone. "He never drinks, not even socially. He kept asking where she'd met him and how this could be happening."

"Ah, I see. And you're surmising that this is the elusive girl that he's been hiding from you. Who is the girl? Do you know her?"

Now the really dangerous part. "Yes. She's the resident witch at the Bruiser joint."

Thomas' eyes lit up with surprise. "Well, well. Why do you think he didn't want you to know about her? Surely that is information a friend would share."

Forgive me, Misty.

"She's into me and he knows it." It was one of the few things I'd said that wasn't twisted in some half-truth.

Thomas inspected his short-clipped nails, his gaze flicking to the image of Alex pinned to the stucco wall. "I see. Did he say anything else? Do you know if they broke up?"

I shook my head. "I know his last partner cheated on him. There are some things you don't forgive."

He plucked up the red marker from the dilapidated desk and I nearly forgot to breathe as he drew a red line across Alex's picture. "You've done well, Matthew. Certainly better than my other 'recruits'." He cast a withering look in the direction the others had disappeared before turning a more appraising one on me. "You are very good at this."

"Thank you sir," I said past the bile steadily clawing up my throat. Why hadn't he completed the X? I needed Alex in the clear, needed to know he was safe. What more would it take?

He recapped the marker and set it aside. "You can report back when you have more information for me. Your... colleagues are waiting." Without so much as a wave, I was dismissed. At least he hadn't called them my friends. But then, maybe that was a bad thing.

I was all set to book it straight out of there when I hesitated.

"Was there something else?" Thomas asked, his expression an unnerving cross between bored and suspicious.

"This Thursday..."

His expression turned decidedly more grim. "What about it?"

"I won't be able to check in as usual. I'll be unavailable the whole weekend, actually."

It was hard to miss the waves of suspicion coming off of him. He glanced once more at Alex's picture with its half an X. "I suppose you've earned yourself some time off."

Careful not to show my relief, I spun on my heel to join the others.

"Matthew."

I froze, every muscle in my body taught, torn between the desire to stand and fight and to flee as fast as the shadow world would let me. "Sir?" I called back, grateful that my voice didn't betray my nerves.

"Be sure this doesn't become a habit. And I'll expect your efforts to reveal the traitor in our midst to double. Understood?"

"Understood," I echoed, my blood turning to ice in my veins as I walked slowly out of the room. I was on the verge of exhaling when Travis stormed up to me, fire burning in his eyes.

He shoved his finger into my chest hard enough that I stumbled back a step. "Why didn't you tell me your roommate was dating that bitch from the club?"

I suppressed a groan and smacked his hand away. Great, now Alex and Misty had an entirely different target on their back. "I only just found out myself."

"Liar," he snapped, getting back in my face. "You knew the whole fucking time. How am I supposed to compete with that?" He flung his arms wide, and I bit my tongue from telling he didn't have a chance in hell with either of them.

"You could be less ugly, for starters," Kyle said, unintentionally coming to my rescue. He propped his elbow on Travis's shoulder and smiled, though it was more of a sneer.

Travis shrugged him off and went to skulk in a corner. I really couldn't take spending *more* time with these assholes. Exhausting didn't even come close, and that didn't factor in the fights at the club. Fuck. That reminded me, I needed to tell Neese I wouldn't be present for the usual pummeling Thursday. That was gonna go over like a ton of bricks, assuming he didn't just hold me hostage like he had the *last* time I'd tried to duck out of a fight.

"What's this I hear about you skipping out on us? Again. Isn't it bad enough you blew us off the other weekend?" George asked, catching the other two's attention.

"I'm allowed to have other plans," I replied, just short of a snarl.

"Like what? What's better than hanging with us?" Kyle asked, plopping on the dilapidated couch they'd dragged in here. Not even fleas would touch that monstrosity, and I sure as hell wasn't planning to either. I'd slept in nicer gutters.

"Some of us are able to get laid every now and again, but it requires actually showing up."

The look on Kyle's face went slack with shock and Travis doubled over laughing. Truthfully, getting laid had nothing to do with it, but it was a language they understood.

"Why Thursday?" George's question blanketed the room in abrupt silence. They swiveled to face me. Shit.

"I can't control the calendar," I said. Now all I had to do was pray that he didn't ask what a calendar had anything to do with it.

He sucked his teeth. "Well, you're telling Neese. I'm not gonna be penalized just because you want to put your dick in something." It took every ounce of control not to bare my teeth at him or, even better, break his face like I'd broken Daniel's. Despite my best effort, though, George noted the reaction and snickered.

"I'll talk to Neese tonight," I managed through gritted teeth, my anger in danger of finally boiling over. I needed to get out of here before I did something I would regret.

"Just be sure not to get too distracted by a pretty face, Matty. We still have a mission to finish."

I froze, damn near white-knuckling with the effort of keeping my fist from burying itself in his smug face. "It's one fucking day, George. Maybe if you spent a little more time focused on the mission instead of blood sport, you could provide some useful information for Thomas yourself." His features twisted into an ominous scowl and I instantly regretted lashing out. This was totally going to bite me in the ass.

CHAPTER 7

FRIENDLY ADVICE

A shadow cast over me, heightening the chill that had sneaked up on the campus. Though maybe sneaked wasn't the right word. It was November. Mother of Night, how was the term already over? And where the hell was my boyfriend? Did I even still have one?

My stomach rolled unpleasantly, and a cough came from above. I glanced up to find Rubio standing over me.

"Took you long enough. Mind if I sit?" He joined me on the bench without waiting for a reply. The late afternoon sun hit his blond hair, momentarily blinding me.

I blinked rapidly a few times, then cautiously glanced at him. "So, uh, what brings you here?"

He leaned back, spreading his arms along the length of the bench. "Figured since you couldn't be bothered to make it to the meeting, I'd bring the meeting to you."

"Shit!" I immediately reached for my bag. "I'm so sorry. I'll head right over."

Rubio placed a hand on my shoulder, stilling my movements. "The meeting was yesterday, Alexi."

I groaned and slumped against the bench. "I'm sorry."

"You said that."

"My head's been a little... messed up lately."

He angled his body to face me better. "That's actually why I'm here."

I tried—and failed—to hide a wince. "Judging by that tone, this is about more than missing a meeting. And... I can't really blame you. I've been a horrific friend and tutor."

Rubio sighed and moved his hands to rest on his lap. "You're not a horrific friend and you're one of the best tutors I've got." He paused, then added, "When you're on point, which you haven't been for a while."

"It's just Matt..." How did I even come close to explaining everything that had been going on between us?

He nodded knowingly. "I suspected as much."

I gave him a sharp look and straightened. "What's that supposed to mean?"

"I get it. He's hot, occasionally sweet, probably fucks like a demon—no pun intended, and he's convenient. But he's not exactly what I would call reliable."

My face burned, though it was a toss up if it was from humiliation or outrage. "You know nothing about him."

"And you do?" he countered with zero mercy.

I held onto my indignation for all of point-five seconds, then shrank back into the bench. "I thought I did."

"Wanna talk about it?"

I scrubbed at my face. "I love him. But he's not talking to me. We were really good there for a bit. Something... changed. I think... I think he's in trouble." To my chagrin, Rubio didn't look even remotely surprised by this revelation.

"You care about him." I opened my mouth to correct him and he held up a hand. "And I care about you. Anyone could take a one look at the guy and know he's got issues longer than the river Ebro. It's not your responsibility to fix them. Please don't punch me, but are you sure he's not just a project?"

I'd push Rubio into the Shadow Realm before he could shout if I didn't value him so much as a friend. Since I wasn't about to potentially murder my friend, I settled for a glare. "Matt is *not* a project."

"I'm just putting it out there. My main point still stands. I'm worried about you." He looked down at his hands. "I think it might be a good idea if you stepped back from the tutoring group for a bit. Take some time to sort yourself, get caught up with classes, prepare for finals."

"What about my clients? They have finals too."

"Let me worry about them. I've already talked to Mariah, Semyon, and Rikka. They've agreed to take on your clients to give you some breathing room."

Despite his comforting tone, I bristled. "You already... So my taking 'time'," I said with air quotes, "to sort my shit isn't a suggestion at all. You've already decided." In a huff, I lurched off the bench, nearly flinging my bag across the lawn.

"Alexi, please."

"I don't want to fucking hear it, Rubio. You pretend to come to me as a friend, but you're really just here as my boss. And instead of supporting me, you just... just..." I threw my hands up. "Cut me off."

He surged to his feet. "Don't you dare. Maybe if you'd come to the meeting yesterday, this would have felt more amicable, but that's on you. Not me. As for supporting you, that's *all* I've done. Seems to me that your so-called boyfriend isn't the only one who's absolute shit at communication."

I gasped, my righteous anger abruptly fizzling into shame. My eyes burned, and I wiped at them brusquely. "I... I don't know what to do."

Rubio's gaze softened, and he rested a hand on my upper arm. "Why don't we go somewhere a little less public and talk through it? The Topaz Lounge? Less chance of campus looky-loos at least and there's booze. But the first round is on you."

I nodded and placed a hand over his, then looked at him with wet eyes. "Don't let go." Before he could speak, I stepped us both into the Shadow Realm. A couple of minutes later, we emerged in an alley across from the retro bar. Walking-walking might have been smarter, but I was on the verge of a full meltdown.

"Whoa, that was..." Rubio swallowed thickly while he continued to look around at the faded bricks and stucco around us. "Different," he finally finished.

I blinked in sudden realization. I'd only ever shadowed Matt before, and that was a heady experience all on its own. But shadowing Rubio had been nothing like that. When he finally looked at me, I gave him a sheepish smile. "Sorry, probably should have warned you a bit more. Now you can say you've walked in the Shadow Realm."

"Is *that* what that was?" He looked behind him as if he could see some kind of doorway.

"You, uh, get used to it. We should probably get inside, though, before someone wonders how we got here." Especially considering the alley dead-ended behind us.

"Right." He quickly checked that the way was clear, then walked across the narrow road. We found a relatively secluded booth and placed an order for two Tequila Sunrises with a passing server.

Once the drinks arrived, my excuse for putting off explaining ran out. I took a sip of the colorful drink and sighed. "I really don't know what happened. We really were doing well. Great, even. I'm not imagining or exaggerating that. He'd finally shared his past with me, and, yes, the sex was incredible. Now, I don't know where he is most of the time. He's certainly not in class, or at least not in the classes we share." I paused for another drink.

"Do you think he's-"

I quickly held up a hand. "Please don't say it. The thought crossed my mind, but when I confronted him about it, he was so earnest that he wasn't." I rolled the glass between my hands and watched the colors blur. "That he would never," I added in a whisper.

"I won't insult you by asking if you believe him." Judging by Rubio's tone, *he* certainly didn't. "When do you think things shifted?"

I abandoned my study of my drink to stare up at the ceiling. *This* I'd had plenty of time to consider. "It wasn't just one thing, not at first. There were lots of little, random bits that didn't add up."

"Like," Rubio prompted.

"Like he came back to the apartment in a state. When I asked what was wrong, he fed me a line. I believe part of it was true," I added quickly in his defense, glancing at Rubio. "But he was clearly holding something back."

He took another drink, keeping his focus on me and my pathetic tale. "Anything else?"

I sighed and finished my drink, then pushed it away. It glided across the table and would have fallen off if I hadn't halted its trajectory with a bump of shadow. "He wanted to stop working on our research project. Not that it really mattered for class, because they ended up scrapping it altogether, but he was so... passionate about it. That he would randomly want to call it quits, especially after we'd made so much progress, was odd."

"If that's the case, why did you go along with it? Why not press for more answers?" Rubio flagged the server and signalled for another round.

"Matt can be cagey. Don't look at me like that. He has his reasons, and they were valid. Plus, he was clearly very upset about it and I didn't think it was worth riling him up further."

He snorted. "And what were these 'valid' reasons?"

I rolled my eyes at his dismissive tone. "Some of them were personal and the other..." I straightened and turned my full attention to Rubio. "Do you know anything about a Bruiser Bar near campus?"

"A what?" He frowned and took a healthy swallow from his fresh glass.

"A fight club. Matt used to go to one before we got together and I'm almost positive he's started up again."

"So, you think that's where he's sneaking off to when he's not with you?"

His word choice was less than stellar. I was positive an actual knife to the chest would have hurt less. "Possibly. Probably." I sagged in defeat. Of course he was. All the signs were there—the unexplained bruises, the late nights. But that still didn't explain his peculiar behavior the rest of the time. And why miss class?

Rubio sat back in the booth. "Well, I can't say I've heard anything about a fight club. Could always ask my roommate."

"The wyvern with the tongue?" I teased, finding a modicum of merriment thanks to the alcohol and an empty stomach.

He chuckled. "Don't knock it 'til you try it. Guy can do truly magical things with that...appendage." He wiggled his eyebrows salaciously.

I barked a laugh, nearly spilling what remained of my drink, which turned out to be not much. We both signalled the server at the same time with Rubio adding an order of chips.

"I'm serious. Neese knows a shit ton of people. Even more than me. If anyone has heard of this Bruiser Bar your man's been popping off to, it'd be him," he offered again before devouring several chips in one go.

I shook my head. "No reason to get your roommate tied up in my mess. I appreciate the sentiment, though." We clinked glasses and fell into an almost comfortable silence. Finally, I let out a heavy sigh. "I just really miss him. We were even sleeping together."

Rubio snorted into his drink. "I knew *that*."

"That's not what I meant!" I shoved him in the shoulder. "Well, I mean, yes, that too, but sharing a room. Sort of." I glanced at him and started. "What's that look for?"

"I think I just threw up a little in my mouth. You're so freaking adorable. I think I might actually die." To lend credence to his ostentatious statement, he mimed a very dramatic death.

"Get off it. Judge all you like, but he was—*is*—very sweet and an absolute cuddle bug."

He pointed at himself. "Seriously, me, dead. Riddle me this, if it was *so* sweet, then why did you stop?"

I worried my lip, then downed the last of my drink, waving off the server's inquiry for another. "Okay, so it might have something to do with the nightmares."

He sat straighter. Even with the shine of inebriation in his eyes, I had his full attention. "This is a new wrinkle. Go on."

"So, um, they were really bad—mumbling in his sleep, thrashing about, the usual stuff. And he maybe, kind of, almost...killed me," I finally finished with a grimace.

"He did what!"

I grabbed Rubio's arm and gave him a severe look. "Would you keep your voice down?"

"Okay, well, way to bury the lead. That sounds as good a reason as any for your beau to ghost you."

"It would. If he knew." I held his gaze until understanding glowed in his eyes and he deflated.

"You didn't tell him?"

I couldn't help but groan at his incredulous tone. I dropped my head into my hands. "No," I mumbled through my fingers.

"Shit, Alexi. How could you not tell him?"

"I don't know. Okay? It just... he'd already been acting weird and even though I was absolutely terrified, I was more afraid *for* him than *of* him." I was regretting declining another drink.

As if reading my mind, Rubio flagged the server. However, the waiter placed two tall glasses and a pitcher of water on the table instead of more tequila. He poured us each a glass and encouraged me to drink. Only once I'd downed half did he ask, "You think he found out?"

"Maybe? But then why not talk to me about it?" And what about the bruises and the rest of the shit he was obviously hiding? "I think you're right about me taking some time. My classes could sure benefit from the extra attention."

He rubbed my back while I watched the condensation slide down the glass. "And your spot with the tutors will be waiting for you next term. Just..."

I glanced at him. "What?"

"Call if you need something. Okay?"

"I will. You're a good friend, Rubio."

He threw his hands up and gave me a wry smirk. "*Now* he says it."

CHAPTER 8

BIRTHDAY PROMISES

M

Fight club was a fucking disaster. Telling Neese I wouldn't be at the club Thursday went about as well as I expected. In hindsight, I should have known there would be immediate retribution. After not one, not two, but *four* fights in one evening, I was dead on my feet. At least I hadn't gotten any marks on me, though my body still felt like I'd subjected it to a meat tenderizer. Too exhausted to even pretend to try, I slept... and slept... *And* missed waking up in time to wish Alex a happy birthday before he left for classes. Determined to make the best use of his absence and glad I'd had the foresight to get everything I needed beforehand, I got to work transforming the dorm.

The spell I'd laid in the hall to alert me when Alex returned tripped. I did a quick scan of the table, making sure everything was in place before laying a cloaking spell. My heart beat a nervous rhythm as I turned to face the door just in time to greet him with a wide grin. He must have had a presentation today, because he was dressed to the nines in a deep blue button down and tan slacks. And just *wow*. He looked stunning. Somehow, he'd tamed his hair, though it looked like it was starting to fight back. In true Alex form, everything was perfectly crisp and well put together. Even frozen in the doorway, he exuded an aura of confidence.

"Why are you looking at me like that?" he asked, setting his things down by the door.

I blinked, realizing I was staring. "Happy Birthday, Alex."

"Oh, uh, thanks."

"Got anything planned?" I pushed on despite his obvious surprise that I'd remembered, crossing my fingers behind my back. I didn't know what I was going to do if he said he was already doing something.

"Um, not really. I was going to go home this weekend to see my mom, but other than that..." he finished with a shrug. I fought to temper my grin into something a little less manic. This was absolutely my best-case scenario.

"In that case, I have a surprise for you." His eyes brightened and my heart gave a little skip. I shooed him toward his room. "You get cleaned up and I'll change."

His brow furrowed. "Why do you need to change?"

"Because it's your birthday, and that warrants something nicer than a sweaty shirt and ratty jeans." Before he could argue, I walked toward my room, dragging my feet just enough to make sure he did the same. Eventually, he rolled his eyes and moved, mumbling under his breath. I shadowed the rest of the way and changed into a gray button down I didn't know I had until the other day and even darker slacks. Then I shadowed back, undid the spell hiding the table, double-checked everything once more, and dimmed the lights.

He was already talking as he came back out. "I guess dressed up means we're not playing pool." He sounded a little disappointed. If that was what he wanted, we could always do that tomorrow, but tonight I had other plans. "You're acting really weird, too. What's..." he finally turned and saw the room. "Up?"

"A tie? Really, Alex?" I laughed, finally feeling relaxed for what felt like the first time in weeks.

He absently straightened it. "You said nice." He glanced past me at the table ladened with plates and the candle in the middle. "Did you do all of this?" I didn't bother to hide my smile.

"You didn't honestly think I wouldn't go all out for my boyfriend's birthday, did you?" His focus shifted back to me. It looked like he wanted to say something. Instead, he shadowed across the room and caught me with a kiss. I sighed into him, loving how he held me so close. The kiss deepened, and I chuckled. "That's supposed to be later."

"Later, huh? What if I said I didn't want to wait until later?" He ran his thumb along my bottom lip, his eyes an intense emerald.

I swallowed thickly. "It's your birthday. I can't exactly tell you no."

He swiped a smaller kiss. "That so? I like the sound of that." He glanced at the spread. "It would be a shame to let this go to waste, though," he said, releasing me.

I joined him at the table, still buzzing with so much excitement it was hard to focus on anything except Alex. Would he like the food? Was everything still warm? Did I remember to turn everything off?

After a while, he waved his fork at me. "I thought you said you couldn't cook."

"Actually, I said that eggs weren't exactly complicated."

"That may be true, but *this*," he gestured at the various dishes, "strikes me as very complicated. And it's good. *Really* good, Matt." My face heated, and I attempted to cover it by taking a drink of water. I'd intentionally left alcohol off of the menu. "Where did you learn how to cook like this?"

That was a fair question, especially given my history. "One of my brief stints in a foster home got me started. There was this grandma that would watch us during the afternoons. She wasn't what I could motherly or even nice, but she was one of the few people who bothered to teach me something. When it was clear I had a knack for it, she taught me more. I even learned a little baking."

"Does that mean I get a cake too?" he asked, as if already knowing the answer.

I bit back the automatic "No". "Do you want a cake?"

"Not particularly." That was a relief. I wasn't exactly sure where to get one on such short notice.

"There's ice cream though."

"Of course there is." He laughed, undoing his tie. It made a soft whisk as it slipped free of his collar. He looped it around his hands so the silk slid through his fingers again and again in a kind of hypnotic dance. When he glanced up, his eyes were the color of midnight.

Heat surged through me. Being able to see how much someone wanted you was downright intoxicating, and there wasn't a doubt in my mind that my eyes were now equally dark. I watched entranced as the tie continued to weave seductively between his fingers.

"Stand up."

I lurched out of my chair so fast I nearly toppled it over. In contrast, Alex flowed effortlessly out of his seat, the embodiment of grace. He walked closer, his eyes once more green, though no less intense.

"Give me your hands."

I held them out, palms up, expecting him to take them. What I did not expect was for him to wrap the tie around my wrists and secure them together.

"Does that bother you?" he asked, a grin teasing the corner of his mouth.

Again, I had to check the immediate "No" and find a different way to answer. "Whatever you want, Alex." He grabbed my arms and leaned close. I tried to close the distance, but he held it.

"You know what I want." His husky reply sent a shiver through me. He didn't give me a chance to respond before moving my arms above my head and then using shadow to keep them suspended. This felt oddly familiar.

"You know that can't hold me," I said with a crooked grin.

He raised an eyebrow. "Then I guess you'll have to maintain it." His slow, sexy smile had no doubts whatsoever that I would, simply because he'd told me to. My heart stopped trying to beat altogether.

"Don't you want your present?"

He hooked a finger at my collar, then traced a line of shadow all the way down my chest. My shirt fell open in its wake and I gasped. "I get more than one?" My breath caught when placed his hands on my bare skin.

"Y-yes. It's still on the table. Are you sure..."

"Matt," he said with a stern expression. "Stop talking."

My mouth closed with an audible snap. Already maintaining the strip of shadow was becoming difficult. It didn't get any easier as he continued his slow, methodical exploration of what he was deeming to be his present.

"I love your body, Matt. I'm glad to see you're taking better care of it."

The earth itself seemed to shatter when he finally kissed me again. I moaned and arched into him, desperate for more. Apparently, I had too much slack, because he casually willed the strand shorter, bringing me to a point where my toes barely scrapped the ground. I stifled my alarm and tightened my hands on the strand, now relying on it to keep me from falling in a puddle at his feet.

"Still good?"

I managed the barest of nods, not trusting myself to speak.

"Good." His fingers danced down my abdomen until they reached my pants. With deft movements, he had my fly undone and my pants pulled free, leaving my arousal completely exposed and entirely at his mercy. His gaze roved over my body as he methodically removed his own clothes, draping them with care over the back of the chair. By the time he was naked, my dick was leaking like a firehose and he hadn't even touched me.

He stepped closer, and I was so enthralled by the way his cock bounced with each step that I gasped when he wrapped his long fingers around my shaft. I struggled to maintain the thin strip of shadow as he lazily stroked me. His thumb glided over my slit, stealing the latest bead of pre-cum, and he brought it to my lips. I obediently opened my mouth, but rather than feed it to me, he sucked his thumb clean. My entire body shuddered and my tentative hold on the shadow binding my arms took another hit. He brushed his hands over my straining shoulders and kissed me again.

I wanted to beg him to let me down, to let me feel him, or at the very least, let me talk. I also didn't want to disappoint him. Not ever if I could help it. And definitely not tonight.

Alex coasted his palms down my quivering sides. He hooked his hands behind my thighs and lifted me higher. I reflexively wrapped my legs around his waist, taking the pressure off of my arms. It seemed to be the appropriate response, because his fingers dug into my hips, causing me to groan. Unwilling to pass up having him within reach, I leaned forward to capture his mouth. It wasn't until I felt a slick finger at my hole that I broke the kiss.

He rubbed his finger in a slow circle along the rim and I worked diligently not to squirm *or* drop my hold. By the time he slipped the digit in, I was positive I'd pass out from anticipation. I moaned as I tried to bear down on him, craving so much more. But the more of him I tried to get, the more he pulled away, until I was whining pitifully.

"That's it, love. I wanna hear how good you feel." He pressed against my prostate as he glided his fingers in and out of my clenching hole. My moan turned into an undignified sound of disappointment when he pulled them free. Then, with no warning, Alex tipped my hips at an angle and speared me in one thrust.

I cried out, immediately tightening my legs around him to keep him there. If he pulled out now, I was positive I'd die. Thankfully, he only pulled out partially, before thrusting back in again and again, until he was fucking me in earnest. I didn't care that I couldn't feel my arms anymore or that I'd yet to touch him. With each thrust, my dick rubbed along his abdomen and the multitude of sensations were unravelling me. He slammed home once more, and I shattered, groaning through an orgasm that seemed to carry my soul.

He caught the sound in a savage kiss that dominated me and stole what little breath I had. Then he panted into my neck while he continued to piston his hips. His fingertips dug into my ass and his breakneck pace faltered. Then he grunted, his body stiffening as his release slammed through him. Finally, he reached up and pulled my arms down. If it hadn't been for already clinging to him, I likely would have crashed to the floor, my legs too unsteady to hold me.

It wasn't until he laid me on a makeshift bed of sofa cushions that he tugged the tie loose. The moment my hands were free, I pulled him to me, every fiber of my being vibrating with need. There was no way to get enough of Alex, but I'd be damned if I wasn't going to try. An exhausting round or three later, plus a break for leftovers, Alex finally gave me leave to talk again.

"Don't suppose you want your actual present now?" I asked, while he trailed his fingers lazily across my abdomen.

"You mean this wasn't it?" He laughed, sending wisps of heat spiraling beneath where his fingers played. "I don't need anything else, Matt." He placed a tender kiss on my shoulder. "Just you."

I smiled, my heart full near to bursting. Had I ever been enough for anyone before Alex? "I apparently got myself into some unnecessarily hot water getting this for you. The least you could do is let me give it to you." He looked away, embarrassment clearly written on his face. I tilted his head up to look at me. "Please."

"Okay, let's see it."

Unwilling to give up the glorious tangle of limbs to retrieve the small box, I shadowed it over. Not exactly easy when I couldn't see it. Thankfully, my selfishness didn't backfire, and I retrieved the delicate box without incident.

Alex shifted as if to sit up.

"Wait," I stalled him and created a thick sphere of shadow around us, making the space extra dark.

He laughed. "How am I supposed to see to open it?"

"Good point." I thinned the sphere enough to let some of the candlelight through. "Lay down." He gave me a look, but I refused to back down. "Trust me."

He shimmied back down into our nest and opened the box. "What's this?" he pulled out a piece of paper covered in colorful words.

"Hold it away from you and tear it in two."

He glanced at me, uncertainty clear on his face. "Matt, what is this?"

"Just do it," I said impatiently. I already knew what was coming, so I watched him to see his reaction instead. After another moment of hesitation, he tore the paper perfectly in two. A series of miniature fireworks leapt from the torn paper to explode above us in tiny pops. I re-darkened the sphere to make the contrast more stark. The reflections of the bursts shone in his eyes. "Do you like it?"

"This... this is incredible." He turned to look at me.

"You're missing it," I scolded. He quickly adjusted his focus. I scooted closer, resting my head on his shoulder so I could watch as well. His arm tightened around me, and I sighed contentedly. "What do you want, Alex?" I whispered between the muted bangs.

He glanced down, catching my eye. "This. I want this feeling to last forever."

I stretched up to kiss him. Someday I'd be able to give that to him.

"Will you be gone in the morning?" he asked sadly.

I barely stopped the "No" before it sprung forth. "I'll be here."

"What about the morning after that?"

"Still here."

"And after that?" he whispered.

"For the next five days, I'm all yours." I saw the disbelief in his eyes, like he was too scared to hope.

"I love you, Matt," he said, rolling us and capturing me in a kiss I'd gladly spend eternity drowning in. My heart felt like it would burst as we made love beneath the fireworks that had been conjured in our living room.

CHAPTER 9

BLENDING

A

Not even a whole day after what was likely the best birthday weekend of my life, everything was back to usual. Matt resumed his disappearing act and left me to wonder if he was attending *any* of his classes, let alone passing them. Apparently, loving him would only be on his schedule, which at the moment was full up with Nyx knew what.

Losing my tutoring job stung, but it meant I had more time to study before the end of term and winter break. It also gave me entirely too much time to think, namely about Matt. If he would just talk to me, then I knew we could sort this out together. But he clearly didn't trust me with whatever had him so preoccupied and that hurt almost as much as the avoidance.

I couldn't fight the feeling that time was running out for us. Which meant I needed to play Matt's game by his rules. I already knew he wouldn't like it, but I needed answers. Despite the pristine condition of his body on my birthday, the bruises had made an almost immediate reappearance. The question was, was he fighting again or had he never stopped? Neither made me happy, but at least the former meant he hadn't been lying to me the *whole* time.

It took some research, but I eventually learned how to set replicate the perimeter alarms he used. They were incredibly handy for determining when he returned to the dorm, as infrequent as that was. Unfortunately, he could give a ghost a run for their money and often had disappeared by the time I realized he was around. At some point, I was going to have to stop letting the distraction of seeing him for the first time in days prevent me from doing what needed to be done. Until then, I practiced the spells until I was sure I had them down. Not that it did me any good—he never tripped them. Considering how outrageously good at practical shadow spells he'd gotten, it was entirely possible he was sidestepping my feeble attempts. Refusing to be deterred, I expanded my web in the dorm, practicing the spell until I could do it effortlessly in my sleep. I also figured out how to mask the spell like the portal-cloaking spell he'd taught me and placed the "trip wires" in creative places. Now, I just had to wait.

I sat on my bed appreciating the pictures from the fair. It had quickly become the only way I could see him for longer than five seconds. They'd found their way into a keepsake box along with the sketches he'd given me, as well as the remnants of the spell for the fireworks. I couldn't help but smile as I fingered the torn paper. That had been such a thoughtful and original gift. It spoke to how he thought and the caring soul I knew was still inside of him, no matter how he hid it.

A wire tripped, and my head shot up. As I suspected, he was sneaking into his room through the wall. I quickly put away the treasures, then rushed into the living room, careful not to shadow despite my urgency. Shadowing would only trip more wires and alert him I knew he was here. When I pushed his door open, he spun around in surprise. He was mid-change and there was no hiding the mottled bruises covering his torso.

"I knew it. You're fighting again." I tried and failed to reign in my anger.

He sighed and finished pulling the shirt over his head. "Alex, not now."

"Then when? You won't talk to me anymore. What happened to being best friends, Matt?" He flinched. "No matter what, remember? You said that no matter what, we would always be best friends. If you've changed your mind about other things, that's fine," I lied, "but at least have the decency to tell me to my face instead of sneaking around, barely even able to look at me. We don't even hang out as friends anymore."

"*Now* you want to be friends?" he scoffed.

"I never did anything you didn't ask me to," I bit back. There were a few liberties with that statement, but the spirit was true.

He opened his mouth, but it took a moment for the words to come. "You and I both know that being *just* friends is out of the question. If I recall, you said it pretty much always was." He turned his back to me and reached to grab his shoes. "Why are you here, Alex?"

"Because I miss you. I miss us. And you won't talk to me about anything. You haven't even denied that you're fighting again."

He shook his head. "What do you want from me? Do you want me to lie to you and tell you everything is fine? I can't do that, Alex."

"You seem to be lying plenty of late." Shock exploded across his face like I'd backhanded him. I softened. This isn't what I'd intended. "I want answers. I want you to trust me again."

"I never stopped trusting you."

"Then why are you hiding things from me?"

"Because I know you. If you knew what was really going on, then you'd try to march off and save the day. I can't let you do that. You'll only get hurt." He clapped a hand over his mouth and groaned. "Damn it, Alex. Just go."

"Why are you so convinced that I can't handle whatever it is?" I closed my hands into fists at my side. "Matt, I'm not a wimp. I can take care of myself."

"I know you can, but this is different."

"Why?"

"I can't tell you that."

"Can't or won't?" I asked angrily.

His shoulders sagged, and he dropped his head back to stare at the ceiling. "I shouldn't have let you spell the dorm."

"Let me?"

"I thought I could avoid them all, but apparently you're getting creative. How many are in here?" He didn't wait to see if I would answer. I reeled from the backlash of all the tripwires disintegrated at once.

"Maybe I wouldn't have to go to such lengths if you would stop avoiding me altogether. Tell me what's going on," I demanded, stepping up to him. I'd avoided outright ordering him to tell me what I wanted to know for a reason: it was practically my last card and if it didn't work, I didn't really have anything else. Much to my shock, he stood frozen in place while a war of indecision and doubt played across his face. Risking it all, I pushed. "Tell me, Matt."

He grimaced. "You don't understand. It's not that simple."

"Then explain it to me." He went to shake his head, and I stopped him. If I lost eye contact, he'd be gone. His eyes widened and I could see the panic as he realized he was caught. "Tell me."

"No." It didn't seem possible to infuse a word with more pain. "They'll hurt you," he added in a whisper, then closed his eyes, clearly having said more than he'd intended. And just like that, I lost him again. When he reopened his eyes, the apathy was back and more solid than ever.

"Stop pushing me away!" I shouted, even though he was still standing there.

Without another word, he shadowed out of the room.

I yelled all of my frustration into the space, resulting in a series of angry knocks on the wall. Despite his slip, I had no more answers than when I'd started—not if he'd been fighting this whole time, *why* he was fighting, were we even together anymore, and who did he think would hurt me? Defeat weighed me down until I sat on the edge of his bed and cradled my head. What was there left to do besides give up, let him go?

My heart gave me a painful reminder that it would never happen. But I didn't know what to do. It felt like I was slowly dying without Matt. Was that possible? It sure felt possible, and honestly, it didn't look like he was faring any better. How much heartache was it possible for someone to endure before there was simply nothing left?

I went to stand when an edge of paper poking out between the mattresses caught my eye. Without a thought for how I'd be violating his privacy, I swung around and investigated. Sandwiched between the mattress and box spring was his sketch book. I glanced at the door before slipping it free, though I don't know why I bothered. He wasn't liable to come back soon, nor was he likely to use the door. I resumed my seat and carefully began turning the pages.

To my amazement, nearly every page was covered edge to edge with precise detail. I now knew why the light was always on—nearly every sketch was of me sleeping. I flipped faster through the pages. None of this made any sense. In my frenzy, something fell out of the book and drifted to the floor. When I picked up the photograph, I saw my face smiling back at me. It was a picture from the house. But how had *he* gotten it? Judging from the state of the edges, he looked at it often.

My level of understanding diminished even more. What did all of this mean? Matt was definitely lying, but now I wondered who he was really lying to. Was it me? Someone else? Himself? I gently closed the nearly full book and replaced it and the picture where I'd found them. One way or another, I was going to find those answers and if he wasn't willing to tell me himself, then I'd have to find them on my own.

Days passed without so much as a sensation of Matt near the dorm. Not that it surprised me after our fight or after he casually undid all the spells I'd spent days placing and hiding. Clearly, he'd gotten far more advanced with his Shadow magic than seemed possible for someone only going to class half of the time.

As I made my way to ballroom class, my trepidation increased. I'd only taken this course because I thought it'd be enjoyable and suspected that it'd be required in the future. Now it was simply a hassle, a drain on my time and annoying on top. I had more important things to do than get fawned over by people I wasn't interested in—like finding out the secrets Matt was trying so hard to hide.

"What's the matter, Roman?" my current partner asked at the end of the set. Amber, that was her name. She was nice enough and one of the few who didn't expect me to grope her.

"Sorry, Amber, just a lot on my mind."

"Girlfriend troubles?" she asked in an unsettling tone.

I looked at her warily. "I guess you could say that." We practiced a few more turns, and she continued the conversation.

"You sure that's all? Your dancing is usually much better."

"I'll try to improve," I replied sardonically.

She shrugged as if it was no big deal to her and spun out. "Anything I can do to help?" Where was this coming from? Sure, Amber and I were on decent terms, but I'd never shared anything about my personal life with her.

"I doubt it."

"Oh, I'm sure there is *something* I could do to at least cheer you up. You seem so melancholy lately." She pouted and while the expression undoubtedly helped her with others, I was unphased.

"Don't trouble yourself," I said as we tried the turn again. This time, when she spun back in, she landed practically on top of me. She really needed to work more on her footwork, but I was in no mood to point that out.

"It's no trouble," she said. Again, there was that hint of something else. Before I could chase it down, though, she reached up on her toes and placed her mouth against mine.

Shock rippled through me. I had to restrain myself from pushing her off. She was just a witch and demonic strength could send her sailing clear across the room. Then, I thought about what Matt had said to me when he forced me to go talk to those girls that night. I needed to blend in. Is this what he meant? That he was perfectly okay with us behind closed doors, but out in the rest of the world he needed me to be more like everyone else? Maybe just me wasn't enough for him. Could I do this for Matt?

Something heavy hit the floor, the sound of it echoing in the open space. Startled, I pulled back. Amber had an almost evil grin and there by the door was Matt. His face was a mix of shock and something he was trying desperately not to let show—hurt.

My heart fell somewhere in the vicinity of my stomach. I looked back at Amber, who was now evil *and* smug. I didn't know what game she thought she was playing, but I wanted no part of it. What was worse, now Matt was leaving. I struggled to disentangle myself. "Let me go. Matt, wait!"

"Come on, Roman, maybe just one more," she teased.

Beyond irritated with Amber's sudden antics, I shadowed out of her clutches, barely remembering to grab my backpack before barreling through the door. I caught sight of his back before he turned a corner and silently thanked Nyx that he hadn't simply shadowed away.

"Matt, please," I called after him. I could clearly see him now, though even at my shout, he didn't turn back. Instead, he made his way into what appeared to be an empty classroom. I followed him and jumped when the door slammed shut behind me. "Matt, I can explain." Actually, I had no idea how to explain what he'd seen. When he rounded on me, I was reminded of when I thought he was going to kill Daniel at the fair.

"I would be very interested to hear that," he said, his voice low and suspiciously calm.

"It wasn't what you think; she kissed me." I could practically feel his rage intensifying.

"It didn't look one sided to me."

"I..." I didn't have an answer for that. "I thought that's what you wanted. You're the one who told me to blend." Something flashed in his eyes. It wasn't anger, but it was gone too fast for me to pinpoint what it really was.

"And you choose now to experiment?" he asked, just shy of shouting.

I flinched. "It's not like that," I tried again, reaching out for him.

He shadowed out and my hand went right through him, causing me to stumble. When he rematerialized ice was warmer than his frigid glare. "I know we've been having issues, but this... this is low even for you. There are some things you don't forgive."

My jaw fell open. I was struck dumb as he angrily walked past me and left. If I'd been confused before, I was even more so now.

CHAPTER 10

THE BREAK

M

I couldn't breathe. The tightness in my chest wouldn't let air in. I needed to find a safe place before I passed out in the hallway. A place far away from Alex. My chest spasmed. I spied another empty room and made a beeline.

I sank to the floor the moment the door was closed, bracing against the wall for support as my legs gave out. I stared at the ceiling, but it did nothing to stop the hot tears from falling unhindered. Even though I'd orchestrated the whole thing, I couldn't stop the pain from welling up. When I'd approached Amber about this, she'd seemed more than enthusiastic. That should have given me pause—hadn't Gilles warned me about witches?—but at the time it had only convinced me it was the right choice. That the ploy would work. I was desperate to get the X completed on Alex's picture, and rumors of him making out with a cute witch from his ballroom class would certainly go a long way toward accomplishing that. But I had no idea that I'd have to witness it.

There was no doubt in my mind that she'd made sure that I'd see, if only so I'd know she'd held up her end of the bargain. But never in a million years did I ever think he'd kiss her back. I bit hard on my knuckle in some vain attempt to hold back the sob threatening to tear me apart.

Why did it hurt so much? This had been the plan—my plan. If anything, he'd made it more convincing. But knowing that didn't change the sickening thud of my heart against my ribs or that every time I closed my eyes, I could see his arms around her, see the moment he kissed her back. It was certainly believable, and that's what I'd needed. Then I'd almost ruined everything when I dropped the backpack. I'd been so surprised that it had just slipped from my fingers. Of course, when I ran, he followed. All I could do was hope that the fight had been enough to put him off of trying to pursue anymore answers from me.

Something tickled at the edge of my senses, and that small hope evaporated.

He doesn't believe I've left. He knows me far too well.

My reprieve over, I pushed to my feet, the abrupt change nearly making me sick. There was no way I could look at him right now, not without completely caving. I stepped into the Shadow World, not caring that doing so would likely result in him opening the very door I hid behind. An actual portal could be tracked, so I walked to another area, stepped out, and opened another breach. It would be harder to follow me if I was playing hopscotch through the Shadow world.

With each step further away from him, I reminded myself that this was the plan. That we'd fought would help to solidify the break. I stumbled, barely catching myself, before crashing into a wall. It felt like I was being torn apart from the inside. My deep breath was less than steadying. I'd do anything to keep Alex safe, even if that meant giving him up. That conviction didn't make it any easier, though.

Unsure of what to do with myself, I returned to the dorm. If this was going to work, then it needed to be believable. I packed a bag full of clothes and a few other items. There was no way I was about to stay at that miserable house Thomas lurked in, but I was no stranger to the streets either. I'd figure something out.

I was already lifting the mattress to retrieve my sketchbook when I thought better of it. If I got caught with literally pages of nothing but Alex, that wouldn't help anything. Then again, I couldn't leave it here either. I'd have to hide it somewhere it couldn't be found. I reached under and, to my surprise, found two books instead of one. I fell to the bed in disbelief. Alex had already found it. I opened the fresh book to the first page. There in his perfect handwriting, was a message. My heart constricted as I read.

It looked like you were running out of room and I thought you could use another. Perhaps I'll even be awake for some of them. You really are a talented artist. I miss you and I want you to know that I'm not done fighting. I love you with all that I am and one way or another, I'm going to get to the bottom of this. Come back to me. I'm not going anywhere; you are my forever.

~ Alexi

I barely got the barrier up in time before I completely disintegrated into sobs.

No. After everything I've done, he's still going to pursue this. He's going to get himself killed.

The sound of my heartache echoed back to me in the bubble I'd created to contain the sound. I clutched the precious gift to my chest as I tried to rein in the pain. What more could I possibly do to keep him from following? I looked down at the empty book. Setting it on the bed felt like ripping off my arm, but I couldn't keep it. Leaving it here would look like rejecting it. Perhaps that, combined with what had happened today, would convince him to let me go.

A quick check showed that he still hadn't returned to the dorm. That was good. I needed to be gone before then. I carefully eliminated all evidence of my breakdown. My hand hesitated when I reached for the other sketchpad with the photo. It was too dangerous to leave those behind. Destroying them would be the smart thing to do, but I couldn't bring myself to do that either. This was already hard enough.

I opened the nightstand and took out the box that had held his present. For a few shining days, things were like they had been before all of this had started. Another sob tried to escape, but I forced it down. I grabbed the book and shadowed it down into a compressed sphere. It would be impossible to maintain it that way, though, which is where the box came in. I willed the inky substance into the box and placed a shadow lock on it. Now the book would stay suspended until the box was unlocked. As an added measure, I put the box in a pocket of the Shadow world inside the drawer, then cloaked it.

I spared one last look at my room. This was the most at home I'd ever felt in a place and I was abandoning it. The book sat on the bed, a clear declaration of my leaving. I considered putting it in the kitchen instead, but that would mean venturing into a space dominated by memories of happiness. I shook my head. There was zero doubt in my mind that he'd check my room when he finally returned. Here was as good a place as any to leave it.

Now I just have to figure out where to go.

After some deliberation, I decided to check out the other forsaken houses on old fraternity row. Then at least I could see anyone they brought to see Thomas. While I hadn't been privy to this event, it was inevitable. Thomas was absolutely the type of guy who'd insist on meeting his target face to face. With over half the class eliminated, options were running low. It was only a matter of time until the stragglers were brought before him to be eliminated.

My stomach heaved. Despite all of my efforts, Alex still made that ever-shrinking list. Not even offering up Gilles and his sketchy past with witches had done any good. Asshole had gone and dropped out, taking my best shot with him. Hopefully, my latest endeavor would be the final piece to clear Alex once and for all.

Resigned in my decision, I laid tripwires much like Alex had. If I couldn't resolve this quickly, I'd likely have to return if for no other reason than to get fresh clothes or shower. Satisfied that it at least *looked* like I'd left permanently, I shouldered the duffle bag. It felt light compared to the weight in my heart as I shadowed out of the dorm.

The first house I checked was in such a sorry state that even desperate, I couldn't bring myself to camp there. Sadly, several of the other options fell into that same category, forcing me further from my ideal vantage. Not that it really mattered if I was at the first house or the last; I'd be spending enough time with the others that I wouldn't be likely to miss anything.

Eventually, I found a place that sufficed. A sweep of my final stop resulted in some halfway decent bedding, surprisingly not infested with fleas or other vermin. That was an unforeseen plus. No running water though, which meant I'd either have to go back to the dorm or find somewhere else to bathe. But that was a problem for later. The day's events had me bone weary and as I laid down on the lumpy bed, I couldn't help but long for the warmer bed clear across campus.

Alex would be back by now, likely have found the left behind sketchbook, and hopefully drawn the right conclusions. He hadn't tripped a wire though, so I could be wrong. As I lay there struggling to sleep, I couldn't help but wish I had brought a sketch or something. Even pretending that I was with him would help. Gradually, the night reached out to claim my abused body. I wasn't surprised when the nightmare started. That's all there ever was now.

Alex was standing in the kitchen when I came in from class. He turned like he always did, and I smiled in anticipation. This was my favorite part of the day. I closed the distance, eager to touch him. Lavender encompassed me like a blanket. I loved that. Lived for it.

He was close enough now that I could practically feel his breath. Just a little further. He stopped just shy, denying me. I caught his eye. There was no happiness or laughter playing in them, just a sadness that made them infinitely dark.

Why Matt?

Why what? I thought, confused, reaching out for him. There was only smoke. Panicking, I tried again.

Why do you want me to hurt you?

Because I have to keep you safe. I can't do that
if you're chasing me.

Why Matt? Tell me why. Why? Why? Why? Why?

I jolted awake. All around me, shadows flailed, inching
across the floor and climbing up the walls, as if looking for
something. I quickly reined them in. I knew exactly what they
were questing for—they were looking for Alex. I'd heard of
demons unintentionally summoning others. This was the last
thing I needed. Now I was going to have to find a way to limit
my powers in my sleep lest I wake up and find Alex beside me.
*Fat lot of good convincing him to let me go will be if I'm
fucking summoning him.*
I grabbed the grimoire the fifth year had given me and
flipped through in the vain hope I could find something. There
had to be a way to keep me from reaching out like that. Finally,
I found something halfway promising. It was like the ward
Vera had placed in the hotel. Hell, it was possible that it was
the same one. There was no real way for me to know beyond
asking her, and that wasn't going to happen.
I worked on perfecting the spell throughout the night,
leaving me bone-weary by the time morning light streamed
through the boarded windows. Once it was cast, I wouldn't be
able to leave or affect anything outside of the sphere of in-

fluence until I properly broke down the barrier. With a heavy sigh, I stood and cracked my back. A little sleep would've been nice, but I had a job to do.

I shoved the grimoire into my bag, lacking the reserves to hide it like I had the sketchbook and unwilling to leave it lying around. While I hadn't seen signs of anyone else attempting to squat in the ruins, I also knew better than to trust what I couldn't see. Shouldering my bag, I stepped into the Shadow world and minutes later emerged on the green, shading my eyes against the unforgiving light.

A quick glance around revealed it was still a little early for the majority of students to be out and about. I briefly debated actually going to Demonic History II. Maybe not into the class itself, but enough to glimpse Alex. My heart constricted. Even thinking about seeing him hurt and it had nothing to do with the contrived fight about Amber.

I shook my head to free the wayward impulse and caught sight of one of my Shadow classmates. A single step back put me firmly in the shadow of the large tree I'd emerged beside and out of sight of Ellie as she walked by. We shared almost no classes together these days, so she'd been a little harder to get a handle on. Maybe this was the universe's way of helping me out. The sooner I could get intel on everyone in class, the sooner I could stop this awful business.

She continued on the path leading to the Witch's college and I fell instep a few paces behind. Close enough to monitor her if she made a sudden turn, but far enough not to raise suspicion. It was honestly scary how good I'd gotten at tracking my classmates. I'd even figured out how to follow them when they'd shadowed somewhere, which was how I knew it left a trail for anyone looking. Luckily, Ellie didn't shadow, as I doubted I'd have the energy to follow.

It wasn't until she was in the castle's shadow that she looked around. I flattened against the side of an adjoining building and kept her in sight. The way she paced combined with the way she kept adjusting her hair struck me as nervous, but I'd yet to deduce why. Then her face lit up suddenly. I followed her gaze and spotted a guy slightly older than us walking toward her. His brown hair was pulled into a bun and his ruddy complexion begged him to spend more time in doors. But his smile appeared genuine as he gathered Ellie into a hug, then planted a kiss on her. When she stepped back, she was equal parts flushed and smiley and oddly still anxious.

I inched closer to hear what they were saying.

"Good morning, dark heart," he said, tucking a stray hair behind Ellie's ear.

She beamed at him. "It's still too early to decide if it's good or not."

"Cheeky minx." He chucked her under the chin. "You ready?"

Ellie's face momentarily fell, then she squared her shoulders and gave a curt nod.

"You're so perfect." He wrapped a hand around the back of her neck and kissed her soundly. I was so wrapped in my own memories and daydreams of kissing Alex, I nearly missed that he'd removed a palm-sized glass vial from the bag at his side. When he broke the kiss, he flicked the mysterious vial open at the same time he seemed to... What? No.

I rubbed my eyes, but the scene remained the same. That was *Shadow* he was pulling out of Ellie. It drifted from her parted lips and into the glass until darkness filled it to the brim. Abruptly, the tendril of Shadow essence vanished. Ellie staggered and braced against the moss-covered stone while he stoppered the bottle.

"Such a good girl," he said as he replaced the now full vial back in his bag.

She gave him a weak smile. "Anything for you." Ellie paused as she struggled to regain her bearings with no assistance from the guy. "Uh, how much more do you think you'll need?"

The guy stepped in close to wrap his arms around Ellie and place a swift kiss on her lips. "Not much, dark heart. I promise. You're so good to help me with this. What other witch in the entire college beside the acclaimed Kyra Hallow herself could lay claim to such an... intimate relationship with a Shadow Demon." The way he trailed his index finger along her cheek made my skin crawl.

I'd seen a lot of questionable shit following my classmates around, but this took the cake. Gilles warning not to trust witches had alarm bells blaring in my head. Even if the guy wasn't a witch, I'd met his type before. A user. Someone who saw others as a commodity to be taken advantage of for their own ends. Thomas would definitely want to hear about this. And maybe, just maybe, this would bring me that much closer to getting Alex cleared.

SURPRISE APPEARANCE

A

After being led on a wild goose chase, I returned to the dorm. I wasn't surprised that he wasn't there, but he clearly had been. I didn't even hesitate to go into his room and immediately wished I hadn't. There on the bed was the new sketch book I'd gotten him. I knew it had been a risk to leave it with the other, but I'd stupidly hoped that it could act as a kind of peace offering. Seeing it so intentionally left out sent a lance through my chest. I walked into the room and picked it up with the vain hope that he'd written something back or left another picture or *some* sign that he wasn't totally lost to me. Nothing. In an inexplicable wave of panic, I yanked back the mattress—the other book was gone. I looked around, a terrifying realization taking hold: everything was gone.

This wasn't be possible. All this over Amber? I shook my head. No. This was something else. While his hurt had been genuine, that fight had been fabricated. Matt was clever, and I was only now realizing just how clever. Everything had a purpose. Every single thing he did had a reason. It might not make sense outside of his own mind, but he definitely had one. Suddenly, I knew he hadn't taken the book or the picture. They were still here. Somewhere.

I reached out with my essence, searching for a pocket of shadow in which he could have hidden the wayward items like he had the liquor bottles in the kitchen. But no matter how many tendrils of shadow I sent exploring, I kept coming up empty-handed. Frustrated, I kicked the nightstand, and the drawer flew open. Almost instantly, I noticed a strange... absence, a void of sorts. I leaned over to investigate, reaching with shadow to determine the confines of the space. The drawer was just that—a drawer. Except for one spot. Curious, I reached into the peculiar spot of nothingness.

My fingers brushed over something small. I pulled my hand back, not sure if I wanted the answer to this riddle. Why couldn't I feel this space? Then it hit me. When I'd cloaked my portal, Matt had instantly lost all sensation of it, but it was still there, still an opening to the other side.

Cautiously, I reached back in to the undefinable space and closed my hand around a small item. In the light of the room, I knew why it felt familiar. It was the companion to my present. I'd wondered where the little box had gotten to, but had been too distracted to care. A smile tugged at my lips.

I scrutinized the box. It should have just opened at a simple touch and yet it resisted. Then I realized there was a faint spell keeping it locked. Refusing to dwell on why it would need to be, I pressed against the spell until it broke. The box sprung open and I just barely caught the oversized item that exploded out of it—his original sketchbook. If I wasn't convinced of the fight before, I was even less so now. And now that I knew what to look for, it was time to uncover any other secrets he might have squirreled away in the dorm.

I reached out, searching for the absence that I now recognized as a cloaking spell against Shadow Demons, and found two more spots. The first was in the middle of the doorway to the hall, the second, my room. I didn't need to break the cloaking spell to know what they were. Tripwires to know when I was here... and when I left.

After several days, I figured out how to remove the cloak. It took asking Vera, who was no less than shocked that I even knew the spell. I neglected to mention where I'd picked it up as well as dodged questions about the location of her secret prodigy. That one I couldn't answer if I wanted to. Wherever he was, he came back twice for clothes and to lay more wires.

I sat on the couch and casually removed the cloak on the latest one. It was in the walkway, in a direct path from the door to the kitchen. At this rate, my only hope was that he'd misinterpret me tripping the wire as leaving and accidentally return while I was still here, either that or grow tired of this horrible game. Final exams were officially here, and it wasn't possible for him to pass Demonic History II or Battle Tactics if he didn't even show up for the test.

The feeling of dying had subsided somewhat at realizing that however much distance he tried to put between us, he still couldn't completely let go. There was still hope. I'd get through to him, eventually. With a resigned sigh, I stopped staring at the latest tripwire and made my way to the kitchen, carefully avoiding three others. I opened the cabinet with no apparent purpose beyond moving. After a few moments of mindless searching, I turned and leaned against the counter, feeling lost.

Abruptly, every shadow in the room warped and twisted, spiraling in on the center of the room. Then, with a painful snap that left me gasping, the inky pool imploded. I blinked several times, not sure I trusted my eyes. The darkness had vanished and now Matt stood in its place looking like he'd been dragged through hell backwards.

"You're here." His voice was like music to my ears, but it couldn't override my concern.

All questions of where he'd been vanished in favor of the most prescient one. "What happened?"

"That's not important." He took two long strides and captured me with a kiss that stole my breath. I tried to put some distance between us, but he was persistent, a blinding firestorm of need.

At last, I managed to at least steal a breath. "Matt, wait. What's going on?" Aside from the obvious looking like hell, something clearly wasn't right.

"Alexi," he whispered, once again ignoring my question, and pressed me against the counter.

"Matt, look at me." When he did, one eye was perfectly blue while the other was midnight. Something was definitely not right.

He leaned forward to kiss me again, and I pulled back as much as our positions would allow. He delicately cupped my jaw and looked up at me entreatingly with his mismatched eyes. "Please, I need this. I need you." His lips ghosted over mine and, much as I knew I should, I couldn't deny him.

"Oh, Matt, I've missed you." I succumbed to his demanding kiss, sweeping my tongue past his parted lips while I tangled my fingers in his hair and wrapped an arm around his waist to pull him closer still. Maybe if I could hold him tight enough, he wouldn't slip away.

Matt moaned into my mouth. But unlike his usual moans of pleasure, it was tinged with pain. He pulled away, wincing as he dragged in a deep breath.

Before he could stop me, I reached down and pulled up his shirt to reveal his side. "What happened?" I shrieked at seeing the condition of his torso.

"I lost," he said matter of fact before snaring me with a kiss that refused to be denied.

Reflexively, I wrapped my arms around him, then caught myself. "Matt, this is wrong. I can't... I won't... I don't want to hurt you." I tried to hold him at bay, but he was having none of it and my desire to have him close again was weakening my resolve.

"I do. I want it to hurt." He leaned in and kissed me again while intentionally putting my hand on his battered ribs. The pain only seemed to spur him on harder.

"But Matt..."

"Alex, please, just give me this," he implored. I could feel myself giving into the inferno that was Matt. No mercy, no prisoners, just pure burning desire.

Against my better judgment, I caved. The feel of him against me felt like summer after an eternal winter. I grabbed his hand and started dragging him to the bedroom. His fingers laced through mine and he came willingly. I'd barely got my trousers off before he yanked me onto the bed. He must have shadowed out of his clothes, because he was already gloriously naked. The lurid bruises on his beautiful body gave me pause, then his hands were on my body, coasting, caressing, kneading. He rolled us so I was beneath him and spent a few minutes conquering my mouth and grinding against me, then stretched across the bed to grab supplies from the nightstand.

Before I could ask if he needed a minute, he'd already rolled the condom on my aching cock and slicked it up. Then he shifted so his back was to me and slowly guided my length to his hole.

I placed my hands on his hips to slow him. "Matt, wait. You need prep."

He glanced over his shoulder, both eyes now mercifully blue. "You're all I need."

The sincere statement threw me for such a loop that my grip slackened and he finished lowering himself. His breath caught repeatedly as he slowly worked me deeper. We both groaned when I was fully buried in his tight ass. Then he moved. Each roll of his hips sent arcs of pleasure up my spine until taking things slow was no longer an option. I shifted so I could wrap an arm around his torso and pressed his back flat against my chest. His needy whine urged me on as I thrust into him again and again.

The rest of the world melted away. There was no room for fear or doubt or worry. Just this impossible connection we had when we were together, our essences bleeding together, uniting us in darkness. I reached for his cock and he twisted to capture my mouth while we writhed together.

At some point, I blinked and had the distinct impression that hours had slipped past. The sun had long since set and the quiet of night blanketed the campus beyond our bubble. I quickly turned the lamp on and looked around. The room was a mess, but Matt wasn't there. Had it all been a dream? Brought on by my desperate desire to have Matt once more in my arms and in my bed? I coasted my hand over the vacant spot beside me, startled to find it warm. Maybe it *wasn't* a dream after all.

A soft thump snatched my attention to the bedroom door in time to see the man himself shadow through it. "Matt?" I asked softly, still not sure if I was actually awake or not.

"Hey, Alex," he slurred as if he was drunk, an observation emphasized by the fact that he was walking in something more like a zigzag than a straight line back towards the bed.

"What happened?" I asked again, unable to ignore the mottling of bruises decorating him from head to toe.

He looked behind him, then back at me, and giggled. "What happened where?" he asked, his gaze sliding as if he couldn't focus.

"Are you high?"

"*That* is an excellent question." He giggled again as he crawled onto the bed and nearly tumbled back off.

I barely caught him in time to prevent the painful fall. His side glowed sickeningly in the light from the lamp. It didn't seem possible that his ribs could look any worse than they had earlier, and yet they did. "Are you alright?"

"Pft, I'm fine. Though in hindsight, *that* was probably not a good idea with broken ribs." He flopped down and continued to giggle.

"You're totally high. What did you take?"

"Oh, dis and dat. There's quite an accumlation of pain kickers in der." He dissolved into laughter at his inability to speak properly.

"How did this happen? Where did you get pain meds like that? How many have you had? Where have you been?"

He rolled his eyes. "I told you, Neese is an asshole. He made me lose." His features twisted into a sullen pout.

"Neese?" Who the fuck was Neese? And why did that name sound so familiar? "How did he make you lose?"

"He's still *super* pissed about me blowing off the fight that Thursday. Totally worth it, by the way." He winked at me and laughed. "Oh, and I'm apparently on his shit list. He bet against me. Can you believe that? Don't matter no ways, he was gonna win one way or t' other."

"Did you throw the fight?" Between the slurring and general gibberish, I couldn't believe or understand most of what I was hearing.

"Haven't you been listening? I've never lost on purpose before," he mused aloud.

"Matt, you need a healer."

"No healers," he said with a surprising amount of force.

I wanted to ask why, but left it alone... for now. "Well, rest at least."

"No can do. Can't sleep with a cunssion."

"Concussion?"

"Yeah. That." He looked at me out of the corner of his eye. "Are you still mad at me? You are aren't you? I don't blame you. I'm awful. And you kissed Amber." His face twisted into a disgusted scowl. "Should've known she was trouble. Can't trust 'itches."

I had no idea who he was talking to or even what he was talking about, so I latched onto the only thing that did make sense—the concussion. "Matt, do you know where you are?"

"Hmm? Sure, I'm... Oh no you don't." He wagged a finger at me. "I'm onto you. I'm not falling for your tricks. You always try to trick me into telling you. At least you haven't asked me why yet. That's a nice change." He let out a contented sigh and settled back down.

"What?" I asked, confused.

"See, no why. Thanks for that. It was really driving me bonkers."

I didn't have the heart to tell him I thought he was already there. "We should wrap your ribs if you won't go to a healer." He glanced down at the marred skin.

"Probably a good idea. They're really starting to hurt. Maybe I should just take the last of the bottle." He made to get up, and I forced him back down.

"I'll get them. You wait here."

He visibly sagged into the rumpled sheets. "You're so good," he whispered. "The best."

"I'll be right back. *Don't* go to sleep."

"M'kay," he hummed with a dreamy smile.

I shadowed to the kitchen and grabbed some candy pieces that I hoped would convince him he was taking the last of the mysterious pills. Then I scoured his room for anything to wrap broken ribs with. I finally found a long scarf that would do well enough and returned to find his eyes closed.

"Matt, wake up!" The candies clattered to the ground as I rushed to his side.

His eyes flew open. "Wha—? This isn't..." He looked at me and I saw true understanding for the first time since he'd appeared out of nowhere in the middle of the living room. He shadowed to within feet of the door and rage incinerated my earlier concern.

"I swear, Matt, you walk out of here and don't bother coming back." He froze mid-step, and I took a step closer. "Now get your ass back over here so I can wrap those disasters you call ribs."

His shoulders slumped, and he turned to face me. I couldn't think of a time I'd seen him look more defeated. But I couldn't give in. Without a word, I walked over to where he stood and began wrapping his ribs.

"Is it too tight?" I asked quietly.

"I shouldn't be here."

"Then why are you?" I finished tying off the last piece, hoping my makeshift bandage would suffice.

"Because I—" he stalled, searching my face. I waited. I wouldn't say it for him no matter how much I wanted to. He glanced away. "I need to leave."

"Not tonight, you don't. Get back in the bed, Matt." He hesitated. "I don't care if you are stronger than me. You're in no condition to fight me on this. In the bed. Now." He continued to stand there uncertainly, so I reached forward and cupped his face. He sighed into the touch and I kissed him. It was gentle, but sincere. He made a noise that sounded like resignation and kissed me back, melting into the embrace. I brushed the hair from his face. "Please get in the bed, Matt. Let me take care of you for one night."

He looked at the bed longingly. "What about the nightmares?" he asked, sounding haunted.

I flashed to the night he'd almost suffocated us both. "You won't have any tonight." It broke my heart to see the hope in his eyes. His resistance faded and he let me help him back into the bed. "How long do you have to stay awake?"

"When did I get here? It's a little fuzzy," he admitted.

I glanced at the clock on the stand. "Several hours at least."

He nodded slowly. "I should be fine."

"Good, now lay down." He did as he was told, and I carefully curled around him. "And Matt."

"Yeah?"

"You better be here in the morning." He didn't respond, but I suspected it was because he was already asleep. I waited a while, still not one hundred percent convinced he was really here or that he still would be come dawn's first light.

CHAPTER 12

THE DREAM

M

How could I have let this happen? I must've hit my head harder than I thought. The last thing I remembered was Neese telling me to throw the fight. It hadn't made any sense, but then, not much of what happened after that did. He'd told me to make it look good and not just like me giving up. While it was true that my fights had been less than stellar of late, this seemed unusually cruel even for him. Of course, that had been the point. After that, it was a blur.

I vaguely recalled my opponent looking unassuming, but nothing beyond that. I didn't remember coming to the dorm or even how. And Alex. I remembered Alex being concerned. I should have known it wasn't a dream when he never asked me why. He always asked me why.

As I laid there trying to figure out what to do, the pain in my chest intensified. One thing was for certain: I had at least two broken ribs and several bruised. I drifted my hand over my chest, fingering the odd bandage. Even after everything I'd put him through, he'd still taken care of me. Pain stabbed through a deeper part of my chest.

"I have to admit, I'm a little surprised you're still here."

The bed shifted beneath me. How long since I'd been in this bed? Days? Weeks? I turned to see Alex staring back at me, no forgiveness in his eyes, though maybe a little concern.

"You really need a healer."

"No healers," I replied by rote, my voice strained and odd to my ears.

Alex scoffed in obvious exasperation. "That's ridiculous. You obviously need one."

"They'll find out. No healers. It's a rule." Given what I'd been through already, I wasn't exactly inclined to find out what kind of retribution I'd face if I broke that rule.

"Is this the same they that apparently want to hurt me?" Alex lifted an eyebrow.

I did a double take. Had I talked in my sleep? I didn't remember having any dreams, but these days it was hard to tell the difference between reality and nightmare. "I don't know what you are talking about."

"Yes, you do. You said something about it last night when you were high as a fucking kite. Where did you get all of those painkillers, anyway?"

I shrugged. "Around." He let out a put-upon sigh. It was past time I'd left. I shifted to get up and the pain that ripped through my side convinced me I'd never broken a rib before now. This was something I would certainly remember.

"What are you doing? You need to rest."

"I shouldn't have come here."

"Why did you?"

There it was, the inevitable "Why". But I couldn't tell him the truth, that even disoriented and blind with pain, I'd run to the only person I trusted. This was why the ward I set up every night was so important. I *wanted* to be here, to be with him, and I couldn't trust myself to stay away.

"I hope whatever secret you feel is so damn important is worth it."

I struggled not to wince at his sharp tone and took a deep breath. That turned out to be a major mistake. My ribs couldn't support that level of air.

"Matt, please," he pleaded, worry eclipsing the edge of anger.

I pushed up from the bed, ignoring the pain lancing along my side. I didn't have the energy for any of this. It had been an epic mistake coming here. It was confusing everything I'd worked so hard to fabricate.

Alex slapped the mattress. "Damn it, Matt, you aren't the only one with abandonment issues."

I rounded on him. "And what would you know about that? You had a mom who loved you and supported you. I just had a long line of strangers that wanted nothing to do with me."

"I am not some stranger!" He surged to his feet. "You have *me*. I don't know how many times I have to tell you, I'm not going anywhere. If you would just talk to me, I know we could figure this out together. But I need you to share."

"I can't." Agony squeezed my heart. "If I let you in, they'll find you. I can't lose you, Alex. I wouldn't survive it."

"And what's this then? You call this surviving? You walk around like some sort of ghost. You used to smile and laugh. Now... now, all you do is lie and run away."

"It's not my survival I'm worried about," I whispered, my shoulders crumpling. Thankfully, it was too low for him to hear, otherwise, I'm sure he would've said something. He stepped closer, and I shied away. I didn't trust myself so close to him and coherent. Every part of my tired, battered body wanted the comfort he was offering, to ease into his touch and believe, if only for a moment, that everything would be alright.

"Tell me one thing." I looked up at him as he took my hands.

"What?" The word was barely more than a whisper. We were entirely too close. Already the pure scent of him was pushing back the aches and pains. I swallowed, my eyes stinging with unshed tears. I missed him so much.

He released my hands to trail his fingers lightly along my jaw, but ensuring that I was looking directly into his emerald eyes. "Will you ever come back?"

I want to, I thought, but I couldn't bring myself to say it out loud. The smart thing would have been to say something hurtful or at least a sharp rebuke, but those died on my tongue as well. I'd already hurt him so much.

"I can see you hurting, Matt." A traitorous tear slipped out. He either didn't see it or chose not to comment. Instead, he leaned forward and placed a lingering kiss on my lips. "I love you."

The ache in my heart tripled as it broke anew. Why was he so understanding? How, after everything I'd done, could he still say that? I kissed him back, unable to stop myself, wrapping my arms around him despite how much it hurt. "Alexi," I croaked in a strained whisper, the pain of it tearing at my heart. I couldn't deny him, didn't want to. I'd spend forever with him if he let me. But this had to be done first. I couldn't rest until I knew he was safe.

"Please stay." His lips were so soft against mine and I sank into the feeling I couldn't deny. I needed him, but needing him wouldn't do anyone any good if he was dead. I pulled away.

"I have to go."

"Where?"

"You know I won't tell you that."

He sighed and rested his forehead against mine. "Then at least make sure you eat. You need to keep your strength up if you intend to heal." I nodded. "Promise me."

"I promise," I said, choking back a sob. How many times was I going to have to say goodbye to him?

"Wait here, I'll get you some fresh clothes," he said and walked out of the room.

I was gone before he could return. Saying goodbye once today was enough. I'd already dallied too long. The others would look for me and I couldn't risk them coming here.

My journey to the place I was squatting was slow going and painful. I wasn't sure if I'd be able to make it in one trip, so I'd stolen a pair of Alex's pants, though I suspected that I'd regret doing so. Having anything of Alex's was a mistake. I changed as fast as I could manage and tried to clean myself up a bit as soon as I was in the hovel I was calling a room. While I couldn't remember much of last night, I had no doubt that some serious reprisals were in store. My report was due hours ago.

At least semi-presentable, I made my way over to the main house. I wasn't surprised at all to find the usual suspects as well as a couple of additional, albeit unfamiliar, faces waiting for me.

"Where did you go after the fight?" George asked. I had a sneaking suspicion he was the one responsible for me getting my ass handed to me.

I showed my teeth, lacking the energy to pretend to be polite. "I went to lick my wounds."

"You took quite the beating," Kyle commented.

"And look at him now. Still standing," Thomas added. Asshole almost sounded impressed. "I hope you didn't spend all of your time assuaging your ego. What do you have for me?"

I looked at him through slitted eyes. "It's a little hard to gather intel when you can't see straight or walk upright."

"I suppose."

"Aw come on, Matty. You still gave him a run for it," Travis chipped in unhelpfully.

"If they'd allowed me to fight, he would've received a lot more," I said, shifting my glare to George.

"Let it go. It's all for the cause." George passed Thomas a wad of cash. "That outta take care of our... dues. Just make sure we get what we're owed." The withering look Thomas gave him was wasted. George was too busy congratulating himself.

"*You.*" I took a step toward him, anger searing through my veins at this confirmation. "You're why Neese told me to throw the fight."

"Watch yourself," George snarled. "You're no match for me healed. I'd hate to see what would happen if you forced my hand while you were in this state."

I tried unsuccessfully to temper my rage. I didn't need to be at full strength to rip this son of a bitch apart. As for the rest of the room, that was debatable. The image of Alex's concerned face flashed in my mind. If I retaliated, George would find some way to punish me. I couldn't take the risk that he'd use Alex against me. My shoulders slumped.

"That's what I thought." This was ridiculous. One of these days, I was going to teach George a lesson and enjoy every fucking second of it. "Get yourself cleaned up, little Matty. You look like shit and there's still work to be done."

I glanced over at the wall. Many of the pictures now sported X's thanks to me. But not the only one I cared about. There was still only the one red line across Alex's picture.

"What's up with you?" Kyle asked. "You look even more depressed than usual. Where'd you go yesterday, anyway? You never said."

I could have killed him right there. Curious eyes swiveled to focus on me. "I got into an argument," I said through gritted teeth.

"I bet it was this girl he doesn't want to share," came Travis' snide remark. For once, his inability to see beyond sex was playing in my favor.

"Like anyone would want to share anything with your disgusting ass."

"Shove it, Kyle. What did she say?" They looked at me expectantly.

Why did they have to be so damn nosy? "Doesn't like all the fighting. Especially when I showed up like this," I said as casually as I could, indicating my ribs.

George snickered. "You tell that bitch you can do as you damn well please."

Thomas caught the flash of anger that passed across my face. "I don't think Matthew appreciates you calling his partner a bitch. Also," he said, pulling out a vial, "you're useless to me if you can't move around. This will speed up the healing process."

I reached out to accept this unexpected gift. I'd heard of healing tonics, but didn't know where to get them. There were plenty of times something like this would've been handy. He pulled it back out of reach, and I quickly checked my snarl.

"I expect you to earn this. No more slacking." Thomas glanced at my asinine companions. "And, George, no more fight club either." I could have sighed with relief at hearing that. George, on the other hand, looked livid.

"And how am I supposed to explain his absence to Neese? The arrangement was that Matt fights."

"You could always grow a pair and step in yourself," Thomas said blankly.

My snicker popped out before I could even attempt to hold it back. Now that was a fight I would pay to see. George shot me a look, and I quickly tried to suppress it.

"I don't know what you're so damn pleased about. Neese will never let you go."

My face fell. He was right. Neese had already proven that any absences would be severely punished.

"I'll take care of Neese." Thomas returned his gaze to me. "You just make sure you stay useful."

I took the bottle of bluish liquid, unstoppered it, and downed it all in one go. Immediately, it felt like I had swallowed sparklers or maybe lightning bugs. The pain in my ribs instantly subsided. They still hurt quite a bit, but I was confident they were no longer broken, at least.

"Should be a lot easier now," I said, walking up to the remaining photos. I resisted the urge to look at Alex. "Who are we looking at next?"

"That's my boy." Thomas clapped me on the shoulder. It made my skin crawl, but I held firm.

A quick look at George showed him staring daggers at me. He was going to be a problem.

CHAPTER 13

REVELATION

A

T he book landed on the table, falling open to easily the most viewed page. I looked down at the picture of the knight leaning towards the demon and thought about Matt's picture safe in my room. His image felt truer than this one. Not to mention, now that we knew for a fact the two ended up together, the sword and full battle armor felt out of place.

I shook my head and scooted it forward to make room for the other books. At least two of them would need translating. Something must have triggered the lamp, because the light slowly came to life. I glanced up to see our book—my book—squarely within the illuminating pool. My eyes widened as I watched the image I'd dedicated to memory change right before my eyes. The demon became less shrouded in darkness and you could actually see her features now; she was smiling warmly and quite pretty. The weapons vanished entirely, and now the knight was holding his helmet instead of wearing it. I stopped breathing altogether as I took in his revealed features.

He was the spitting image of Matt, from the feathery hair and pouty mouth to the brilliant blues that practically shone on the page. But it didn't just look like Matt, it *was* Matt. I became faint as dozens of puzzle pieces clicked into place. Matthew was a derivative of Matthias. A family name passed from father to son. Matt didn't like his full name was because it *wasn't* his name. He was a Warde.

No wonder Matt was obsessed with all of this. Some part of him must have instinctively recognized that this was *his* history, not just some random family. It also explained his dueling nature: the light and the dark, forever at odds with one another.

Holy. Fucking. Hell. Matt was a Warde.

I quickly closed the book and shoved everything back into my bag. The last book was nearly in when I hesitated. I needed to find out what happened to that child. How many generations removed was Matt from this? I thought again about the picture. They could have been twins. The knight even had that same lost expression. The gray history practically flew back onto the desk as I yanked it back out, pages flipping past in a whirl until I found a time frame that applied to what I needed.

I stopped my frantic search when I saw a passage that said Matthias—our Matthias—had gone missing. What? No, that didn't make sense. Unless, of course, he ran off with Sopteală. But that didn't feel right either. Taking a deep breath to calm my racing thoughts and heart, I read line by line until I found something that made me pause. Matthias had been found nearly dead, protecting a newborn boy. They'd taken one look at the infant's eyes and known it to be Matthias' son. The family took the baby to raise as one of their own in the true Warde tradition and buried their fallen brother. No one knew who the mother was, only that the battle was nearing an end. The commander of the scouts, Sopteală, had been caught on the fringes of camp and her execution was to serve as the final blow to end the war.

A breath escaped me as if I'd been punched in the gut. We'd been looking for a child we assumed was missing and the entire time he'd been securely within the family's grasp. We'd searched for a demon baby. Yet, if he hadn't manifested, no one would have known that this seemingly mortal infant was of mixed lineage. And without a surviving parent, no one would be the wiser.

I skipped whole chunks of pages, seeking the resolution of this grizzly tale. Without the scout's organized efforts, surveillance fell apart. She'd apparently found the blueprints for how to make shadow lights and carried the secret to her grave. Generals and commanders on the demon front were captured and executed without mercy or distinction. As the leaders fell victim to the remaining unstoppable weapons, the rest of the gathered forces dissipated. Most notably, any remaining Shadow demons vanished without a trace. The Wardes immediately set to eliminating all evidence that any such battle or race had ever existed, determined that the world would never again know the fear and evil that resided in the night.

Matt was right. The histories were scrubbed. There was no way that humans could have possibly erased everything, though, not with so many supernaturals involved. Which meant Shadow demons had played an active part in disappearing themselves from history. They became myths, hiding in the night and never revealing their power. For the Warde family to stop hunting them, they had to make them believe there weren't any left.

I sat there, shocked at my revelation. Between this horrible family and my kind, we'd almost led ourselves to extinction. If it hadn't been for Vera forcing us into the limelight, then Shadow demons around the world would have continued to fade until we really were nothing more than a story in some long forgotten history.

The book fell with a sickening thud into my bag. I knew there was a reason I hated this thing—it was genocide told by the victors. I finished putting away my things, then glanced over at the stacks where Matt had said the librarian had taken him. Stealing my resolve, I made my way over. He'd said it was like the books didn't want to be found. As I got closer, my trepidation increase. I pushed against it until fear sprouted like an unruly weed.

Matt wasn't just acting out, he realized this was a mistake. Another step.

He was waiting at the dorm to tell me he'd changed his mind and was leaving. This wasn't him. It never had been.

I gasped at the very real pain in my chest. How had he done it? I was still yards away from the shelves and I didn't feel like I could go on. This spell was more than any reasonable aversion. There wasn't a doubt in my mind that I'd die before I ever reached the shelf. The school would never have put such a drastic spell in a public place. That gave me pause. If not them, then who?

I took a few steps back so I could think more clearly. The only people I could think of who wouldn't want the world to know about these wars were the demons that had lost. But that didn't make sense either. If demonkind knew what the Shadow demons had faced and what they'd done, it could have been a rallying cry. That only left the humans. Of course, what better way to eradicate your foe than to delete them from history? Including any record of your own great victory. It was insane. How was it possible that the Warde line was still around? How would they even have known that they hadn't wiped out Shadow Demons once and for all? Once again, the answer was Vera. She was simultaneously our salvation and would likely cause our ultimate demise.

Suddenly, I remembered something I'd read long ago in the Shadow Chronicles. I raced through the shelves in search of a copy, earning me several reproachful glares and numerous demands to be quiet. When I found them, I struggled to remember which volume had what I was looking for. The most I could scrounge up, however, was that it was towards the end of the Rebellion.

I skimmed volume after volume in search of my elusive answer. Surely I hadn't imagined Vera being captured and tortured. There! I almost dropped the book in my excitement. The entry was small, as if intentionally understated. A pair of brothers had held her captive for weeks and tortured her. They'd used science and magic to create something they called a Shadow light which could burn a Shadow Demon's essence.

I closed the book and slipped it into my bag with the others. Only one brother had ever been caught, despite relentless searches using every available resource. I'd bet my life that those brothers were members of the Warde family, and thanks to Vera, they'd rediscovered how to make the most dangerous weapon known to Shadow Demons. My first instinct was to ask her how she'd escaped, but first I needed to tell Matt what I'd found. This changed... everything.

My journey out of the library took me back by the entrance to the restricted section. I shuddered. How had he done it? Then it dawned on me. Matt was part Warde, and Wardes had placed the spell. It was the only explanation that made sense. The spell would have recognized one of its own. But Matt wasn't pure Warde. I swallowed hard before turning away. He'd literally almost died for me.

I was almost to the dorm when I remembered he'd still be in class, assuming he'd gone. If I waited outside of his classroom, then he couldn't avoid me without drawing too much attention. At this hour, he should be at his Advanced Spells class. He actually liked that one, so I was optimistic he'd be there. That left me thirty minutes to get there and find an inconspicuous place to wait.

Luck was with me, and there was a sort of nook with a water fountain around the corner from the door. From there, I should be able to hear when people started leaving. Now I needed to figure out how to break this life-altering news to Matt. My phone ringing sliced through my thoughts and made me shadow right out. I pulled it together and answered.

"Hi mom."

"Everything alright dear? You sound a little excited."

"Yeah... everything is fine," I side-stepped.

"Alexi Roman, do not lie to me."

"Okay, everything is not fine," I corrected, almost rolling my eyes. She had a knack for knowing when I did, even when she couldn't see me.

"Is it Matt still?" *Still...*

I sighed. "Yes, I mean, no. It's hard to say."

"I take it y'all have yet to sort things out?"

"Sorting things out would require him actually talking to me, which he isn't doing at present. And don't tell me to make the first move. That's all I've ever done." She tried to offer some condolence, but I was on a roll. "I love him so much and I still don't know if he feels the same. What if this is all my fault? What if I pushed him into something he never wanted?"

"I don't believe that, Lexi. I've seen the two of you together. Matt loves you even if he can't say it."

"But why? Why can't he tell me he loves me?" I was so absorbed in our conversation, I didn't realize I had an audience.

"Aww, are we having boyfriend problems?"

I looked up to see none other than George from class. Behind him were two of his lecherous followers. My mouth went dry. I knew for a fact that almost all of them had barely passed Intro to Shadow Magic, so there was no way they could have gotten into Advanced Spells. Which meant they were here for some other reason. Maybe they were also here for Matt. He'd been spending a lot of time with them lately.

"Mom, I'm going to have to call you back." She was still trying to ask what was wrong when I hung up. My gaze darted between the three of them. Nothing about this situation felt right... or safe.

"And he's calling his mommy for advice," one of them snickered. I wasn't sure if it was Travis or Kyle. I didn't bother trying trying to distinguish between the two.

I shifted to grab my pack and stand, keeping George in my line of sight. He altered his stance, cutting off my exit.

"Told you there was a fag in our class," George sneered.

"Yeah, but is he the one Thomas is looking for?" That was definitely Kyle. Spineless weasel.

"Does it matter? One queer is much like another," Travis chimed.

"Just think how pissed Matty is going to be when he finds out we found him first," Kyle said, high-fiving Travis behind George. Matty? Matt? *My* Matt knew about this?

"First things first. We take him to Thomas." Something that resembled a thin baton slid from George's sleeve. He flicked a switch on the handle and it sprung to life with an eerie purple light that seemed to buzz with electricity. I didn't need him to name it to know what I was looking at—he was holding a Shadow light.

I shadowed to my feet, forgetting my bag and tried to knock it out of his hand, suddenly grateful Matt had never taken it easy on me in training. The demented weapon skittered on the floor, still fully functioning. George floundered at the loss, his venomous gaze shooting to me before he lunged for the weapon. Pain blossomed on my back as if someone was searing my soul. I screamed as waves of agony forced me to my toes, then collapsed into darkness.

When I came to, they'd tied me to a chair. A look around revealed nothing more than a dark room. My lower back felt like some had beaten me with a super-heated metal pipe. I didn't see George or his crew, nor any other signs of life. No telling how long that would last. It was now or never.

I shadowed to escape the bonds and excruciating pain radiated from my wrists and ankles. My scream could have woken the dead. The agony refused to abate until I released my hold on the Shadow world. I sat there gasping for air. The pain may have relented, but the memory was still there. Fear blossomed in my chest as the gravity of my situation fully sank in.

"Good, he's finally awake. Go get Thomas." The voice could have belonged to George, but I was too out of it to investigate.

In hardly anytime at all, someone was forcing my head back. I groaned and tried to open my eyes. A light came on and I instinctively flinched.

"See, boys, it doesn't take much to teach them fear. A little more of that, and I doubt he'd ever shadow again or even crawl out of whatever abyss spawned him." That voice sounded familiar. But why? Where had I heard it before? It wasn't one of my classmates.

I tried to focus, but I didn't recognize the man who swam into focus. The one behind him, however, I did. It was the weaselly TA from the seminar that Matt didn't like. I looked back at the man in the lead. His beard was black instead of white, though it retained the severe cut, and he no longer looked to be of such indiscriminate age, now appearing decidedly mid forties. "Professor Warden?" The inquiry was barely audible.

"I told you he was a smart one, Douglas," Professor Warden said to the TA.

"But is he the one we are looking for?"

"We will find out soon enough. Carmen and Matthias were delusional to think they could hide their abomination from us. They paid for that crime with their lives. If he isn't the one we seek, I bet he knows." He picked up my bag, dumping out its contents, and I vaguely wondered how it had gotten here. Professor Warden snorted as he examined the collection of books. "This explains some of your rather impertinent questions." He picked up Volume Six. "How did you get your hands on this, I wonder? No demon should be able to go anywhere near these. Look into it, Douglas. We can't have others sticking their nose where it doesn't belong. And what do we have here?" he asked, bending down to pick up our book. I struggled uselessly against my bonds, mindful not to shadow even the tiniest bit. The book fell open to the same page it always did. "Well, I'll be. Look at this, Douglas."

"What is it, sir?" Douglas asked in a nasal voice, stepping closer.

"This is the journal of Matthias Warde himself. You know, he almost lost the war for us? I guess now we know why." He held out the picture for his comrade to see. Mercifully, without the lamp to illuminate the spell, they couldn't see the true identity of the knight. George, at least, would instantly recognize Matt.

"And only they had the power to harness light itself and burn back the darkness," I quoted to distract them from the book lest they put it together, anyway.

"Very good," Professor Warden rumbled.

"You're a Warde." It wasn't a question, it was a fact. Matt's instincts had been right about not wanting to share what we'd found. I turned to face my classmates in disbelief. "How can you be helping him? His entire family tried to wipe out all Shadow demons!"

"It's just a shame we weren't as successful as we were led to believe. As for them." The professor indicated the disgusting excuses for Shadow Demons. "They would do just about anything to ensure their place at the top of the pyramid." Naturally, the goons were busy congratulating themselves in the background.

"How stupid do you have to be? They won't let any of you live." My argument fell on deaf ears.

"Douglas, you and your... creatures find out what he knows. If he *is* the one we've been looking for, then our search is over and we can finally wipe this taint from the Warde bloodline. If not, don't kill him just yet. There's someone I want to see him before he dies." The malicious gleam in Professor Warden's eyes sent a fresh wave of fear crawling over me.

CHAPTER 14

UNWANTED GIFT

M

Over the following week, I became the epitome of a shadow following and reporting after my remaining un-cleared classmates. With the almost perfect exception of Alex, I supplied information that would make their mother's blush. My guilt grew with each check in with Thomas, as did my suspicion that there was more going on than I was being led to believe.

As upsetting as that was, though, it wasn't what had me worried. Alex hadn't tripped a single tripwire in days. At first, it was easy to assume he was studying or taking a final or shadowing through the wall, but as more time went by, those excuses fizzled away. There was only so much I could take not knowing. I began stopping by the dorm regularly, not even caring whether I bumped into him. Not that it made a difference. Even the hope that he'd simply gone home felt like an empty dream. I'd have called his mom to find out, but I didn't have her number or even a phone. Finally, I got desperate enough to go into his room.

Bracing myself, I opened the door. The smell of lavender was like a blanket on my aching heart, but it was getting faint. That wasn't good. I scoured the room for any sign of where he could have gone. Distantly, I imagined that he'd likely done much the same when I hadn't come back. I rubbed at the ache in my chest at the thought of how hurt he must have been to see his loving gift so callously disregarded. I dropped my hand. There wasn't time for guilt; I needed to figure out where he was.

When nothing immediately sprang to attention, I tore the place apart. However, despite my frantic search, no clues were forthcoming. His things were still here, even something that looked a bit like a keepsake box. He wouldn't have left that if he'd truly gone, which meant he intended to return. I'd even stumbled across my sketchbook. Because, of course, he'd found that. I paused my search to flip through the nearly full book, wishing for more pictures with his eyes open. I loved his eyes.

Stealing myself, I took out the keepsake box and inspected that as well. It wasn't likely, but there might be a hint as to his whereabouts hidden within. Inside, I found several things that tugged at memories of a more carefree time when my only concern was passing class. That certainly wasn't happening now. Smaller trinkets, like a beer bottle cap and a spoon, got set down on the bed so I could examine the drawing I'd given him what felt like a lifetime ago. The darkness reached out like a lover's touch across the page. My heart clenched as I thought about how nervous I'd been to give this to him and how excited he had been to receive it.

I sighed and set it aside, revealing the two strips of photos from our visit to the fair. Looking at our happy faces, I couldn't help but wonder when the last time I smiled was. But it was the second strip that really caught my attention. I'd had no idea he'd started a second series when he kissed me in the booth. His wonderfully ridiculous grin looked back at me, full of joy. I just barely didn't crush the delicate material as I fought back a tide of worry. Where was he?

After days with no clear sign or trail, I simply came back to the dorm full time. I had no desire to sleep in my bed and couldn't bring myself to go into his room again, so I stayed camped in between. All the keepsakes I'd found got moved to the living room, where they remained spread out across the coffee table. They felt like my only remaining connection to him. A lifeline of sorts. I was beginning to fear that I'd grow roots into the couch as I waited impatiently for him to return. After a while, I had to turn the clock off because I kept uselessly checking the time like it somehow bore any relevance to when he'd return. Assuming he ever would.

Even though I was back in the dorm and loathe to leave it, I didn't dare risk avoiding my checks-ins with Thomas. So I continued to report, although the information I was bringing arguably became less useful in clearing anyone. The only good news was that I'd heard nothing from Thomas about people being brought in. I could feel it, though. Any day now, they'd decide questioning suspects face to face would be easier than this hide and sneak game we'd been playing the last few months. I didn't relish that day.

I opened the new sketchpad to add yet another rendition of the photos I had at my disposal. All I could do was hope that Alex really was at his mom's and that all of this worrying was for nothing. As the pencil moved across the page, my mind wandered to a better place. It always did when I sketched Alex. Focusing on his pronounced cheekbones and the curve of his mouth calmed me; although getting his eyes right was a source of endless frustration. Time slipped by with nothing remarkable to measure it and the page gradually filled with more and more details.

I was adding contours to his face when there was a loud knock on the door that shook the dorm and fractured the peace I'd struggled to cultivate. I glanced at the locked door in alarm. No one came here and Alex could have gotten in with or without his key. Anxiety and adrenaline coursed side by side through my veins. Out of habit, I shadowed to hide everything on the table before getting up.

I cautiously approached the door, sharpened pencil in hand like some sort of last ditch weapon. My free hand opened and closed nervously before I finally turned the handle. I tried to brace myself for whoever or whatever could be on the other side. But when the door opened on ever-silent hinges, there was no one there. I blinked and glanced down the hall. Not a trace of anyone. The hall appeared completely deserted. Then I looked down.

"Alex!" My anguished scream ripped through me to echo down the deserted walkways.

The entire world stopped as I stared down at his still form. I could barely even make out his face amidst the matted blood. It bore no resemblance at all to the image of him not ten feet away. How had this happened? This wasn't happening. It couldn't be. I'd fallen asleep on the couch while sketching. This was just another nightmare. A really, *really* bad nightmare.

I couldn't... I couldn't breathe.

Darkness crept in on the edge of my vision. I let it. Dream or not, I couldn't take this. What was the world, my life, without Alex? The darkness inched closer. I'd finally find out what happened to Shadow demons when they got swallowed whole. I wasn't afraid. The night could take me. There was nothing without Alex.

A tiny sound like air through a small tunnel drifted up. All the darkness fell away when I realized it was coming from Alex. He was moving.

"Matt?" My name was a barely audible rasp. I crashed to the ground, too afraid to touch him. A glance down the hall showed that my outcry had drawn attention, though, and there was no telling who else may have been watching the tragic scene. I didn't care. He was still alive.

"Alex, it's okay. I'm right here. Everything is going to be fine."

He tried to move and was racked with coughs. It sounded like there were bubbles of blood coming up, but there was no way to tell amidst the already crusted fluids. That wasn't good. I needed to get him inside and cleaned up so I could see the worst of the damage.

As carefully as I could, I slipped my arms beneath him and carried him inside. I didn't even think as I carried him to his room and laid him on the bed. His breathing resembled someone scratching up and down a washboard. At least he was still breathing. I shoved down the desire to heave uncontrollably and retrieved a cloth that I dampened with warm water. As gently as I could, I cleaned his face.

One eye was almost perfectly sealed shut with bruising, making his beautiful skin a horrible mottled purple. Scratches and breaks canvased every stretch of visible skin. He winced when I touched his cheek. It looked broken. My stomach tried to heave again as I took in the sight of the unbelievable damage covering him from head to toe. No part of him had been spared. Even in my worst fight, I'd never come out looking like this.

"Matt, I..." he trailed off, unable to gather enough air and disintegrated into coughs that made his wounds bleed again.

"Please, don't talk," I sobbed. My chest spasmed, and I dropped my head to rest beside him as agony wracked my body. Against all odds, his hand fell to the side and touched mine, where I was white knuckling the now blood-stained cloth. I broke. "Alex, I'm so sorry. I should have tried harder. I should have stopped this. I can't... I can't..." My blubbering prevented me from continuing. "I don't know what to do."

"Healer."

I looked at his face, barely even believing it. Looking back at me was a sliver of green. Of course, a healer. I sprung up, ready to track one down, then stalled.

"How?"

"Phone." He tried to move his hand, but only managed a vague indication of direction. His phone was in his back pocket. There was no way I could get to it without causing him immense pain.

"This is going to hurt," I cautioned. "A lot."

"Do."

I took a deep breath and wiped my face. The quicker I was, the less I'd have to move him. He cried out when I shifted him and my heart shattered, but I didn't roll him back until I had the device. Mercifully, it was unscathed. I shadowed to the kitchen, tripping practically every sensor in the dorm. I dispelled all of them in one sweep and ripped open the drawer with all the emergency school numbers. As I dialed the Healer Station on campus, I prayed they would answer.

"Healer Services. What is your emergency?" The voice was perfectly professional, bordering on mechanical.

"He's hurt. We need someone now."

"Sir, I'm going to need you to take a deep breath. How extensive are the injuries? Where are you? Do you know what happened?"

"I don't have time for this," I snapped. "We're in Starling Hall. Room 2708. He needs help now."

"I understand your frustration, but this is information we are going to need."

I tried to take a breath and slow down. "The injuries are bad, really bad. But I can't see the extent."

"Without better information, we can't put your case as a priority. We are completely booked. All our healers are currently out at the moment on other calls. It may be quite some time before we can get anyone there."

"He doesn't have time!"

"Sir, I'm going to need you to stop shouting. That will not help the situation. Give me your information and I will add you to the list. In the meant time, do what you can to make your friend comfortable."

I gave her the address again and hung up. Help would come—eventually. I ran back to the room, taking the last of the pain pills with me, thankful I hadn't finished the bottle. "I'm going to help you sit up. Then I need you to take these."

He groaned.

"I know, but they'll help with the pain. Someone's coming to help." I couldn't bear to tell him how long he might have to endure this pain before that help arrived.

Gently, I shifted him so he wouldn't drown trying to drink the water. He bit back a cry and I saw the effort it took on his face to keep it to himself. Finally, I had him more or less propped up. The faint sound of bubbles punctuated his wheezing breaths, and there was blood on his lips again. The unfeeling machine was right. I needed to know more about the injuries, and cleaning him up would go a long way towards that. In a move I would come to regret, I peeled back the sticky mess that was his shirt. Beneath the oozing wounds were burn marks, but they didn't look like any burns I'd ever seen. It looked like some kind of acid or allergic reaction had literally disintegrated the skin, leaving it puckered.

"What... what are these?"

"Shad—shadow," his words gave out as did his breath. It looked like he was going to be sick. I shouldn't have moved him so much, I fretted. Then what he was trying to say sunk in and I knew.

"Shadow lights." It felt like the world around me imploded. He'd been beaten and tortured within an inch of his life with nothing less than a mythical super weapon. Unadulterated rage swept through me, burning away any doubt or hesitation in its path. "I'm going to kill them," I snarled. They'd pay dearly for what they'd done. When I finished, there'd be nothing left of their miserable corpses.

"Don't," he said, the word barely a whisper.

"I'll be right back." The lie came easily. An iron grip held me back when I attempted to stand up. A look down revealed Alex's hand encircling my wrist. I caught his eye and held firm. I was practically vibrating with anger. They had done this to him.

"They'll kill you." Already I could tell that his strength was waning. An inkling of doubt tried to worm its way in. Then he coughed and blood seeped from the vicious cut on his lip.

"You need to rest. A healer is on the way." His grasp slipped, and I shadowed out.

CHAPTER 15

SHADOW LIGHTS

A

My world became one long series of painful breaths. I gave up trying to see, but that could have been due more to the fact that my eye wouldn't open. My only reprieve was when I passed out, though that never lasted long. Shadow lights were truly an impressive weapon and exceptionally effective. I could see why generations of Shadow Demons had chosen to hide rather than risk facing them again. Douglas was ruthless in his pursuit of answers. But try as he might, I wouldn't let them have Matt.

My throat became raw from the screaming until it became apparent that I lacked the ability to talk at all. That's when they started tipping drops of what had to be healing tonics down my throat. Never enough to repair any actual damage, only enough so they could start again. George and his minions lost the stomach for outright torture early; however, Douglas seemed to relish in his work. He'd used the searing agony of a Shadow light against my abused flesh many times, without even asking a question. I was coming to peace with the knowledge that I'd likely die here when he inexplicably stopped. Someone cut my bindings, and I slumped forward without any support.

"You know where to leave him?"

"Yeah, we've got the just the spot. He hasn't left the dorm since his last report." That sounded like George, but who was he talking about? The question evaporated in the blinding pain that consumed me when I was picked up and the world fell once again into darkness.

It wasn't until I heard a scream that any level of awareness returned. Something about the sound struck a chord. I struggled to focus, but all I could see were fuzzy feet. Then a face came into view. Matt? Absolute devastation twisted his angelic face and though his lips were moving, the only sound I heard was my labored breathing. The world swam back out of focus again.

When I next opened my eye, I was in my room. The soft bed beneath me was a stark contrast to the pain. Something touched my face, bringing the distant aches back to the surface full force. Finally, it stopped, and I returned my focus to just trying to breathe normally. One plus to the fresh wave of agony was that it had caused one of my eyes to crack open. I was rewarded with an image of Matt. Seeing him made my heart hurt every bit as much as my body. His eyes were bloodshot, his nose was red, and I could just make out tear tracks. He was falling apart. But I needed him to pull it together. The Order of Light was real, was still active. And it was only a matter of time before they came for him. I needed to warn him, but the words didn't want to work.

"Healer," I finally croaked. The suggestion seemed to surprise him. Of course, Matt never went to healers. Now that he knew what needed to be done, there was just one problem: I was lying on his only way to reach them. No amount of care could diminish the flood of agony when he moved me. Pain defined every aspect of my being and, like so many times before, death felt a hairsbreadth away. Except this time, there weren't any healing tonics. Not even the dribbles they'd afforded me. My only consolation was that at least I was with Matt.

Abruptly, I was moving again. I gritted against the excruciating pain. As suddenly as it started, I was still once more. Then he held a glass to my lips. I reflexively refused to drink.

"I know, but they'll help with the pain. Someone's coming to help."

Tears I didn't think I had left welled in my eyes, making the already hazy image of Matt even harder to distinguish. I parted my lips as much as I could, given the swelling in my face. He pushed small somethings—pills maybe—into my mouth and I fought the urge to spit them back out. By the time my throat stopped throbbing from swallowing, I was spent.

A squelching sound had bile clawing up my throat. Unable to stop myself, I glanced down to find Matt had pulled back my blood-soaked shirt. Compared to the rest of the pain I'd endured, breaking the seal on my open wounds barely even registered. I shifted my gaze to Matt's face to find him looking as green as I felt.

"What... what are these?" The horror in his voice broke my heart, but also lent me a renewed sense of urgency.

I needed to warn him they had Shadow lights. That the Order was real. That they were coming for him. "Shad-dow," I wheezed. I watched his horrified disbelief turn to understanding, then into a fury that frightened me.

No. Matt, no. You can't. They'll kill you. You're the one they want. If you go, they'll know it's you.

He looked at me as if he hadn't gotten any of that. It was getting harder and harder to focus, to feel. As if the world and I were suddenly made entirely of cotton. It could have been the painkillers he'd forced upon me, but I suspected something far more sinister.

Before I could try again to convey my worry, Matt disappeared in a blink of shadow. I shouted in dismay at the place he'd been standing and surged forwards despite the debilitating pain. There was no way I could bring him back myself, but there was someone who could. Unfortunately, my lurch had caused the phone to tumble to the floor. I fumbled for it as best I could, ignoring how my arm didn't to want to work properly or that hot blood was seeping into the comforter. At last, my fingers closed over the tiny piece of salvation. Now she just had to answer.

The ringing sounded overly loud and harsh, but it had to be the most beautiful sound at that moment. "Hello?" a man's voice answered and all of my hope crumpled to dust. Had I really just used the last of my strength to dial the wrong number?

I struggled to get my words together and hoped against hope that I hadn't. "Vera there?"

"May I ask who is calling?" he asked absently. I didn't know how long I'd be able to talk, so I needed to make this count. Already, darkness crept along the fringes of my limited vision, reaching up to drag me back down. I longed to give in, but fought it back the best I could.

"Matt in trouble. Shadow lights. Old fraternity row. Needs help... can't... please..." I dug deep to stay conscious for a few more precious moments. "Please... don't let him die." The darkness won, and I fell into oblivion.

When I came to again, it was to the distant sound of arguing. As I gradually regained awareness, I realized they weren't far away, just lowered.

"I already told you. Gabriel didn't say anything else." The woman's exasperation was palpable and her voice was eerily familiar.

"Get a healer is pretty cryptic, even for him," an unfamiliar man responded sardonically.

I struggled to make sense of the hushed conversation. Gabriel... That rang a bell. But what did Vera's husband have to do with anything? Then it hit me—*The phone.* I shot forwards and immediately cried out as I was reminded that virtually every part of me was beaten, broken, or burned.

"Oh my god."

I cracked an eye at the declaration of disbelief. Unliked the muffled conversation earlier, the voice was crystal clear... and close. The man standing in the doorway seemed vaguely familiar, like someone I had seen a picture of. Maybe in a book? Try as I might though, I couldn't push past the throbbing in my head to place the tanned open face, hazel eyes, or sandy brown hair. However, I absolutely recognized the fiery-haired woman attempting to push past him.

"You can't come in here. Doctor/patient confidentiality," he declared, forcibly shoving Vera back.

"Dorian Valens, I know you are *not* pulling that bullshit with me. He is *my* student and I have every right to be in there." Dorian? *The* Dorian? I had no idea when Matt said a healer was coming how well he would deliver.

"Unless you're a spouse or a parent, you wait out here." He scowled, contorting his otherwise stunning features, and pointed back into the living room. "I mean it, Vera. Sit." He closed the door, then walked to the side of the bed. "Jesus Christ." A gentle touch on my forehead accompanied the whispered exclamation. Then a warmth spread through me as if I was sinking head first into a bath. "You'll need more for sure, but this is going to take a while. But first, I need you able to talk to me. Do you think you can do that?" He peered at me with intense hazel eyes and waited.

"Yes." My eyes widened with shock at how easily the word had come, and without blood bubbling up either. The rest of me still hurt like hell, but my face and throat were at least tolerable. This revelation in hand, words rushed out of me. "You have to help him. They'll kill him as soon as they know. He's walking right into a trap. Why isn't Vera with Matt? Is he here? Have you seen him?"

"Easy, easy." Dorian made soft shushing sounds and placed a hand on my shoulder that made me wince despite how feather-light the touch was. "That was only a minor healing and you overdoing it is just going to make this take even longer than it already will," he said, then did a double-take. "Wait, you're not Matt?"

I nearly shook my head, then thought better of it. "No. I'm Alex, I mean Alexi."

"If you're Alexi, then where is Matt?"

A keening sound I didn't even recognize came from my throat. "I told you on the phone. Matt went to the old fraternity row. You don't understand, they have—"

"Shadow lights," he whispered, cutting me off. He glanced quickly at the door. "And keep your voice down. Vera can*not* know. Understand?" I nodded numbly. "And you didn't talk to me," he said as he carefully removed the rags that used to be my clothes. "You talked to Gabriel. He's with Matt."

"But..."

"Don't worry. He'll keep him safe."

"What if he can't find him?" I asked, terrified that he'd never get there in time.

Dorian shook his head, as if musing to himself. "If anyone can find your missing friend, he can. And he's dealt with," he paused and glanced at the door again, "what they have before. He'll keep him safe."

I relaxed slightly; it wasn't like there was anything I could do about it now. "So, um, why are you here?"

He looked at me like that had to the most ridiculous question he'd ever been asked. "Gabriel told Vee to bring a healer to the dorm. All he told her was that Matt was in trouble. She assumed he was the one who needed a healer."

"But why you? She could have brought any healer."

"She always calls me first," he sighed before stepping into the bathroom to grab some towels and hot water. "This won't be pleasant. The last time I had to do this, it took days. To be fair, I think you might actually be in better shape. Also, I doubt you're pregnant."

I frowned at him, not really following. "You have a strange bedside manner."

"What is it with Shadow Demons and constantly criticizing my methods? I'll have you know that no one else ever complains."

"That's probably because you're attractive." He looked up sharply, and I gave a sort of shrug. "Plus, you're healing them."

He shook his head. "Back to the task at hand. We're going to focus on the more severe burns and open wounds first, then move on to breaks and bruises. I say 'we', because this is going to take from you as well. While normally I could use just my energy, your injuries a far too extensive for that and I imagine when the others return they'll need help as well. Shadow Demons always need help, bunch of troublemakers makers," he mumbled under his breath. "Anyway, that means the rest of the energy has to come from somewhere. I'm not about to let Vera in here, which leaves you." He paused and softened his voice as he met my gaze once more. "I understand you're tired and in a lot of pain, but I'm going to need you to be strong. The good news is, as bad as this is going to hurt, you're not dying anymore." I tried to ignore the casual implication that I would have died if he'd gotten here any later.

"You're still in love with her," I said as a way of distracting myself from the awful feeling of his fingers probing the wounds on my chest.

His jaw tightened, and he didn't respond.

I fought the urge to sick up as a blistering cold radiated out of a burn. Then it stopped, taking some of the pain with it. I gasped for breath. That was easier now, too. I no longer felt like I was trying to breathe underwater. "Is he going to be okay?" I panted.

He looked at me, his hazel encouraging. "If he's half a strong as Vera says he is, I'm sure he will be. But *you* should really be more concerned about yourself right now. I don't have time to clean every wound to find the worst. You'll need to guide me."

"Don't have time? I thought you said I wasn't dying anymore."

"Not actively dying doesn't mean you still couldn't. I suspect the drugs in your system, combined with the initial minor healing, are helping you to ignore the acute agony your body is in. Anyone of these wounds could turn fatal and if I don't get to the right ones in time then..."

I scanned his face and fought to get my sudden shaking under control. "They shoved a rod of Shadow light between my ribs."

"Excellent." He shifted around to address the wound. The sensation of ice being stabbed through my chest reached a blinding height and stopped. "What else?"

"There's a cut on my leg. It was really deep." It took him a few minutes to find it because he had to cut away the fabric first. A warmth much like the bath feeling from earlier emanated from the gentle touch. "Why... why is that different?" I asked, closing my eyes and forcing myself to take deep breaths.

"Hey, stay with me. You can sleep when we're done. It feels different because something mundane versus magical caused the damage. I've been told that the magical wounds are the worst." He saw my confused look as I struggled to stay awake. "I heal a bit differently." That made sense.

I continued walking him through as many of the major injuries as I could remember, my body becoming increasingly numb. The tips of my fingers tingled and needles raced up my arms. If I'd had the energy to move them and restore circulation, I would have, but exhaustion weighed me down. Then Dorian touched my broken cheek. I screamed and passed out. It wasn't until a fresh round of pain from him shaking me that I came back to. I blinked at him, but everything was fuzzy and indistinct. I was fairly sure he was scolding me. He really had a terrible bedside manner.

"S-sorry," I mumbled.

He let out a sigh that held a worry that wasn't present in his words. I got the distinct feeling that he was lying before and I was definitely still dying. There were simply too many wounds to get them all and without me being able to guide him, there was no telling if he'd gotten all the major ones. Not to mention that for every inch of skin he cleaned, fresh blood covered it. He glanced back at the door nervously. I could practically see his indecision to have Vera help. His mouth set in a grim line of determination and he turned back to me.

"I'm just going to assume that the worst has been addressed. Okay, Alexi, this last bit won't be easy. I'll do what I can to prevent too much energy coming from you—you simply don't have it to spare." He placed one hand on my forehead and the other on my now exposed knee. "I'm totally going to regret this," he muttered to himself before saying louder, "Brace yourself."

A torrent of ice and fire swept through me, relieving the last of the aches and pains. The tide ebbed. Then there was darkness.

GABRIEL

M

The moment I arrived at the house I'd been squatting in, my scream ripped into the dilapidated room. The expulsion of sound felt like someone tearing me apart from the inside out. After everything I'd done, they'd still gotten Alex. Had beaten and tortured him. And shadow lights. They were real, not some really messed up fiction. All myths have roots in reality; Alex had told me that. But the truth was so much worse than the story. Just remembering what his skin had looked like made my stomach turn.

Alex—*my* Alex—they'd done that to him and I was going to kill them for it. But I had to be smart. I couldn't just barrel in, not the least of which, because I didn't know if they were actually there at the moment. I should've known challenging George would come back to bite me in the ass. Except it hadn't been me, it had been Alex, which was so much worse.

I looked around the room, trying to focus. Ideally, I'd have snuck into the house and waited, then taken each of them out as they arrived so I could draw out their agony. However, there was one huge problem: the house was shut up tight. I'd never located any entrance besides the front door. Without stealth as a viable option, that meant they'd definitely see me coming.

I glanced around the room for something clean. It wouldn't do any good to show up covered in Alex's blood. I got as far as removing my top before my frenzied movements stalled. I stared down unblinkingly at the stained shirt in my hands, a sense of emptiness rising. How had I let this happen? He'd suffered so much and it was all my fault. I hadn't protected him. I'd promised his mom I'd keep him safe and then... then.... The shirt crumpled in my hands as I fought the urge to dissolve into a sobbing mess. I couldn't live without him.

The presence of another shadow demon tickled my senses, effectively snapping me out of my downward spiral and putting me on high alert. Out of reflex, I pulled on all the nearby shadows, prepared to rip apart whatever unfortunate soul had stumbled across my hiding place. Whoever thought that trying to sneak up on me was a good idea was going to be sorely disappointed. I couldn't help but hope it was George, though it certainly didn't feel like him. Getting a jumpstart on my retribution would be great. I tightened my grip on the darkness and settled into my customary fighter's stance.

"Easy there. I am not here to harm you. Quite the opposite."

I oriented on the deep velvety voice, but didn't see anyone. The sensation I got from the presence wasn't like any I'd ever felt before. Closest comparison I could think of was Vera, but it definitely wasn't her. Who or whatever this was, I didn't think my odds were good. I relaxed my hold on the neighboring shadows, but I didn't completely drop my guard. Just because I didn't feel confident that I'd win, didn't mean I wouldn't fight to my last breath. I owed Alex that much, at the very least.

"Who are you?" I demanded. A long, lean figure stepped from the darkness, slowly solidifying from shadow to physical. I did a double take. His dark hair and complexion reminded me of Alex, though he was decidedly older. I took an involuntary step backward as I registered the waves of raw power emanating off of him. He noted my reaction and quirked an eyebrow the same way Alex did when he thought I was doing something strange.

"Interesting that you don't know. After all, you called me." He meandered around the room, taking in its shabby state with a disinterested expression. "At least you know you are outmatched, though I suspect that wouldn't stop you from fighting if you thought I would prevent you from reuniting with your lover."

I narrowed my eyes. The only people I'd called had been the campus healers, and this guy was no healer. "Alex," I said, realization sinking in, then the rest of his casual statement sank in. He nodded in agreement. "We're not lovers," I added belatedly, though the defense sounded hollow even to my ears.

"Aren't you?" His slow, purposeful movements were making me nervous. They reminded me of a snake waiting to strike. The fluid motion was reminiscent of the way Alex moved, except significantly more sinister.

"He's my best friend."

"Does he know that? Because he is absolutely in love with you." The mysterious demon's gaze flicked to me. "He's the one who told me where to find you, by the way. Even made me promise not to let you die." He ran a finger along some dilapidated shelving, then flicked away the dust. "Says something that he never asked for help for himself, despite his obvious condition. That being said, you seem exceptionally determined to seek vengeance for someone you only deem a friend—best or otherwise. What *is* your plan exactly?" he finished, catching me with startlingly gray eyes.

I resisted the urge to shrink from his penetrative stare, squaring my shoulders. "What's it to you? Who the hell even are you?" For all I knew, he was one of Thomas' creatures.

He released a long, exasperated sigh. "I swear, they don't even pretend to teach proper history anymore. Of all the Shadow Demons in the world, I end up dealing with the two most insufferably stubborn, blindly ignorant, anger-ruled..." He stopped himself and took a deep breath. "I am Gabriel Xiander."

I stared blankly at him. The name sounded vaguely familiar, but nothing more.

"And that means nothing to you." He sighed again. "I am Vera's husband. Alex called her a short while ago. Thankfully, *I* answered. He didn't sound in good shape. I can't imagine he had very long left, and that was before he used so much energy to make that call. I suspect it is far less now."

I blanched. "Wha- What do you mean?"

"Honestly, he sounded like he was moments from death. You didn't know?" That eyebrow again.

The room tipped and swayed alarmingly. I was going to be sick. Alex wasn't fine. I'd been deluding myself. He was *dying, and* I'd left him all alone. I hadn't even told him...

"Does he know you love him?" Gabriel asked, as if reading my mind.

I looked up at him amidst the tilting room.

"What?" he inquired passively.

"I'm not..." I began.

He scoffed and rolled his eyes. "Why today's generation is so preoccupied with sexual orientation, I'll never understand. When you live long enough, it is a trivial matter. Everyone tries everything. Judging by your expression, I'm going to assume that you haven't told him. That's a shame. I'm sure he would have liked to know. I would have." He sounded so calm, so matter of fact, about something that I hadn't even been able to admit to myself.

I clutched my chest, struggling to breathe. "He's going to die, and I never told him, not once. I just... I just..." I gasped for air, darkness creeping in on the edges of my vision. Alex was going to die all alone, not knowing that I loved him with everything that I was. That I'd do anything to see him smile. That he was my whole world. That he was the reason I knew what happiness felt like. I had to get back. I couldn't let him die without knowing.

Except... it was too late. In my blind rage, I'd left him in immense pain with the vague promise of a healer that would never arrive in time. He was probably already dead. Alex was gone, and I'd never hear his laugh or teasing comments again. He'd never hold my hand under the table while we studied. Wouldn't kiss me so deep I felt it in my soul. All of it... gone. Without him, I was nothing. There was only the void opening up beneath me. An immense chasm ready to swallow me whole. Unshed tears stung my eyes as the gaping emptiness within me yawned wider. It wasn't worth fighting. What had fighting ever gotten me?

"Shit." The hissed explicative barely registered. Then hands were gripping my arms tight as if they could somehow save me from falling into the abyss. But what was the point? There was no escaping the darkness.

"I have to go. I can't..."

The firm grip forced me back a pace. "You need to take a deep breath and focus. He won't die."

I glanced back at Gabriel, barely registering his sincere, albeit concerned, expression. He really reminded me of Alex. The world steadied ever so slightly.

"I know what I said, but I told Vera to get a healer there as soon as possible. She won't dawdle, and she'll bring the best one she knows. For the record," he added, releasing me as the darkness finally retreated to where it belonged, "that was a major sacrifice on my part. Not that you care. Your... friend will be fine. Now, back to the task at hand. I can't allow a fresh cache of shadow lights to exist, not when I know where they are for a change. I've spent too long chasing these people to give up this opportunity."

"What are you saying?" The last thing he'd said that had made any sense was that Vera was bringing a healer. Alex wouldn't have to wait.

"What I'm saying is that we are already here. We might as well finish what you planned. Which was what again?" The condescension was hard to miss.

"I...I don't really have a plan. Yet," I added quickly, to which he rolled his eyes. "The use the last house on the row as a base of operations, but I don't know if anyone is there yet."

Gabriel scowled, his dark brows snapping together. "Why haven't you shadowed inside already?"

"Wards are everywhere. The main entrance is the only open way in, and even that alerts Thomas when someone arrives." He nodded, receiving the information without comment. "They know me though, so it won't be unusual if I walk in unannounced."

"That sounds like the makings of a plan that would make Vera proud." He grinned and shook his head. Something told me that wasn't a compliment. "The two of you are alarmingly similar. No wonder she likes you." That was news to me. Last I'd checked, I was nothing more than an irritating thorn in her side. "Let me make sure I have this correct. The entirety of your plan is to walk through the front gate and see what happens."

I shrugged. Sounded about right to me.

He laughed. "This should be interesting. From what I can tell, there are already a handful of other Shadow demons that have already passed this way."

My rage returned two-fold as an image of George breaking Alex's cheek came to mind. It was possible it could have been one of the others, but my gut told me it was definitely him.

"Easy," Gabriel admonished. "I take it those are likely the people who will face the brunt of your wrath. In that case, there is no need to wait any longer. Finish changing and we'll go."

At his command, I realized I was still standing there half-dressed, clutching the bloody shirt. I tossed it aside and picked up a clean one. "Pretty sure the spell on the front gate is Shadow Demon specific. If you walk in, he'll know I'm not alone."

"It's no matter." He waved a dismissive hand. "You will go in the front as expected and I will find another way in." I was about to ask how expected to do that when he once again responded to the unasked question. "There isn't much that can keep me out." Well, that was vaguely ominous. "Lead the way. I'll follow at a distance and see you inside." He slipped back into the shadows, leaving me to make my way out to the main street, where I then proceeded on foot.

I hesitated at the door. Leaving Alex had been a mistake. My heart constricted. If he died before I told him how much I loved him, I'd never forgive myself. Of course, I doubted I'd live much longer myself. I was walking blindly into a hornets' nest with little more than the distant expectation of unknown backup. If Gabriel didn't find a way in, I was fucked.

A noise from within the rundown house and anger seared through me. They were going to pay for what they'd done. I took a fateful step forward, hyperaware of the spell that would alert Thomas to my arrival. Step by step, I worked my way through the ruined building until I reached the cavern of the main room. A sense of anticipation seemed to fill the room, making the hairs on the back of my neck stand on end. I glanced around, noting the presence of too many people in the gloomy space. My anxiety spiked. When had so many joined Thomas' ranks? None of the additions were other Shadow Demons, either. The suspicion that had started weeks ago intensified. There was a lot more going on here than George's homophobia.

"Hey, Matty, you made it!"

I nearly shadowed out at Kyle's sudden speech. *Focus, this is no time to be caught off guard.* Per usual, where there was Kyle, there was Travis.

"Did you hear? We totally caught him." I could have punched Travis in his stupid, excited face. He caught the anger that flashed across my own. "No need to be bitter, just because you missed it."

I walked past him silently, barely restraining myself from throttling him right there. Striking out now would ruin everything, and I didn't know how long Gabriel would need to get inside. So I did what I could to reign in my mounting fury. Already that seemed like an impossible task as I caught sight of my true target. My feet carried me the rest of the way across the absurdly open space to where George stood on the far side. Kyle and Travis were by no means innocent, and they would certainly get what was coming to them, but George was the instigator.

"Where's Thomas?" I asked, barely keeping the sharpness from my voice.

"What's your deal, Matty?" Kyle asked, flanking me.

"Yeah, just because you didn't find him first. Though how, I don't even know. He was right under your nose the entire time." Travis was a special kind of stupid. I kept my focus on George and suppressed a growl.

"Yeah, Matty," George sneered, narrowing his eyes. "Did you like your present? We left it special, just for you." Travis and Kyle laughed like it was the best joke ever while my fists clenched by my side. "How long did you know he was the one we were looking for?" The cage on my temper thinned. "Were you hiding him this whole time?" he asked, like I'd committed a heinous breach of trust.

"I want to talk to Thomas," I insisted.

George glanced over his shoulder at someone I didn't recognize. "Tom did say he wanted to know when Matty finally got here. Go get him."

At last, the presence of extra people made sense—this was a trap. They'd been expecting me. I glanced around warily, taking stock. They wouldn't let me walk out of here in one piece. Hopefully, Gabriel was halfway decent in a fight.

"You should have heard him scream," George said, recapturing my attention. "He was a lot stronger than I would have expected from a fagot." His lip curled and the thin reign on my temper completely snapped.

"That *fagot* is my boyfriend and I'm going to fucking destroy you." The words fell with the effect of an atomic bomb, ricocheting off of the distant walls and coming back as shrapnel.

Surprised fury dominated George's face while Kyle and Travis shared a confused look. I advanced, ready to knock George's head clean off his shoulders, when the sensation of something dangerous buzzed into my awareness. I looked in his hand to see a thin baton crackling with purple energy. All I saw was black.

Without thinking, I used shadow to lift Kyle and Travis, who were advancing behind me, and slung them clear across the room. There was a loud crack as they smashed into the flaking plaster. George growled and took a step toward me, weapon in hand. I'd waited a long time for this moment. Every horrible thing I'd endured because of him—every hateful statement, how he'd kept me from Alex, how he'd left him dying at my door like some demented calling card—all of it fueled my arm as I hauled back and slammed my fist into his face. He didn't have a prayer of getting that flimsy weapon up in time to stop the assault. An immense satisfaction washed through me at feeling bones crush beneath the impact.

Unfortunately, my victory was short-lived. A searing pain the likes of which I'd never experienced in any of my countless fights spread across my back. I shouted and spun around to find that Kyle and Travis had both recovered and were wielding their own batons. The eerie purple light leapt and danced while it burned into my flesh. My teeth ground together as I fought back the shout. Someone tossed what felt like a rope around me and pulled it tight, unleashing a wave of unbelievable pain.

I attempted to Shadow away, and the agony increased tenfold. The instant I released the Shadow world, the pain subsided. Right, so shadowing was off the table. That was fine by me. I'd fought plenty of fights without it. Ignoring the burning on my hands, I tore the flimsy binding off and tossed it at Travis and Kyle. They squealed in terror as the remains fell on them. Their desperate attempts to avoid the painful material only resulted in them getting more tangled. That was perfect; I needed time to deal with the rush of people coming at me from the edges of the room.

In the gloom, it was difficult to get an accurate picture of just how many bodies were hurtling toward me. Not that it mattered. One or a million, none of them were innocent and none would be spared. Chaos and pain swirled around me, fueled by my anger and grief. I barely even saw faces as I dispatched each one. Yet for each body I sent flying away, another was already there to take its place. I leveraged the Shadow World as much as possible, but with the presence of so many shadow lights, that was increasingly difficult. Even without being physically touched by the weapons, the mere glow on my skin was like being brushed with acid.

I fought through the onslaught, but the tide was never ending. Abruptly, I realized I wasn't fighting on my own. Somewhere in the melee, Gabriel had joined me and was dispatching opponents with equal indiscrimination. A gap opened in the flood and I caught sight of George making a break for it. I barreled through two nameless faces and slammed into his back.

"Not so fast, you son of a bitch." I smashed his face ruthlessly into the ground. "You're going to suffer like he suffered." I could hardly distinguish the red painting the ground amidst the black clouding my vision.

"Tell me, Matty," he laughed through bloody lips. "Did you wait for him to die before coming here or just abandon him?"

I growled and twisted his arm.

He laughed again. "When did you realize no healer was ever going to come?" My grip loosened slightly, and he took advantage of the hesitation. Somehow, he'd kept his hold on his Shadow light and it burned ruthlessly into my stomach. "That's right, Matty. We made sure no healer would answer your call. You fucking queer. You condemned him to die miserable and alone. Just so you know, I enjoyed shoving this in him." He pressed the light harder until it broke the skin.

I gasped at the horrible feeling of my insides bubbling. If he pushed any harder, the other end would push through the other side. The thought of him doing something similar to Alex sent me over the edge. I roared and reached down, taking hold of the unforgiving light. The urge to be violently ill rose as I pulled it out. I grimaced through the pain, and at last, the light was free.

George's eyes widened as he fought and lost to keep the light where it was.

"I'm going to end you, you night-forsaken, miserable waste of life." Terror filled his eyes when I snatched the baton from him and raised it overhead, ready to plunge it into his chest.

"Matty... Matt... please. Don't. I'm begging you."

I snarled at his desperate pleas for mercy. There would be none. I braced myself to drive the flimsy weapon down with enough force to pin him to the ground permanently. A hand rested on my shoulder, not restraining, just firm.

"Matt, stop. You don't want to do this." At the sound of Gabriel's voice, I realized the din in the room had subsided. Besides the muffled groans of agony, there wasn't a single sound beyond my own harsh breathing and George's whimpering.

"He... he... Alex is dead, and it's *his* fault!" My entire body shook with the effort of remaining steady. "He deserves to suffer for what he's done. Let's how you like it, *Georgey.*" With every ounce of strength I had left in me, I drove down.

Gabriel's grip on my shoulder tightened, halting my progress. "He wouldn't want you to do this."

A sob wracked my body. "He was all alone and now he'll never know. They blocked all the healers. I'll never get to tell him." My grip on the evil baton was failing. George watched the wavering shadow light with wide eyes while the world crumbled around me.

"He's not dead, Matt, not yet. There is still time."

Was it true? Was there still a chance? I stared down at George, my desire to destroy him warring with my need to see Alex. Alex won. Alex would always win.

"Let's go," I said, flinging the baton as far as I could.

CHAPTER 17

THREE WORDS

A

"I don't understand. Why did they take you in the first place? How is Matt involved in all of this? I swear that boy," Vera added, rubbing her temples.

I didn't really have answers for her. After Dorian's warning, I was afraid to say too much, but she needed to know Matt was definitely still in danger. The moment he arrived, the Order would have known he was the one they were seeking all along. Exhaustion weighed heavily on me, but I refused to rest for even a minute until I knew Matt was back safe and sound. Except with each second that passed, that seemed less and less likely.

I shot Dorian an anxious look, which he noted. He gave a barely perceptible nod. At least he understood I had to tell her something. "They're looking for someone, but they don't seem to know who exactly. They asked a lot of questions."

She raised an eyebrow. "Asked?"

"Demanded," I corrected myself. Memories of the agonizing burn tried to resurface. I closed my eyes against the phantom pains and pushed them as deep into the dark recesses of my mind as I could. There was no time to fall apart. Not when Matt was still in danger. "I'm pretty sure it's actually Matt. I didn't tell them anything, though." Nothing they could have done would have gotten me to give them him. However, that hadn't stopped them from trying.

I absently rubbed the spot on my chest where a Shadow light had forced its way between my ribs. According to Dorian, it had barely missed my heart. He said it was lucky; I suspected it was skill. Douglas had known exactly what he was doing every step of the way. He'd never have "accidentally" killed me.

I noticed Dorian watching me and snatched my hand down. He wasn't pleased at all about my refusal to rest. Vera, however, had no qualms in pursuing her inquiries while I was awake. Not that I blamed her for being confused. Thanks to Dorian, she was only getting half the story.

"Why do you think they're looking for Matt, of all people? How did he even get involved?" She threw her hands up in exasperation. How Matt got involved in the first place was something I, too, very much wanted to know.

"I think he thought he was protecting me." That much I'd been able to cobble together from his slipped comments over the last few horrible months. "As for why, I believe he's the one they are actually after—he fits the bill."

"What do you mean?" she prodded.

I gave Dorian another nervous look. Just how much was I not supposed to say? At this rate, she'd never know why Matt was in so much danger. *They'll never let him leave that house.* I smashed the dire thought down with a violence that surprised me. I couldn't think like that, not if I wanted to keep standing. The hope that he was alright was the only thing that had gotten me through the healing process at all. I took a moment to pull myself back together and attempted to answer her. "Well, they had certain criteria that needed to be met and.... I found something."

"You're being awful vague, Roman. Out with it." Vera put her hands on her hips, her eyes burning into me.

I swallowed anxiously. Did Gabriel get there in time? Did he ever even find him? There'd been no word from either of them. Yet, Vera didn't seem worried—at least, not about that. I took a deep breath and chose my words carefully. "They're looking for a missing member of their family." This subterfuge was giving me undo stress. I just wanted to know if Matt was okay and I doubted that all of this questioning was good for me after my ordeal—healed or not.

"That doesn't answer anything." Damn woman was persistent.

"Matt's a Warde," I blurted in complete disregard to Dorian's very pointed glare. Vera stared blankly back.

"I know he's a ward—he's my ward—but that doesn't explain why you were harmed or why he's in trouble."

I stood there, dumbfounded. She didn't know. All my caution not to say too much and she didn't even know who the Wardes were. Did she know anything? Surely, she of all people would know the truth. "Have you ever heard of the War on Darkness?" I asked tentatively.

"No. Should I have?"

At that moment, the door to the dorm flung open with enough force to hit the wall. I immediately stood up and nearly fell right back down from the head rush.

Matt walked in with the same the purpose he did everything. He looked a little worse for wear, but he was alive and walking. I'd never seen anything more beautiful.

"You need healing."

"I'll be fine," he argued with the voice behind him.

"I didn't say you wouldn't be," the deep voice countered.

"I need to talk to Alex." His gaze finally fell on me standing there. He froze in place, his eyes going wide as they swept up and down me in what could only be disbelief. I tried not to think about what I probably looked like the last time he'd seen me.

I gave him a small wave, inexplicably self-conscious. "Hey, Matt."

The moment he stopped, Dorian stepped forward to proceed with the aforementioned healing while who I assumed must be Gabriel followed Matt into the room. The two words seemed to snap him out of whatever trance he'd fallen into. He surged forward at the same time Dorian reached out to stake hold of him. "Let go of me. I need to talk to Alex."

"You can talk to him in a minute. We need to see to your injuries first."

"I can wait. This can't," Matt insisted, struggling to free himself from Dorian's grasp.

"Why do Shadow Demons always have to be so damn difficult?" He shot Vera an accusatory look. Though whether it was because she too was a troublesome Shadow Demon or because she wasn't helping him restrain Matt was anyone's guess.

"I need to talk to Alex," he repeated, continuing to fight Dorian, who was proving very unsuccessful at keeping him still.

"Then talk to him," he replied, sounding irritated.

"In private." It looked like he was going to resort to actually hitting Dorian if the healer didn't release him soon.

"I strongly suggest you let him," Gabriel offered, sounding bored. Vera looked from him to Matt and then to me. Dorian simply threw up his hands in total exasperation.

"Fine, have it your way. I get called out here in the dead of night and then no one will let me do my job. What about you?" He gestured to Gabriel.

He held up a polite hand. "I think I'll pass."

"Of course," Dorian grumbled, though he didn't seem surprised. I was so absorbed in the scene that I didn't even realize Matt had finally liberated himself.

"I'm going, I'm going." I laughed as he practically dragged me into my room, then closed the door. I could hardly dare to believe it—he was okay and his usual pushy self. "What did you want to talk to me about?" I asked, turning to face him.

"It's impossible. There's not a scratch on you," he said, not answering the question while he commenced what amounted to a full pat down. "I was so worried. I never should have left. They said such horrible things and I... I... " he trailed off. Meanwhile, his hands continued to rove gently over my body, presumably in search of the aforementioned scratches.

As much as I was enjoying hearing how much he cared, he really needed healing. "What did you want to talk to me about?"

His response was to snare me with a kiss, once again avoiding the question. After days of torture and then hours of wondering if he would come back alive, I gave in completely. I knew he had to be hurt and had no idea how severe those wounds might be, but his lips worked just fine. As suddenly as he caught me, he let go, returning to his ceaseless inspection. "Its incredible," he mused softly as his fingers brushed gently across my face.

"If kissing me was what you wanted to tell me, I really don't think the others would have minded."

Confusion flashed across his face. "What? No. I don't care if they see me kiss you." That was certainly news to me.

"Then what is it? You need healing." I brushed a smudge of something on his face and tried to ignore the fact that it was probably blood. My fallen angel looked like he'd walked through hell itself. He stared back at me as if searching for something. Surprisingly, there didn't seem to be a hint of doubt or trepidation in his clear blue eyes. I was about to prompt him again when he spoke.

"I love you." The world went completely still. "Alex, I'm *in* love with you. I'm so sorry about everything. I should have told you how I felt every single day. Leaving was the dumbest thing I've ever done. What if I hadn't gotten back in time?"

The tide of words flowed over me and seemed my heart had finally given out. I was pretty sure I hadn't blinked or drawn a breath since he'd uttered those three fateful words. He opened his mouth to keep talking, and I stole the next words with a kiss. Awareness returned in an explosion of feeling. I cupped his face and kissed him harder, desperate for an outlet for the emotion threatening to overwhelm me. Matt loved me. It didn't matter what I'd been through to get to this moment, that was all I needed.

He let out a sigh and melted into me. Raised voices in the other room threatened our beautiful bubble, but he didn't pay it any mind and neither did I. Matt placed his hand over mine and kissed me deeper. We were absolutely falling, and the best part was that we were finally doing it together. I wanted this perfect moment to last forever.

"I will not sit here and just twiddle my thumbs! Certainly not while someone is still in need of healing. No, I've had it with you Shadow Demons and your weird demands! Oh."

At the exclamation of surprise, I cracked an eye to find Dorian standing in the doorway, turning an interesting shade of red. Beyond him, Vera was hiding a laugh behind her hand and Gabriel looked like he was trying very, *very* hard not to say "I told you so". Reluctantly, I pulled back and found Matt's stunning eyes looking back at me with such openness I thought my heart would burst.

Dorian cleared his throat awkwardly. "I, um... I can come back."

"It's okay, Dr. Valens. Matt will sit still now," I said, without taking my eyes from Matt. Dorian gave a nod and retreated to the other room. A hint of curiosity touched Matt's unblinking gaze.

"Valens, like Dorian Valens?" he asked in a whisper. I nodded. "When Gabriel said that Vera would get the best healer she knew, I had no idea it would actually be *the* best healer. Wow. And I was so rude," he added, looking a little ashamed.

I rubbed a thumb across his cheek. I loved him so much. Him and his quirky mannerisms and strange sense of right and wrong. "And now it's your turn to get healed. I'm ready to have *my* Matt back."

His small smile touched his eyes. If he kept looking at me like that, he wasn't going to get any healing at all. Despite his assertion that he didn't care if they saw us kissing, I fully suspected he might have an issue with them being in the other room while I performed my own thorough inspection.

I smiled and turned him around. He allowed me to steer him back towards the living room, where he sat on a chair in the middle of the room. His eyes never left me, going so far as to crane his neck around when he was facing the wrong direction. He didn't even glance up when Dorian placed his hands on his shoulders, presumably to do an examination like he'd done on me. I watched, fascinated, as the minor scrapes and bruises disappeared from Matt's skin as if being erased.

"What on earth?" Dorian exclaimed. "What the hell have you been doing? You feel as if you've been in a fight nonstop for months. It's a wonder you can walk at all." He gave Vera yet another accusatory glare.

"Don't look at me like that. Tonight's the first I've heard of any trouble. Albeit, Matt has a history. Maybe that's what you're sensing?" she offered hopefully.

He shook his head. "No, all of this is more recent. Come on, I'll need to get a better look at what you've done to yourself." Dorian nudged him back towards my room. When Matt stood, I knew he had no intention of walking in there.

"It's fine. You can look here," he said as he removed his abused shirt.

Simultaneously Dorian, Gabriel, and I all shouted for him to stop. But it was too late. Matt stood there with his shirt in his hands, looking confused. The entire upper half of his body was a canvas of abuse, the shadow burns eerily clear in the yellow light.

"What?" he inquired innocently.

It was like someone sucked all the air out of the room. The moment Vera's eyes lit on the horrific marks, it felt like all the shadows began collapsing. It was as if there was a black hole in the middle of the room and she was the epicenter. The pull on my essence was so strong it was a wonder I was still standing. Everyone's eyes went dark save Dorian's, who looked appropriately alarmed. The sensation of the Shadow world being torn in two made me want to vomit. The violence of it was overwhelming. I was completely powerless to fight against what was happening.

My knees crashed into the ground, and Matt stepped towards me. It was like he was moving in slow motion or more likely, fighting a pull he had no chance of resisting. I looked at him, feeling helpless, and saw my fear reflected back. The room was quickly becoming darker than midnight and the pull was only getting stronger. Whatever she was doing, she had complete control over both of us.

Gabriel stepped towards Vera and wrapped his hands around her arms. She didn't seem aware of him at all, her eyes still riveted on the burns. "Vera, my love, you have to stop."

I'd have screamed if I thought I could. As it was, I felt captive, held in place, waiting to do the bidding of a far more superior demon. This was something for stories, not something that could actually happen in reality. Our essence forced into a shadow state, possibly never to return to a physical form. I focused on Matt, who didn't appear to be faring any better. He'd finally come back to me and now I was going to lose him forever.

Without warning, the pull and the darkness both disappeared. I fell forwards. Matt's own momentum from trying to reach me brought him close enough in time to prevent me from face planting. I gasped for air and kept my head down, too afraid to look at Vera. Matt's arms encircled me and I held onto him for dear life. One of us was shaking, maybe both.

"I... I'm sorry," Vera said hesitantly after several tense moments while she leaned into Gabriel's comforting embrace.

"I didn't know," Matt whispered shakily in my ear. I wanted to console him, but was struggling myself to come to terms with what had just happened. How was that even possible? I was beginning to think that the horror stories regarding her escapades were grossly understated.

"Right. Now that the cat is out of the bag, let's get a look at you." Dorian was the picture of professionalism, though he still sounded shaken.

"Go," I told Matt as he helped me to my feet. The world spun as if it was untethered. I took a steadying breath. "You still need healing." Even saying that much was difficult.

Matt looked back at me, his eyes clouded with concern. For a moment, I thought I'd have to march him back to the chair myself. Then, thankfully, he did as I asked. Dorian shook his head and quietly began examining his patient again. As I'd said he would, Matt sat perfectly still while Dorian began to heal, first one wound and then another.

While he still didn't have as many burns as I'd had, he had enough, not the least of which was where it looked like one had nearly to skewered him. Once again, I envied Matt his exceptional control. He didn't cry out or fidget, he barely even flinched. The whole time he kept his eyes locked on me like he was afraid that if he blinked, I'd disappear. I didn't think I'd ever be able to bear telling him how close that had actually been.

"You're strong, kid, but I'm going to need a lot more energy to take care of some of the older wounds."

"Leave them," Matt responded, clearly unconcerned.

Over my dead body, I thought, then immediately reconsidered my choice of words. "What do you need?" I asked, remembering how he'd said he could take energy from someone else.

"Absolutely not. You don't have a speck of energy to spare after what you've been through. Neither do I." Fear flitted across Matt's face as Dorian confirmed his suspicion that he almost hadn't made it in time.

"This is ridiculous, Dorian. You don't have to ask, just..." Vera said as she stepped towards the pair.

"Take mine," Gabriel said, cutting her off and capturing everyone's attention. Even Matt blinked. Vera looked at her husband like she couldn't believe what she was hearing. Then the light of understanding blossomed in her eyes and she stepped back.

"Are you sure?" Dorian asked, gazing at Gabriel with no small amount of trepidation. Gabriel gave him a level look. Dorian shook his head again, like he wasn't sure how he got himself into such predicaments to which I could whole-heartedly relate. "Fine, but I don't want to hear anything about you getting healed by proxy."

Gabriel nodded and placed a hand on Dorian's shoulder, then turned to Matt. "You might want to brace yourself."

This time when Dorian placed his hands on Matt, Matt gasped, his eyes going wide. I couldn't help but relive the acute sensation of being shoved under a bitterly cold waterfall with no apparent hope of relief insight. Matt arched back, the force of the intense healing literally lifting him from his seat. Then Dorian released him and he fell back. He swayed in the chair and tilted forwards.

I raced to catch him, but Gabriel beat me to it. I caught his brown eyes, and he gently released Matt into my care. He sagged into me, his breathing shallow. Carefully, I shifted my hold to ensure he wouldn't fall off of his perch. True to form, he'd passed out. No sooner did I realize he was out cold, then his eyes blinked open. Panic shimmered in his blue eyes as he scanned the immediate area, vanishing when his troubled gaze settled on me.

"We should let them be for the night," Gabriel said.

"But..." Vera started.

"Fine by me. The lot of you are insane," Dorian said at almost the same time.

"You can talk to them again later," Gabriel reassured Vera, who in turn pouted. It was impressive to see someone handling her for a change. "For now, I think they have earned the right to a peaceful night. They need to rest."

"That at least I can agree with," Dorian said, turning to face us. "Be sure to eat something substantial to restore your strength," he said, then promptly exited the room. Man really did have the *worst* bedside manner.

CHAPTER 18

FORGIVENESS

M

After some vague statement about reconvening later to debrief, Alex and I were finally alone. And I didn't know what to say. He'd almost died, and it was *my* fault. If I closed my eyes, I could still see his broken body bleeding on the bedspread. I watched Alex move restlessly about the room, putting it back in order. Not that it was a mess to start, but that didn't deter him. He'd also probably been the one to change his bloodied sheets after being healed. He silently ventured back over to where his backpack was sitting on a table. I couldn't recall how it had gotten there or even if he'd had it when I found him in the hall. The horrific image of his busted cheek and blood frothing at his lips flashed through my mind. My fault. It was all my fault. I curled inward on myself with a whimper.

Alex's head whipped around from whatever he was scrutinizing in his backpack. "Matt? Are you okay?" He stepped toward me and I nearly fell in my rush to vacate the chair. "Did Dorian miss something? I'm sure he can't have gone far. I'll call Vera," he said, already reaching for his phone on the coffee table.

"Don't do that," I said, the words thick in my throat.

His eyebrows snapped together as he looked up from the device. "Do what? Call Vera?"

I squeezed my eyes shut and shook my head, but none of it could erase the way he'd wheezed my name or the sharp metallic smell of his blood sinking into the carpet.

"Matt," he said again, softer, his bare feet making a light whisk on the floor as he continued to move closer. I took another step away, my hands tightening by my side. "Do what, Matt?"

My eyes flew open and the burn of tears I'd been fighting stung as they filled my vision. "Try to take care of me," I said with an anguished cry.

Alex stopped walking and stared at me in shock. "What... I don't—"

"No, *I* don't," I cut him off. "I don't deserve your compassion or even your love. Don't you see? I'm a *monster*, Alex. And I almost got you killed."

"Matt. Love," he said gently, resuming his approach.

I side-stepped him. "No. You don't know the things I've done. I may not have physically hurt any of the others, but it wasn't like I didn't know what they were in for. What could happen." I sobbed, no longer able to delude myself into believing that they'd been okay. "I might as well have done all of that to you myself." My hand shook as I pressed the heel of my palm into my face to scrub away the tears that kept falling. Suddenly, Alex was in front of me, holding both my wrists.

"None of that. Whatever you got wrapped up in was *not* your fault. Those people's actions are *not* yours. They used you, manipulated you."

I tugged to get free, but he wasn't letting up. "But they didn't. *I* got George to introduce me. *I* walked in of my own free will. *I...* I reported on our classmates," I finished in a whisper. "It was all me. I was so afraid of losing you I... I would have done anything, Alex. *Anything.*"

He released my wrists, which fell limp and defeated to my sides in order to cup my face. His thumbs brushed lightly across my cheeks as he wiped away the latest tide of tears. "That doesn't make you a monster, Matt. *None* of that makes you a monster."

"But—"

"But nothing," he snapped, his emerald eyes flashing. "You are *not* a monster. Say it."

I stared into his eyes, eyes that had captured me the first time I'd seen them, though I hadn't realized it at the time, and tried to see what he did. But I couldn't. I'd done unforgivable things all because I'd been a coward.

"Matt," Alex sighed and rested his forehead against mine a moment before leaning back. "Say it. Say 'I'm not a monster'."

I didn't think it was possible to shed more tears, yet more spilled free.

"Say it, my love."

"I'm not a monster," I croaked, my voice weak.

He brushed the hair back from my face with such delicacy that it nearly broke me. "That's right, you're not."

I squeezed my eyes shut once more. What right did I have to this tenderness? I should be consoling him, not the other way around. But after what I'd done—ghosting him for months, lying, breaking up, leaving him to die alone—I didn't even deserve to touch him, let alone talk to him. "I'm so sorry," I whispered.

"Shh, shh, we're safe now. I'm safe. You're safe. And we're going to get through this... together." He paused, running his hands over my hair. "Speaking of which, I need to tell you something." His serious tone cut to the quick of my insecurities. We might be safe now, but it wouldn't stay that way. Thomas was still out there and after the stunt I'd pulled, I was walking with a target on my back. With any luck, they assumed Alex *had* died and wouldn't come for him.

I stepped back and looked him over for the hundredth time, still unable to accept that every single injury was gone. Sure, I'd endured the same intense healing, but my wounds had been nothing compared to his. "Are you okay?" I cupped his formerly injured cheek, now blemish free, then ran my hands gently over his shoulders and arms.

"Yes, Matt, I'm okay. In fact, I think Dorian might have even healed some of my childhood scars. That healer does *not* fool around. Terrible bedside manner, though," he added with a chuckle that was a balm to my bleeding heart.

My lips twitched with an echoing grin. "No kidding. Pretty sure he's not our biggest fans."

"To be fair, I don't think it's *us* personally."

"Oh?" I responded absently while I continued to run my hands over him. A large part of me still wasn't convinced any of this was real. Odds were higher that I'd gotten cracked pretty hard at the old frat house and this was a fever dream fueled by delusional hope.

"Yeah, definitely more about demons always getting into trouble or some such." He grabbed one of my hands and I glanced up. "I really need to tell you something."

While I heard the words, all I could see was the way his mouth formed them. Not an hour ago, I'd believed I'd lost him forever. Now, he was standing in front of me, warm, safe, *alive*, and all I wanted to do was get lost in him. I pulled him into an embrace, tightening my arms around him. He hesitated a second, then wrapped his arms just as tightly around me. I sagged into his chest, burrowing my face into his neck, where I could inhale his wonderful lavender scent. When was the last time I had just held him? It felt like something inside me was breaking, or maybe it was already broken and trying to reform. "I thought I'd never see you again," I said, squeezing him tighter.

"Hey, it's okay. I'm fine. You can't get rid of me that easily."

I'd never heard anything more beautiful or tragic. I pulled back and kissed him. His return was equally soft as he stroked my cheek with the backs of his knuckles. "I don't expect you to forgive me," I whispered, sadness weighing on my heart.

"Matt, look at me."

I lifted my head to meet his stunning gaze.

"There is nothing to forgive. You did what you thought was right. I can't fault you for that. Now that morning you left after you promised not to.... that's a different story." His lips quirked into a smile.

The band around my chest tightened. I didn't deserve this tenderness, not after what he'd been through because of me. How could anyone be so forgiving, least of all him? The memory of the shadow lights searing my flesh was still just as fresh as if it was happening now and his... his had been so much worse, and none of it would have ever happened if it hadn't been for me. "Alex, I don't know how I can make this better. There's no way to undo the awful things I've done, the people that suffered because of me. You, you suffered because of me. I'm so sorry," I finished, looking down. I couldn't bear to meet his gaze, to see that gentle understanding peering back at me.

"Matt, you have to stop apologizing." Even his voice was gentle. Guilt sat heavy on my chest, steadily gaining weight.

"But..."

"I mean it, Matt. Stop." The whispered command silenced me. His fingers were gentle yet firm as he moved my chin up to look at him. My heart stuttered. How was it possible to care so much about one person?

"How can you still say that after everything? After what they did to you? After what I did? The way you looked at me..."

I could still see with perfect clarity the expression of abject horror as I shadowed away, leaving him to die alone.

He frowned, but didn't release his hold. "What are you talking about? What look?"

I took a shaky breath. "When I returned to the house after seeing... after seeing..." I squeezed my eyes shut, it was too much.

Alex's warm laugh washed over my face. "Matt, my love, shade of my heart," he punctuated each endearment with a soft kiss on my lips, my cheeks, my nose. "I wasn't afraid *of* you. I was afraid *for* you. You were so furious. I was terrified that you'd leave on a reckless suicide mission and I'd never see you again." He ran his fingers lightly through my hair and gave me a small smile.

I blinked, taken aback. He wasn't wrong: it had absolutely been a suicide mission. "Oh."

"Good. Now that we've gotten that out of the way, I need to talk to you about something." He glanced toward his discarded bag.

I nodded and caught him in a kiss. As much as it didn't make sense to me, he'd forgiven me. What was more, he didn't believe I needed forgiveness.

He pulled away slightly. "I really need to tell you something."

I loved him so much. I claimed his mouth with another kiss, letting my feelings for him fuel it. More than anything, I just wanted to drown in him. That, and never let him out of my sight again.

"I'm serious," he persisted.

"Uh huh," I replied noncommittally, snaring him again. I needed him, and I wouldn't deny that longing anymore.

"It's important," he said breathlessly.

"Tell me later."

"But Matt..." His words got lost in a deeper kiss. He let out a moan and the last of my doubts disappeared. All wasn't lost. We still had each other.

"Later. Right now, all I want to do is make love to you. I almost lost you, Alex," I added for emphasis, slipping my hands beneath his shirt.

"Matt," he gasped when I pulled him tight against me. I missed touching him and couldn't seem to decide where to start. All of him. All of him seemed like a good place to start. "I don't really think this can wait," he stubbornly insisted.

"I want to be surrounded by you, Alex," I whispered, running my hands down the length of him. He arched into me and groaned, effectively contradicting his insistence that he needed to tell me something first.

Without preamble, I shadowed us both to his room, where the smell of lavender and *home* immediately enveloped me. Shadowing us had the expected result. The control Alex tried so hard to have completely dissipated and he unleashed all the demanding passion I craved. His kiss was harsh and filled with a need that rivaled my own. I helped him pull his shirt over his head as he rid us both of what remained of our clothing. I trailed my fingers down the beautiful, unmarked canvas of his chest. For a moment, visions of shadow burns blazing across it overrode reality. Delicately, I traced the line that one of the worst had taken.

"Matt, don't." He took my hand and brought it to his mouth, where he brushed a light kiss on my palm. I stared back at him, feeling so lost. "It's okay, I'm right here. Everything is going to be fine."

My breath caught. He'd heard me. When I'd thought he was all but gone, he'd heard me.

He used my captive hand to pull me back in close, and I went. I needed him on levels that defied reason. There was no me without him. The next kiss held its own burn, sweeping through me with all the fierceness of a firestorm. There had always been an undeniable heat between us and for the first time, I wasn't afraid of it.

"I'm so sorry," I managed between kisses.

"Stop. Apologizing," he growled, then snared me with a kiss that sent heat curling all the way to my toes. It was all-consuming and seemed to claim my very essence. The force of his ardor propelled us until my back hit the wall. I gasped at the cold contrast and his mouth closed over mine again. He hoisted me up to straddle him, and I groaned as his fingers dug into my hips. I was never going to let go of him again. He abandoned my mouth to work his way along my neck and collar, each touch a brand declaring me his. "I love you." The low, heated words sent a shudder through me.

"Alexi," I moaned, tangling my hands in his hair. I arched into him, desperate for more. I'd missed this so much, missed *him*. He shifted, and I realized he was reaching for the nightstand. With a cheeky grin, I let my eyes go black and reached into the Shadow World. "Looking for this?" I asked, holding up the bottle of lube.

"You." He smashed his mouth back onto mine as he took the bottle. I twined my arms around his neck, adjusting our angle to give him better access to where I wanted him most. His finger brushed my rim and electricity raced up my spine. He pressed inside and my head dropped back with a loud moan. I rocked into each thrust of his fingers, unabashedly giving into my desire for him.

"Now, Alex. Please," I panted.

"Need a condom," he panted right back, his mouth barely leaving mine long enough to form the words.

"Fuck the condoms. I want *you*. And I'm pretty sure that whatever Dorian did took care of any and every ailment we could have had."

He laughed as he snatched another kiss. "Fair. I was going to suggest we get tested soon, anyway."

"Yeah?" I asked, squirming with impatience now that his fingers were gone.

"Yeah. I'm tired of there being anything between us." He stopped kissing me and stared deep into mine as if he was seeing my soul and not the blue looking back at him.

"Me too," I whispered, momentarily forgetting about my clenching ass and the need coiled around the base of my spine. "I love you."

Something feral entered his eyes as he shifted his grip and lifted me. "You're mine," he growled and then sank into me in one thrust.

"Alexi!" I cried, throwing my head back. I dug my fingers into the back of his shoulders, giving over wholly to the mind-blowing sensation of having him inside. He was right, I was his, always had been.

He pressed me into the wall as he continued to thrust, magically hitting that perfect spot again and again until my brain was more liquid than solid. I stole what sloppy kisses I could while he alternated between nipping and sucking on my lips, neck, shoulders. I squeezed around him and the feel of him bare was pure fucking ecstasy. Every move brought fresh sensation that conquered me, body and soul. Eventually, he gave up the wall and walked us over to the bed where he still didn't slow. I was completely his and reveled in every touch, caress, and kiss.

When we were somewhere near satiated, we simply lay there staring at each other. His green eyes seemed so peaceful as they looked back at me. For once, I felt content; a feeling

I'd been waiting on for a very long time. Alex was my friend, my lover, my everything. I couldn't imagine life without him, and I hoped I'd never have to again.

I traced the contours of his back while he continued to watch me. Visions of the horrible burns kept trying to reassert themselves. Between each blink there was the brown of dried blood mixed with the bright crimson of fresh bleeding. I shuddered. There was no way to unsee the gruesome damage caused by the shadow lights, no matter how perfect his skin looked now.

"What are you thinking?" he asked quietly.

"I don't think I'll ever be able to forget the way your breathing sounded." I could almost hear it now, the way each bubble had brought a fresh paint of blood and that night awful rattling. My stomach twisted.

He snaked out a hand to cover my free one. "You can't keep blaming yourself." Yes, I could. "Matt, I mean it. You aren't the one who did any of that." He was wrong. None of it would have happened if I'd protected him better.

I trailed my fingers down his back and along the perfect curve of his ass. Then a new horrible thought occurred to me. What if they'd done more than just torture him? I couldn't even formulate the heinous thought as my hand stalled. "They didn't... they didn't..." I swallowed, pretty sure I was going to be sick. I couldn't bring myself to say it out loud. It had been a mistake to spare their lives. One I was fully prepared to rectify.

He blinked back at me, then seemed to realize what I was trying and failing to ask. "No, they didn't. Lots of other things, but not that." I looked into his perfectly green eyes. They seemed haunted by the memory of what had happened in that place. "Did you kill them?" he asked.

"No," I said, doubt creeping in. What if Gabriel had been wrong?

His face relaxed. "Good. I don't want something like that following you around for the rest of your life." Suddenly, I had a new doubt. Would he lie to make sure I didn't?

"Would you tell me the truth? If they... they..." I closed my eyes against the awfulness.

He paused a moment, as if weighing his answer. "Yes. There's no reason to lie to you, Matt, no matter the consequences. I'd tell you everything they did to me if I thought it would make you feel better, but I don't think it will."

I stared back down at him, not sure if I could trust this. Did I want to know? "Who broke your cheek?" The question simply popped out. I was pretty sure I already knew the answer, but I needed him to confirm it.

"George. He is definitely homophobic."

I flinched. I was right. He definitely should have suffered more. If Gabriel hadn't stopped me, then he would have. What else had he done to my beautiful Alex?

He looked pensive for a moment, then continued on without encouragement. "They found me while I was talking on the phone with my mom. I was actually waiting for you outside of your advanced spells class." I blinked. He'd been so close. "Unsurprisingly, I was talking to her about you. She wanted to know if we'd worked things out yet."

Guilt stabbed through me. He never would have been there at all if it wasn't for me.

He gave my hand a gentle squeeze and went on. "I'm pretty sure they missed that though, otherwise I doubt they would have just taken me. Thanks to you never taking it easy on me in training, I was able to knock George's weapon out of his hand before he could use it. Lot of good that did me." I gave him a curious look, and he answered the unspoken question.

"I didn't expect his lackeys to have their own as well. They are the ones that burned my back first. I'd never felt anything like that. I'm a little embarrassed to admit I passed out. Maybe if I hadn't, I could have fought them off long enough for your class to get out. At any rate, when I came to, I was bound by shadow lights to a chair."

The thought of what he must have endured to learn that was sickening.

He sighed and continued. "Travis and Kyle lost the stomach for it almost immediately. George didn't hold out much longer. When Douglas started stabbing me with the shadow lights, he gave up as well. For all his bluster, he really is a coward."

"He said you begged for your life," I said, recalling his goading from earlier in the night.

Alex snorted. "He didn't stick around long enough to know what I did or didn't do."

I glanced down at him, seriously doubting he'd begged. Despite his self-deprecating statement of being weak, he was far from it. Alex really was the strongest person I'd ever known, certainly stronger than me. "I love you." The words seemed to find their own way out of my mouth. They were no less true now than they'd been the first time I'd said them. His face almost immediately broke into a stunning smile, and I raised an eyebrow. "Are you going to grin like an idiot every time I tell you that?"

"Probably," he said, rolling onto his back and effectively trapping my arm. Then he pulled me down for a kiss. Undeniable heat and desire curled through me. There really was no way to get enough of him. Already I could feel the fire flaring to life inside of me. "I love you too, Matt."

I sank into him, letting the kiss get deeper, and used my trapped hand to pull him in close.

Suddenly, he pulled back. "Wait. Are you going to be here in the morning?"

"Yes," I replied with a laugh, kissing his collar.

"What about the next day?"

"Yes."

"And the day after that?"

"Yes," I said, trying to hold my laughter. He opened his mouth, no doubt to add another day, and I cut him off. "I'll be here every day. I'm yours as long as you'll have me."

He scanned my face. "Are you sure? Forever is a long time." There was no suppressing the smile that dominated my face. My heart felt like it was flying.

"Not long enough," I replied, pulling him back to me.

CHAPTER 19

LEGACY

A

The next couple of days slipped uneventfully by and Matt hadn't let me out of his sight for more than a couple of minutes. It was wonderful. After waiting for him to come back to me for so long, having him be his old self again felt more like a dream than reality. Every morning that I woke up to him curled beside me, I had to pinch myself to prove I wasn't still asleep. Aside from the random times when he would look at me and I could tell he was actually seeing the wounds, things were wonderfully normal. I didn't know how to help him with that besides giving him time. Then there was him telling me he loved me. Every time he said it, I felt giddy. Shamelessly, I'd been counting how many times he actually said the words and I was running out of things to count on. It was incredible, like telling me had opened up a whole new side of him, like all of his reservations and hang-ups disappeared over night.

But our perfect bubble couldn't last. Selfishly, I refrained from telling him about what I'd discovered before I was taken. We deserved this feeling of happiness and I wanted it to enjoy it as long as possible. But I also knew it was wrong to keep this from him. Once again, I glanced over at my bag and considered showing him the picture. Surely the magic of the spectacles would be strong enough to see through the spell.

"What's this?" he asked, interrupting my internal struggle.

I turned to find him holding up a piece of paper he'd presumably picked up off of the table. "I don't know. It's not mine." I knew for a fact nothing had been on the table before. "What's it say?" I asked, joining him. His arm slipped absently around my waist as I leaned over to examine the page. It looked like a handwritten note, except it was in some other language.

"Grab the glasses," he said, giving me a light squeeze before letting me go.

"Bossy. Why don't you grab the glasses?" I fired back.

He laughed under his breath and kissed my shoulder. "Because I don't know where they are."

"Oh. Right." I stepped over to the bag and rifled through until I found them. When I straightened, I was holding both the spectacles and the memoir. Apparently, not telling him was really weighing on my conscience. He took the glasses and immediately put them on, briefly derailing my brain with how incredibly hot he looked in those. Then I remembered the book. I swallowed. "Hey, Matt, I still need to talk to you about something."

"It will have to wait. We've been summoned."

This was it. I was officially out of time to come up with a better way to break this to him. My heart fell. I'd hoped for a little more time, but time was not on our side. "It really can't," I said, trying not to sound like it was terrible news. He looked up at me over the glasses with a curious expression. For a moment, I forgot to breathe altogether. I didn't care what his lineage was. He was still Matt, and he was mine.

"Okay, Alex. What is it?" he asked quietly, taking the book like he knew it had something to do with it.

"I found something. Look at the picture," I said awkwardly.

He chuckled, "Alex, I can sketch this picture in my sleep. I don't know what you expect me to see that I haven't already. We've literally looked at this image at least a thousand times."

"Not with the glasses we haven't." That piqued his interest, and he opened the book. Suddenly, I didn't want him to see it, didn't want him to know. Something told me he wouldn't take the news well at all, and I couldn't bear the thought of him shrinking away again. "Wait," I said, obscuring the image.

"Alex, come on." The smile on his face suggested he thought this was a game, and it about broke my heart. I couldn't bear to lose him, not again. "What's wrong?" he asked, his face clouding over.

I stepped forward and kissed him. Once more, his hand snaked around my waist and he pulled me in tight, deepening the kiss. I easily slipped into the ever-present desire.

"We really don't have time for this," he said, his voice low as he returned several smaller kisses. Despite the statement, he didn't much sound like he cared, letting the heat build unchecked with each brush of his lips against mine. As much as I now didn't want to tell him, that didn't change that he had a right to know. Not talking to each other is what had led to this whole mess in the first place.

"I need you to know that I love you no matter what," I said with another kiss.

"I love you too," he replied, caressing my face.

My heart fluttered, and I felt sick. His eyes were so blue it hurt. "No matter what," I emphasized. There was merriment dancing in the crystal like he thought I was being silly. It would have to be enough.

"Alright, let's see what all the fuss is about."

I stepped away to give him more space.

He repositioned the glasses and looked down at the fateful page.

I held my breath while I waited. What was taking so long? Maybe the glasses weren't strong enough. This was a mistake. There had to be a better way to tell him.

Then his eyes went wide, and he looked up sharply. "What is this?" he asked with a distinct edge, as if *I* was somehow responsible for altering the image.

"That is a picture of Matthias Warde and his lover in 1218 BCE," I said as matter-of-fact as I could.

He shook his head. "This can't be right."

"Matt, what did you think George and the others were looking for?" I asked, suddenly curious and not sure why I hadn't asked sooner.

He immediately turned pink, then cleared his throat and looked down. "George led me to believe they were looking for someone pretending to be someone else. And he's... you know. I just assumed..."

I thought back to what George had said when he found me. "You thought they were looking for a gay kid in class." His blush deepened. "You do realize that would include you," I said with a smile. He finally looked back up at me.

"What? No. I'm not—"

"Maybe not gay, but also not entirely straight." I simply raised an eyebrow when he opened his mouth, no doubt to continue arguing, and his blush returned two-fold.

He cleared his throat awkwardly. "I hadn't... I didn't... . You're different."

"You think Gabriel is attractive, don't you?" I asked, taking a stab in the dark. He looked like he was going to swallow his tongue. I laughed. "At least you're consistent. We can go over the myriad of sexualities another time, but the point stands."

"He's still not you," he grumbled. "Anyway, back to what you were supposed to be telling me."

I rolled my eyes. When Matt didn't want to talk about something, he *really* didn't want to talk about something. But that was a concern for another day. Right now, we had bigger issues to tackle. "They were looking for the same thing we were. Except where we were looking for a story, they were looking for an actual person." He frowned, his face the picture of confusion, and I pointed back to the picture. "They are looking for you, Matt. You don't like your name because it *isn't* your real name. You are the legacy of Matthias Warde."

He stared blankly at the page. Unfortunately, his silence wasn't giving me any clues how he was taking this.

"You're a Warde, Matt. The Order of Light is real."

He stood there frozen in silence for a solid, tense minute, then dropped the book on the table like it had burned him. It landed with an exceptionally loud thud that seemed to echo through the room. "No, I'm not. I don't know what I am, but I'm not that. I'm not one of *them*." The loathing with which he said it tore at my heart. I reached out and pulled him close. He melted into the embrace and clung to me as if he was afraid that if he let go, he'd simply drift away. "They lost any claim to me when they abandoned me," he mumbled into my shoulder.

I hugged him tighter. "None of this changes who you are or how much I love you. Now you just know more about where you come from."

He snorted. "A line of bigots and assholes. Awesome. To think this whole time.... I *knew* something was off about Thomas."

"That reminds me. I'm surprised you didn't recognize him."

"What do you mean?" he asked.

"Thomas is Professor Warden. He must have been using a spell to make himself look older than he was, but it's definitely the same guy." His eyes brightened with realization, then darkened with sorrow. He leaned forward and rested his head on my shoulder. I rubbed the back of his neck, grateful that he was finally willing to let me comfort him.

"I'm so sorry, Alex. I was so blinded by my need to keep you safe I never even... I should have seen it. Can you ever forgive me?"

"I already told you, there's nothing to forgive." I placed a kiss on the top of his head.

After another moment, he let out a sigh and straightened up. "We really should get going. They'll be waiting for us." He looked at the book on the table. "We should probably bring all of this, too. They'll need to know the whole story, if they don't already."

"I think you're right," I said, picking it up to add it to my bag with the others. Vera, at the very least, didn't have a clue about any of it. I paused, considering the book, and smiled.

"What?" he asked, folding the missive and putting it in a pocket. The glasses he tucked into his shirt.

"I was just thinking about how I've basically been in love with you for the better part of my life." He gave me a quizzical look, and I waved the book for emphasis. His smile was small, but still shone in his eyes. Perhaps some part of me had seen past the spell and that was why I'd reacted to Matt the way I had the first time I saw him. I'd just *known*. He studied me a moment longer, then swiped a quick kiss and out we went.

It felt strange to be out in the real world. So much had happened in such a short amount of time. I was grateful for remembering to grab a jacket as the frigid air hit me. The holidays would be over soon and the smattering of people still around would grow until the place looked overrun. The day was beautiful with the sun glistening in a perfectly blue sky, which only added to how surreal everything felt. Odd how the world kept turning even when yours was falling apart.

"Hey," Matt said in greeting to someone. I looked up to see Sam and Lucas adjusting their course to meet us.

"You guys stuck here for the holidays, too?" Lucas asked.

"Yeah," Matt replied.

"Totally boring, right?" Sam said as he stopped beside his friend. "You look in better spirits," he added.

"Something happen?" Lucas asked.

"You could say that," Matt replied with a smile.

"Like what?" Sam asked, sounding genuinely curious.

Matt laughed, sounding wonderfully carefree and relaxed, then held out his hand to me. I looked down at the extended appendage not sure what he expected me to do with it. I searched his face for a clue and he quirked an eyebrow. Hesitantly, I took the proffered hand. This broke all of the rules. *His* rules. His fingers tightened around mine and he pulled me in close, where he stole a kiss. That broke even more of them.

I leaned back, shocked. "What are you doing?" I hissed under my breath.

"I won't ever let anything stop me from loving you again," he whispered and placed his lips against mine once more. I nervously returned the kiss, convinced this had to be a dream. He released me in time to see Lucas smack Sam.

"Told you so. Hand it over."

Sam rolled his eyes and took out a twenty. "I knew it was weird. You're not that good with girls and *never* take one home," he huffed, passing it to Lucas. Matt simply chuckled and released me. I caught the barest hint of a blush before he ducked his head.

Lucas admired his prize a moment, then asked, "You guys up for pool later?" Sam brightened.

"That sounds like fun. I've been helping Alex with his form, so it should be more interesting." Matt slid an arm around my waist. It was borderline possessive, and I was still struggling to believe that any of this was actually happening.

They groaned in unison at this news. "Great, but you're buying your own drinks," Sam said.

"What do you say?" Matt asked, turning to me.

I blinked, and he stared back, patiently waiting. In fact, they were all staring at me, like what was happening was perfectly normal and didn't go against everything I'd been led to believe over the last semester. At last I found my voice. "Yeah, I'd love to."

"Then it's settled. We'll see you guys later. What..." Lucas looked at Sam.

"Tomorrow?" Sam finished for him, looking back at us.

Matt nodded, and we went our separate ways. My head was spinning, and the day had barely started.

CHAPTER 20

THE MANOR

M

We made our way through Mysterio College to Vera's office. The note had said to take the portal. Considering how cagey Vera could be, I doubted that it'd just be sitting around for us to walk through. Thankfully, the door to her office was unlocked, so there was one hurdle we didn't have to jump. However, a glance around did not immediately reveal the promised mode of transport. I let out a sigh and began searching along with Alex, who'd remained stoically silent for the better part of the journey here.

I suspected his silence and the looks he kept giving me, that he clearly didn't think I'd noticed, had something to do with what had happened with Sam and Lucas. While I was a little surprised that they'd placed bets on whether Alex and I were together, it really wasn't a big deal. I didn't care, and neither did they. Did Alex?

"Are you alright?" I asked after checking beneath Vera's desk, which, in retrospect, was a little dumb. Who would put a portal there?

He glanced up from his search of the wall with a calendar as if he'd been caught writing naughty things on it. "What? Yeah, of course."

I sighed and walked around to sit on the edge of the desk closest to where he was doing a shit job of pretending to be okay. I hooked a finger in his belt loop, gave a sharp tug, and he stumbled into my waiting hands, letting out an "oof" as I caught him. "I won't apologize for loving you. Nor will I hide it. Not anymore," I said earnestly before he could speak. Despite my words, he remained stiff and uncertain. I shook him by the hips. "Talk to me."

"There's nothing really to talk about. I... It's just adjusting to a new set of rules, that's all."

"What do you mean?"

He let out a huff that I wasn't sure what to make of and crossed his arms over his chest. "Matt, you made it very clear from the beginning that I wasn't allowed to touch you outside of the dorm. Out here," he gestured to the general space, "we were strictly friends."

Guilt lanced through my heart. Had I really done that? "I'm sorry. I never meant to make you feel that way." He shrugged and looked away. "Hey, that's my thing," I said, tugging on him again so he lost his balance and fell against me. His lips molded with mine and I barely checked myself from sliding right into the fire. "It won't happen again," I assured him.

He kissed me deeper. "You could always make it up to me."

I groaned as his fingers dug into my thigh, positive my eyes were solid black. "I want you," I whispered against his eager lips.

"I know," he responded huskily and rubbed against me. My breath caught as he worked his way down my neck. Night I loved this, loved him and the way he made me feel. I'd gladly be his play thing forever. Just one thing was getting in the way: we were supposed to be somewhere else. As if reading my mind, he whispered, "This really isn't the best place for this." I mumbled some sort of agreement as he snared my mouth again. He pressed into me and I arched back, loving the feel of him against my body and letting out a moan as his hand left my thigh to grab my ass and pull me closer. "Or time," he said, his breathing ragged.

"Except," I said, still struggling for air, "we can't find the damn portal. It has to be here somewhere, but I can't sense a thing." Despite his declaration that this was neither the time nor the place for our... extracurriculars, he was already kissing along my neck. Definite lack of conviction in stopping. I was half a heartbeat away from sliding my hands beneath his shirt and suggesting he lock the door, when I felt him chuckle along the sensitive skin. I shivered at the delectable sensation. "What's so funny?"

"You mean I know how to do something you don't?" Laughter danced in his eyes as he leaned back to look at me.

"You usually do," I grumbled. He gave a half shrug, not disputing it. I was seriously contemplating bringing him back by wrapping my legs around him, then he spoke again, and I could have groaned in frustration. He did this on purpose. Insufferable tease.

"Think about it. If *you* had to place a portal that you didn't want anyone to find, where would you put it? How would you keep it hidden?"

"That's easy. I'd put it behind the door and cloak it."

He raised an eyebrow. "Did you check behind the door?"

"Yes," I replied, with no small measure of attitude. It really wasn't very nice to leave someone hanging. "But there's nothing there." He chuckled again, and cold air rushed between us as he added more distance. Damn it.

"Think outside the box. How do you think I found all your trip wires and squirrel holes?"

Squirrel holes? I stared back at him, waiting for him to answer his own rhetorical question.

He rolled his eyes. "If the portal is cloaked, then you can't feel anything." I nodded. We'd covered this before. "Anything at all." I frowned, but it did absolutely nothing to temper his enthusiasm. He swiped a kiss, then stepped toward the door. "It creates a void, Matt. That's how you find something cloaked."

I thought about that for a moment and focused on feeling the shadows around where I'd have hidden a passage. Nothing. Alex waited with an expectant smirk. I pushed harder and discovered a very distinct absence. There was only one spot that the shadows didn't behave normally, almost as if they just stopped existing altogether. My eyes went wide. "You're a fucking genius," I pronounced, hopping off of the table.

"I am pretty good," he said humbly.

I shook my head and reached up to feel the space where the portal must be. There was still something off. Then it hit me. "There's a barrier spell."

"Can you break it?"

I gave him a look.

"Of course you can."

"But I'm not going to—you are."

He gave me an incredulous look. "Matt, we are already unbelievably late."

And we'd have been even later if I'd gotten my way. "They'll wait. Now come here. Take your time and look for a part of the spell that feels like it's coming off. We don't want to break it, just... loosen it. Once we are through, we'll need to tie it back. Can't very well have someone wandering through by accident." He gave me a look that said I'd officially lost it. "You're wasting time," I prompted.

He huffed, but moved closer to inspect the barrier. Abruptly, he spun back to me and grabbed my hips, pulling me flush against him. Maybe he wasn't going to be such a tease today after all, I hoped, as his hand slid into my back pocket. As suddenly as he'd grabbed me, he let go.

I stumbled and wasn't able to stop my sound of disappointment. "What the hell?"

He held up the folded note with a smug grin, and I scowled. "You could have just asked."

"Where's the fun in that?" he countered with a maniacal grin. He was going to be nothing but an endless source of frustration. I just knew it.

"So what are you thinking, then?" I asked, trying to rein in my denied hormones.

"You and Vera are both very crafty. I doubt she would have told us to come to a locked door without giving us a key to open it." He unfolded the note and held it up to where we assumed the portal was. It still felt like a safe bet, although I didn't sense any change. I shrugged and his mouth tugged down into a frown. He looked back at me. "Put on the glasses." I sighed and did as he asked. For a second he just stared at me, then seemed to shake off whatever had distracted him. "Here," he said, pointing to a word that didn't seem to fit the rest, "What does it say?"

"All it says is 'into darkness'. Doesn't make much sense with the rest of it, though."

"Huh. Maybe it doesn't need to be translated. *In tenebras*," he said with damn near perfect pronunciation.

Immediately, I felt a shift. "It's opening," I said in disbelief.

"And you wanted to do things the hard way," he said, passing me back the paper. He took a step forward and half of him disappeared. "Are you coming? I doubt it will stay open for long."

I hastened to follow and felt his hand close around mine as I stepped into a world of pure darkness. For all the times I'd ventured into the Shadow world, this felt infinitely deeper, making the office we'd just been standing in feel like a distant reality. "Now what?" My words barely traveled at all, like we were standing in a vacuum instead of another layer of the world. I felt more than saw Alex gesture to the ground where there were faint illuminations that resembled footsteps.

Without another word, we followed them. Out of reflex, I sent my essence out to explore this strange place in which we had found ourselves and could sense Alex doing much the same beside me. Turned out, the door we'd come through was one of many. Some had similar barriers that made the world look and feel extra muted from this side, while others felt like they would simply dump you out. We were heading for such a one now. As we crossed the invisible threshold, bright light from all sides greeted us.

"I told you they'd figure it out," said a familiar woman's voice.

"And you were right," a man replied.

I blinked to bring the world back into focus. It was entirely too bright.

"So, which one of you figured it out?" At last I could make out an excited-looking Vera and an exceptionally bored look-ing Gabriel.

"Matt knew where the portal was, but he wanted to crack the spell. I assumed you gave us the key," Alex said beside me.

I glanced around, taking in shelves upon shelves of books. We were in the library? Why not just say: hey, go to the library?

"Well done, Alexi," Vera said, walking forward. Gabriel gave me a nod, which Alex unfortunately did not miss.

I quickly adjusted my focus. "Where are we?" I asked, pray-ing that I wasn't turning as red as I thought I was.

"Welcome to the manor." Gabriel stood from the wing-backed chair he'd been occupying and held out his hands. We both turned to look at him. As long as I didn't think about how much he reminded me of Alex, I was totally fine.

"The Manor?" Alex repeated in awe.

Vera's laugh rang out into the space. "It's just a big house."

"A big house filled with a ludicrous amount of history," he said, rushing over to one of the many tables strewn about the space. Since he hadn't released my hand yet, that meant I got dragged along in his wake. "I mean, right here is where the Shadows sat to devise a plan to overthrow the Regency."

"Only because the War Room is too crowded," Vera replied casually. "What happened to your neck? I thought Dorian healed you."

It took me a moment to realize she was talking to me. I absently reached up. "We were making out in your office," I said, still trying to take in the room. Her jaw fell open, and Alex looked mortified.

"On that note, we really should get down to business. While I'm pleased to see you've brought what notes you have, I doubt they will be of much use," Gabriel said, sinking into a seat at the table.

Alex gave him a searing look and dumped out the contents of his bag onto the table. I looked between the two of them and took a seat beside Alex. I was beginning to suspect that my apparent hickey was not an accident. Meanwhile, Vera seemed to miss the entire exchange and took a seat opposite us.

"Here's what we've uncovered." He lined up the books we'd brought and organize the notes. The history immedi-ately caught Gabriel's attention, and he reached forward to grab it. Alex surreptitiously moved it out of his reach before he could. "During the War on Darkness, the Warde family attempted to wipe out Shadow Demons using what we call Shadow Lights." Vera's face darkened at the mention of the weapons, but she held her peace. "One of them had an affair with a general on the other side. While neither survived, their child *did*. Somehow, over the centuries, this child grew and unknowingly passed on his Shadow Demon heritage beneath the watchful eye of a family determined to erase all existence of said heritage. Now, it seems they've realized the betrayal and are looking for that progeny." He gestured to me. "They are looking or *were* looking for Matt."

I shifted uncomfortably in my seat. Hearing it again didn't make it any easier to swallow.

"But how do you know that? And who are the Wardes? I've already asked Gabriel about this supposed 'War on Darkness'," she said with air quotes, then shot Gabriel a nasty look. "Do not get me started there."

He let out a sigh. "How many times do I have to tell you? It was a joint decision. All Shadow Demons went into hiding. We just did it for so long that many forgot what they were hiding *from*. As for the Wardes, that's the name of the family that founded the Order of Light," Gabriel offered by way of explanation.

"Douglas and Cane," she said, her voice dripping with acid.

Gabriel nodded and reached out to her. I could clearly see her anger fighting for control and braced for a repeat of what had happened at the dorm.

Out of nowhere, a small child burst into the room and raced over. Vera immediately snapped out of her fury-induced funk. "Lelana Isabel, what do you think you are doing?" Vera scolded the young girl. She couldn't be more than four. "You are supposed to be with Aunty Kyra. And where is DJ?"

The child pouted. "She's taking a nap, and DJ won't let me play with my powers."

Vera picked up the child and let out a sigh. "Sorry, Kyra was supposed to be watching her while we had our meeting. I'll track her down." The little girl immediately began squirming, her long dark hair swirling around as she fought Vera's grasp.

"She can stay," Alex said. I looked at him. His eyes were bright as he resisted the urge to laugh at the young girl's antics.

Immediately, the girl turned to Vera. "Mama, please, please, pleeeaase..." she begged.

Vera looked anxiously around the table, then she gave a resigned sigh. "Alright, but you have to be on your best behavior. Understand?" The little girl nodded enthusiastically until Vera set her back down. She then raced over to where Alex had scooted back from the table.

"What's your name?" she asked her benefactor.

He laughed, "My name is Alexi, and this is Matt."

I gave a small wave, not really sure what else to do.

"Uh-lex-e," she said, accentuating every syllable. "I like it! It's pretty like mine," she beamed up at him before scrambling into his lap. When she turned back to the others, she looked like a proper, miniature adult, complete with a super serious face.

Alex laughed again and resumed what he had been talking about. The memoir and glasses he slid to Vera so she could see the unbearable likeness between me and the infamous Matthias Warde. Then we talked at length about what to do next. Which amounted to a lot of nothing. It felt like they were really just talking in circles, rehashing things we already knew. None of it getting me any closer to punishing Thomas.

Eventually, Lelana decided it was time to share her attentions. She calmly extricated herself from Alex's lap and ventured over to me. She looked up expectantly until I picked her up. I'd never dealt with children outside of the orphanage and was a bit at a loss. Alex gave me an encouraging look, and I sat her down on my lap, much like she'd been before with him. Vera looked borderline mortified, while Gabriel looked like it was the funniest thing he'd ever seen. Alex, however, was giving me an entirely different look that I didn't understand in the least. I let it go and tried to refocus my attention on the current topic. They were saying yet again that there was no lead where the Order could be hiding or if they were even still around to be found. I rolled my eyes and tried not to look as bored as I felt.

Abruptly, I jerked and realized I'd been dozing off. Reflexively, I made sure the small child curled against me didn't fall. She too had fallen asleep and the sound of her faint breathing drifted up. Something about that innocence was reassuring. I blinked the sleep from my eyes and tried to figure out where we were at. Vera and Gabriel were talking animatedly, or maybe they were arguing. It was difficult to tell. Alex, on the other hand, was smiling at me. I returned with one of my own nervous ones.

He turned back to the others and interjected, "We should probably get going. It's getting late." Vera and Gabriel looked up, then back at each other. Something told me this battle of words was common for them.

"He's right." Vera stood and walked around the table.

I looked down at the little girl nestled like some kind of baby bird in my arms and gave Alex a beseeching look. He chuckled and moved over to help. She mumbled in her sleep as he scooped her off of my lap. She really was precious, if a bit feisty. I watched as he walked her over to her mother, looking totally comfortable holding the small child.

"I'm sorry about that," Vera said as she took the child from Alex. "She can be quite insistent. And without her powers being bound, sometimes it's more trouble than it's worth fighting her on things."

"It's no trouble," Alex whispered, gently rubbing Lelana's back. "As a matter of fact, if you ever need a babysitter, just let me know. We'd be happy to." He looked back at me. What? How had I gotten volunteered? He smiled and gave me a wink.

CHAPTER 21

PLAYING FOR KEEPS

A

I finished getting dressed to go out and was trying in vain to get my hair to do something resembling decent. Matt had vanished to his own room to change and was likely already waiting for me in the living room. I let out an exasperated sigh and gave it up as a lost cause. My hair would do whatever it wanted, no matter what I did. Defeated, I made my way to the door and hesitated. On the one hand, I was super excited about getting to play pool again. While admittedly, I wasn't very good, that didn't make it any less fun. On the other, though, I literally had no idea what to expect from this evening, especially after Matt's blatant display of affection the other day. Quite frankly, I wasn't even sure what the rules were anymore. Were there rules?

I shook my head and stepped through the door, forgetting to actually open it. Startled, I blinked at the still closed door behind me. Amazing how second nature shadowing could become. And I made fun of Matt, I mentally scolded myself.

"It's about time." I looked back to the room to see Matt waiting impatiently, the hint of a smile playing around his mouth. "Let me guess," he began, walking towards me, "you were fussing with your hair. Am I right?" He ran his fingers through the rebellious strands for emphasis.

"Seriously, Matt?" I admonished as I tried without success to flatten it back down.

He chuckled and let it be. "It looks fine. *You* look fine." Heat colored his words, and I dropped my hand.

"Um, thanks," I responded after clearing my throat. "We should really get going or we'll be late."

"Pft, I feel like it's almost impossible for a Shadow Demon to be late," he scoffed, shadowing out for emphasis.

"Vera does it all the time," I countered. "Besides, while walking through the Shadow world expedites the process, it still takes time."

"Fair point," he conceded.

"At any rate, we should leave," I tried again, attempting to move around him towards the door.

"What, no kiss?" he asked, raising two curious brows. The question may have sounded innocent enough, but there was a devilish glint in his eye.

I narrowed my eyes at him. This was a trap, I could feel it.

"Just one," he offered reassuringly. I'd believe that when they brought cheese down from the moon.

"Fine. One." I gave him my best serious look, which didn't faze him in the least. I licked my lips nervously. There really was no telling what he would do. He'd been fairly unpredictable before and this new Matt was a whole other level. He was attentive, affectionate, open, possessive, and absolutely insatiable. To be fair, he had been most of those things before, only now he wasn't shying away from it. In truth, I had no idea why I was so anxious as I leaned forward to press my lips against his; I loved the way his molded perfectly to mine. However, that did nothing to prevent my heart hammering loud enough to echo in my ears. To my infinite amazement, he gently kissed me back without doing anything else. I leaned back, still feeling dubious about the whole affair. "Better now?" I asked, quirking an eyebrow at him before taking a step towards the exit. I only made it two before his hand on my arm stopped me.

"Wait a sec."

I turned back to him. "What?"

In less than a blink, he'd pulled me back to him and snared me with a substantially less sedate kiss. His arms tightened around me, pressing me hard against him. I let out an involuntary squeak, and he stole the opportunity to deepen the kiss. I instantly got swept up in the pure fire of Matt's passion. My fingers tangled in his hair as the torrent of desire poured through me. And his hands felt incredible as they roved relentlessly beneath my fresh shirt. I moaned and leaned into him. At last, he pulled back to give me an absolutely evil grin. The sigh that escaped me at the release completely contradicted my earlier assertion that we needed to go. I now very much wanted to stay.

"Just that," he said

I struggled to get my breathing and my heart rate back under control. There was zero doubt in my mind that I looked 'peeked', as my mother would say. He, on the other hand, was barely even breathing hard. "You are absolutely insufferable," I said at last.

His grin widened. "You know you love it." He took a step back, giving me more space to breathe. "Now we really should stop stalling. The guys will wonder what we're getting up to." The look in his eye suggested he already had several ideas in mind.

My jaw barely didn't drop. Who was this person and what had they done with my awkward roommate, who could hardly admit he wanted to kiss me?

I followed Matt in a daze to the pool hall and likely would have drifted aimlessly off if he hadn't been holding my hand. A part of me wasn't sure if I could handle this completely unreserved version of Matt. Another recognized that this was always who he'd been and was the exact person I'd fallen in love with. Either way, it was proving to be a little unsettling. The entrance rose unexpectedly before us, snapping me out of my fog. The place really looked like a total dive, and contrary to what he'd said our first visit, the inside *did not* look better.

"It's about time," Lucas said, straightening up from his shot as we joined them at a table. Sam looked over and waved in greeting.

"Sorry," Matt said as he grabbed two cue sticks. He passed me one and leaned on his own.

"Would someone please explain to me how people who can shadow walk can always be late?" Lucas asked aloud as Sam leaned down to take his own shot. Matt slid me a sidelong look. I didn't even want to think about what sort of disaster would result if he'd shadowed us here.

"Shadowing isn't always the best idea," Matt replied.

"Just because you have powers doesn't mean you should use them for everything," I added.

"Speak for yourself." Sam passed Lucas the cue ball, and suddenly, there were two Lucases. The real Lucas leaned down to line up his next shot. As he was working on getting his angle just right, other Lucas slid the cue stick up his leg. Original Lucas scratched. Matt snickered, and Lucas spun around to face himself.

"Cut it out, Sam. How many times have I told you? It's creepy to play with myself." It wasn't until the rest of us erupted in laughter that he realized what he'd said. He groaned and rolled his eyes, then promptly smacked Sam back to normal. Perhaps Matt *hadn't* been exaggerating when he said how people messed with each other when playing.

"Don't be such a sore loser," Sam poked, once more, his usual blond self.

Lucas soured. "The only reason I'm losing is because you're cheating."

"I am not."

"You are too."

"Alright, alright, either break it up or get a room," Matt interjected. They both rounded on him, and I looked at him in total amazement. "What? Look, how about we mix this up a bit? Which one of you is the better player?"

The question had the effect of tossing a match into petrol. Eventually, after some very loud quibbling, they resorted to flipping a coin.

"Ha!" Sam declared at winning the toss. "What's my prize?" he asked Matt.

"You're on Alex's team."

"What?" Sam and I said together.

Matt shrugged and bumped my shoulder. "You'll be fine. Just remember what I showed you." There was nothing innocent about the smile he gave me.

"Surely you don't mean *everything*," I fired right back. Two could play this game.

"You're welcome to remember that too, but I don't think Sam will appreciate you being so distracted," he responded with a sly grin. Sam immediately began having a coughing fit, and I thought Lucas was going to pass out from laughter. The devil.

"Right, so the game," Lucas finally managed. He set the table and stepped aside so Sam could break.

It wasn't bad, but I was definitely getting a better understanding of just how good at this Matt was. Luckily, I still recalled enough of the actual instruction from last time that I wasn't totally deplorable. I even sank a few shots. Once the game was truly under way, the shenanigans resumed. Matt leaned down to take his next shot. I was appreciating the view of him completely laid out on the table when he suddenly jerked his head and snatched his hand up to his ear. His intended shot went wide, and he ended up sinking one of ours instead.

"The hell, Sam! No spells, that's cheating."

"It's only cheating if you can prove it was one of us," Sam responded, gesturing between us. Matt barely spared me a look before returning to glare at Sam. I was a little offended that he didn't think it could have been me. We'll just have to see about that. Sam then confidently walked up to take his turn. I watched as Matt stepped forward, no doubt to return the favor, only to have Lucas hold him back. They smiled at each other, and Lucas stepped closer until he was almost right beside Sam. From my angle, I couldn't quite make out what he was doing, but judging by the feral grin, it was nothing good. Sam was just about to take his shot when he let out a yelp. The ball bounced off the table and Matt had to run after it as it continued to roll halfway across the room, disturbing several other patrons. Matt sat the cue ball back on the table, still laughing.

"What was that?" I asked.

"Oh, we forgot to mention. Best not to get on Lucas's bad side. Things can get hairy," Matt offered.

I looked at Sam in the hope of some clarification. "Yep, he's a real howler when he gets mad," he teased.

"Would the two of you knock it off with the cheesy puns?" Lucas griped.

"What are you guys even talking about?" I asked.

"I guess it's time we fessed up. So, Lucas is a werewolf and I'm a witch. My specialty is illusions if you hadn't already figured that part out," Sam added. Lucas glanced up from his unhindered shot to give me a smile with a few too many teeth.

A tad surprised I hadn't picked up on all the wolf puns, I shifted the shadow nearest Lucas to slide down the neck of his shirt. He squirmed wildly and sank the eight ball by mistake. Matt's jaw dropped in total disbelief.

"You've got to be kidding me! Seriously, Lucas? The hell was that about?"

"How should I know? Ask those two," he said, still trying to rid himself of the shadow that had long since dissipated.

"Don't look at me." Sam held up his hands and Matt's shocked gaze turned to me.

I shrugged. "What? I'm just playing the way I was taught."

Lucas smacked the table. "I call do-over."

"It doesn't work that way," Sam argued.

"House rules. We can call a do-over if everyone agrees," Lucas insisted. "I demand a vote."

Sam rolled his eyes. "Fine. What do you say Alex?"

"Doesn't matter to me."

"There, you have your bloody do-over. Put the ball back, but your turn is forfeit."

"Sold," Lucas said as he carefully replaced the eight ball roughly where it had been. I shook my head. These guys were a mess. "Okay, newbie, you're up."

Now that it was obvious what sort of game we were playing, I was not looking forward to my turn. My mind rebelliously kept flashing back to the last time I'd played pool with Matt. Consequently, I remembered quite a bit that had nothing to do with pool, resulting in the very distraction Matt had alluded to before. Damn him. I lined up my shot and took my time, making sure I had the form right. In a brief moment of hope, I believed I might actually make it through the turn with no one messing with me. Sadly, hope was a fickle mistress. I smelled

Matt before I felt his hand on the back of my leg. But I was determined not to lose focus. I would not mess up this shot. By some miracle, I was doing halfway decent and I wanted to keep it that way. As I prepared to take the shot, his hand drifted towards my inner thigh. *Focus, Alexi.* Suddenly, his hand shifted *much* higher and I let out a squeak of indignation. Unfortunately, the cue was already in motion and there was no way to adjust the very wrong course it was now on. The stick skittered off the top of the ball and Sam gave his own indignant squawk.

"Foul play."

"You're just saying that because we got a do-over," Lucas countered.

"That's not even fair. Alex barely has a poker face, let alone the experience to stand up to—" He waved wildly at Matt, who didn't look the least bit ashamed.

"Don't be deceived. Alex has an excellent poker face," Matt calmly defended me.

I glanced at him. "What is that supposed to mean?"

"I'm just saying you're not a guileless as you're leading them to believe."

"That's ridiculous. I would never," I responded with a crooked grin.

"I'm done. Matt, it's your shot. I'm going to get a drink. Anyone want anything?" Sam asked as he walked backwards towards the bar. Matt and I declined, while Lucas requested a refill.

Matt assessed the table before choosing his intended target. He seemed to be trying to determine the best angle to take when he glanced up. Whatever he saw made him do a double take. The angle was all wrong and, while I was pretty sure he hit the right ball, it knocked into the eight ball on its skewed path. Lucas watched in horror as the black ball slowly rolled towards a side pocket, hesitated at the cusp, then fell in.

"You have *got* to be kidding me," Lucas cried.

Matt didn't seem to notice. He was still riveted on whatever had caught his attention. "What the fuck is Alex doing?" he asked, his voice dangerously low.

"I'm standing here watching you lose like a pro. What the hell do you think I'm doing?" I quipped. Matt and Lucas both looked back at me, then across the bar.

"Oh shit," Lucas said.

"What?" I still couldn't figure out what they were looking at.

"I'm going to fucking murder him," Matt hissed as he threw his cue on the table.

"Murder who? Why?"

They both ignored me. "What the hell does he think he's doing?" Matt asked again.

"I'm pretty sure he's using your boyfriend to pick up chicks," Lucas supplied, shaking his head. I reevaluated Matt's obvious anger and the direction of his murderous rage. Then I saw him—or more appropriately, I saw me—and the two girls from the first time I'd been here. I was blatantly flirting with them. Oh fuck.

"Matt," I cautioned. "Take a deep breath."

He looked at me and stuttered, unable to put words in anything resembling a coherent sentence.

I glanced back up in time to see me gesture towards our group. This had disaster written all over it. The girls giggled and turned back to the bar. I gave a small sigh of relief that he wasn't escorting them over. I had no idea how we would explain *two* of me. Another glance at Matt said I wouldn't have one for long. Sam then began walking back, looking exceptionally smug and more like himself. He made it all the way to the table before he realized we were all staring at him. He froze mid-step and glanced around at the accusatory glares.

"Uh, hey guys. What's up? Is it my turn already?" he asked nervously.

Matt made to advance, and I held him back, having caught sight of the girls now making their way over. Sam caught the move and quickly scrambled out of the line of fire. Matt barely wiped the scowl off of his face before they stopped in front of us. They both smiled and waved at me. For lack of any better ideas ideas, I did the same. I felt Matt tense, but it couldn't be helped. Hopefully, Sam hadn't promised anything too outrageous.

"Are you sure it's alright if we join you and your friends?" the girl with blond hair even paler than Sam's asked.

I looked at Matt and sent up a silent prayer that he wasn't scowling. Much to my surprise, he was the picture of confident ease. I quickly checked my own facial expression. The girls gave each other an anxious look. When Matt didn't answer right away, Sam not so discreetly nudged him in the back. I was beginning to think Sam had a death wish. Somehow, Matt refrained from reacting to the obvious prod, aside from finally deigning to speak.

"I don't see why not. The more the merrier, right?" They looked relieved. "My name is Matt, by the way." They gave him a once over that was a little too thorough for my liking. I definitely hadn't imagined that they were hoping for a package deal the last time. Now, thanks to Sam, that hope was alive and kicking. "That there is Lucas, and that dork is Sam," he finished mercilessly. Sam made a strangled sound, but I had zero sympathy for him.

"I'm Taryn," the blonde said, pointing to herself, "and this is Hannah." Hannah gave a small wave and glanced behind us at Sam.

Matt nodded at the information and gestured at me. "I'm assuming, of course, you've already met my boyfriend, Alexi," he added, cool as a cucumber. Both of their faces fell. They definitely hadn't expected that when they made their way over.

Lucas took in the situation, glancing between those gathered as if waiting for all hell to break loose. Finally, he asked in an obvious attempt to break the ice, "So you ladies play?" Their focus shifted immediately to the less hostile member of the group. The second their attention was on Lucas, Matt spun around and smacked Sam.

"What the hell is wrong with you? You can't pick up girls on your own, so you hijack *my* boyfriend?" he hissed under his breath.

"Ow. What? I thought you'd be more upset if I used you. Besides, you did it the last time," Sam tried to defend himself.

"Wait a minute. Last time?" I interjected. "What's he talking about?"

Matt waved it off. "That was different."

"How so?" Sam persisted.

"Yeah, how so?" I mimicked. I'd been exceptionally inebriated at the time, and most of the conversation was a blur, though I had a distinct memory of pink.

"I knew he wouldn't come back with anyone."

Sam blanched and finally had the decency to look guilty.

"Now get your ass over there and save Lucas before he puts both feet in his mouth."

Sam quickly scurried to obey, if only to get out of range of Matt's wrath. A glance showed the girls were sufficiently amused by their bait-and-switch partners. I shook my head and followed Matt over to the stool he'd acquired.

"Did you really put me up as bait last time?" I asked, in an attempt to divert his anger.

He gave a half smile. "We've already talked about this." He spun me around so that I could lean my back against him.

"That doesn't make it better," I prodded. "What would you have done if I'd been more successful or if they'd been more interested in you?"

He chuckled. "I think I've made it pretty clear by this point that I have no intention of sharing." His thumbs slipped beneath the hem of my shirt and began rubbing the small of my back.

I sighed into the intimate gesture. "You know what I think?"

"Hmm?" he responded as he ran his nose along the back of my neck.

"I think you're a bit possessive."

"Your point?"

"Just an observation." He placed a small kiss at the nape of my neck and the heat of his breath sent a shiver through me. I felt him smile and the next kiss was adventurous enough that I had to work to school my features.

"You taste amazing," he whispered in my ear. I shuddered as he followed the statement by tasting my skin. "All of you."

"Matthew." I straightened and turned to face him. He flashed me a wicked smile. Unbelievably, his eyes were perfectly blue, without so much as a hint of black. The damn things should have been midnight after a heated statement like that.

"What's going on over there?" Lucas asked while Hannah took her shot.

"Nothing," Matt answered, once more looking like an innocent angel.

I scowled at him. These last few days proved that Matt was about as far from innocent or angelic as it was possible to get. One thing was for certain: I needed a minute to cool down. I politely excused myself. In the men's room, I stared at myself in the mirror and wondered when our cat-and-mouse dynamic had shifted. *Probably about the time that Matt owned up to actually being in love with you*, I helpfully answered myself. *This will never do. It doesn't matter how much more open he is now, he's still Matt, and I still have his number.*

When I returned, it was like I'd lost again before I could even start. I could hardly believe my eyes. Matt was *dancing*. He smiled and laughed as he spun, first Taryn and then Hannah, much to their delight. It was clear he was trying to get the others to join, but they were pointedly refusing. Despite their earlier disappointment, the two girls seemed to have accepted the newly corrected perception with an impressive amount of ease. Even they were trying to coax the others to join them as they grooved along to the music. Though I doubted this latest turn of events was diminishing their belief that they still might walk away with both of us. I walked up and crossed my arms while I waited for Matt to notice I was there. He eventually spun far enough around that he caught sight of me. His smile stretched from ear-to-ear, and I could feel mine trying to surface. I carefully schooled my face. I loved seeing him happy and carefree, but I was on a mission.

"Come on. Don't tell me you're not going to join either," he teased.

I raised an eyebrow. "I thought you said you couldn't dance. You seem to be doing just fine to me." I swept my eyes over him, none too subtly.

He laughed self-consciously and danced closer. "I said I couldn't dance ballroom. Besides, I wouldn't exactly call me flailing about like a bobolink that's lost its tail dancing." I had absolutely no idea what on earth a bobolink was, but I didn't think he was doing all that bad.

"Didn't you say something about wanting me to tutor you in ballroom?"

He hesitated a fraction of a second.

That was all I needed. I used shadow to push him towards me and grabbed his hand. Before he knew it, I guided him through the box step, a ball change, a heel turn, and several spins before landing him in a dip. His eyes were wide with alarm as he stared back at me from his precarious position. A chorus of appreciative "Oohs" surrounded us. He gave a nervous swallow. Without warning, I spun him back up and caught him with a kiss. The "Oohs" turned to whoops. When I pulled back, he looked totally shell-shocked, his face a wonderful shade of pink and his eyes completely black.

That's more like it.

CHAPTER 22

Q&A

M

I quickly concluded that going out with Alex was danger-ous. Beside the fact that now that I had no qualms about who knew that we were together, he'd made it clear that if I got out of hand, he'd very decisively set me down. Not that I minded. That was fun on its own.

I smiled up at the ceiling. My whole life, I'd never known it was possible to be this happy. Being in love with Alex was like getting to have my cake and eat it too—but like one of those really *fancy* cakes. He was the best friend I'd ever had. He was funny, understanding, attractive, and phenomenal in the sack. He was too good to be true, is what he was. I couldn't help but wonder when the other shoe would drop. Good things like this just didn't happen to me. Eventually, the universe would realize its error and that would be the end of everything.

I tried to shake off the negative thoughts. It was easy enough to do, considering the scent of lavender still surrounded me. I pulled the comforter over my head to make it more complete. Despite the warm cocoon of contentment, my mind rebel-liously refused to be silenced. There was still the whole Warde issue. Vera had yet to say anything more past the absolutely nothing we'd covered at our one and only meeting. The covers flew back down. Thomas wouldn't give up. I knew that just like I knew that neither would I. He'd threatened something I held more dear than life itself and I would never forgive him for that.

"What are you scowling about?" Alex asked, flopping onto the bed practically on top of me.

I let out an oof. "Nothing."

"Liar."

I looked at him. His green eyes danced with humor, but there was an edge to them. I let out a sigh. "I'm just tired of waiting to hear from Vera. I want to know what's going on. Haven't I earned the right to be kept in the loop?" Alex's sigh was as heavy as mine. I knew he didn't enjoy hearing about what had happened, but he'd asked, and there was no sense in lying about it. We'd already established that I sucked at lying to his face, anyway.

"I wish you could move past this," he said softly. He cut me off before I could do more than open my mouth. "I know you can't, but that doesn't change that I wish you would. Why can't you simply appreciate where we are now and enjoy our time together?"

"I *do* enjoy our time together." I sat up. "I love our time together." He smiled, and I went on before he could interrupt. "I'm just afraid it won't last. That something will happen." He reached up to cup my face and I leaned into the caress. I didn't know what I would do if I lost him again.

"Matt, together we can handle anything thrown at us. Try to remember that." He punctuated the statement with a kiss. It was small, but I caught him before he could pull away and deepened it. Colors burst to life in fireworks of sensation. The familiar burn grew until flames were actively licking up my insides. I could kiss him forever. Reluctantly, I let him go. He looked back at me, shaking his head, his eyes still clouded with heat. "I'm serious. One of these days you really are going to kiss me stupid."

I gave him a lopsided grin. "Pretty sure I already have... a couple of times."

He gave me a look and shifted to a better sitting position. "Anyway... Are you planning on staying in bed all day or are you actually going to get dressed and be a productive member of society?" It wasn't until he mentioned getting dressed that I realized he already was. By the looks of it, he was planning on actually going somewhere other than the living room.

"Where are you off to?"

"In case you've forgotten, school is due to start back up soon. I'm going to go out and get some supplies for the new semester. I was going to ask if you wanted to join, but I suspect I already know the answer."

I made a face. It didn't escape my notice that we were both pointedly ignoring the fact that I hadn't taken most of my finals. There was no telling if I was even still enrolled.

"That's what I thought. Fine, you stay here and be a laze-about and I'll get extra supplies for you." He stood and straightened his outfit.

"You're the best," I said, enjoying the view. He really was a work of art. I recalled the only semi-full body sketch I had of him. At the time, it had been almost pure extrapolation. I could do better.

"I know. Oh, there's still some breakfast in the kitchen, if you're hungry."

At the mention of food, I scrambled out of the bed and was pulling on pants by the time I heard him laughing. "What's so funny?"

"I figured that would motivate you. Maybe I should've led with that."

I frowned and stopped my flurried movements.

He chuckled and walked up to me, then snagged my belt loop and dragged me closer. "I'm not criticizing. Honestly, it's comforting to know that you're eating again." He snagged a quick kiss before adding in a low voice, "You're looking more like yourself." Familiar heat curled inside of me. My eyes must have betrayed me, because he released me and stepped away. "I'll be back in a few hours. Try not to get into too much trouble while I'm gone," he finished with a wink.

"Yeah, yeah," I said, then he made his way out of the room. The door closed behind him and I instantly regretted not stealing another kiss. I raced into the living room, but he was already gone.

I pondered what to do while I devoured the leftovers in the kitchen, which amounted to a full meal. Oatmeal wasn't really my favorite, but it was my own fault for over-sleeping. I considered the options available to me. I could read. Nah. Play a game. I glanced at the neglected console. It brought back memories that just made me wish I had gone with Alex instead of being a bum. Hmm, what else? Could always draw. But if I was going to sketch Alex like I wanted to, I'd need him here. Still at a loss, I cleaned the dishes. I could always wander around the campus. That was probably the least appealing of the options. Then my gaze landed on a small piece of paper lying forgotten on the counter. It was the note with the directions on how to get to the manor. Could always get some answers. I immediately shoved the paper in a pocket and finished getting dressed.

Rather than shadow directly to Vera's office, I opted to walk, if only to take up more time. The thought of the college being locked or under a boundary spell only vaguely crossed my mind.. Neither really concerned me. The air was beyond cold and I was seriously debating shadowing back to the dorm to add a few more layers when Mysterio College came into view. I quickened my steps. Part of me hoped she was in her office, but judging by the lack of bodies on campus, that seemed unlikely. To my amazement, the doors were neither locked nor warded. Admittedly, I was a little disappointed at the lack of challenge, but shrugged it off.

Inside, it was substantially warmer. I rubbed my hands together and wondered if Jeffrey had included some decent gloves in that comprehensive wardrobe he'd put together. How it could be so damn cold and not even snow was beyond me. At last, I made it to the classroom. Unsurprisingly, it was vacant. Sadly, so was Vera's office. Unlike the last time, the door was locked, but still no barrier. I shook my head as I shadowed through. Maybe she wasn't worried because the portal wasn't here anymore. That would really suck.

I sent out my essence, searching for the void Alex had so ingeniously picked up on before. As I explored the area, it occurred to me that was why he'd never tripped a wire. Crafty bastard played me, and I couldn't be more proud. The tendrils of my essence suddenly fell into nothingness. I let out a triumphant whoop and walked up to the portal. "*In Tenebras.*" The words felt strange in my mouth and weren't nearly as eloquent as when Alex had said them, but they worked. It wasn't until I stepped through the inky door that it even occurred to me to check for a trip wire. No help for it now.

As I followed the same dimly illuminated path as before, I couldn't help but wonder where the other doors led. I resisted the urge to explore, more determined to get answers than to satisfy a vague curiosity. No sooner than I stepped into the massive library, I felt another demon materialize out of the shadows. Definitely needed to remember to check for trip wires from now on.

"What are you doing here?" Gabriel asked as he stepped into the light, his uncanny resemblance to Alex messing with my head.

"I'm looking for Vera."

"Why?" he asked, sounding bored, though I detected a hint of defensiveness.

"Because I'm tired of waiting around to find out what's going on. I've earned my stripes, now I want answers." It was getting difficult to maintain my righteous stance in the face of his blatant apathy. He raised a speculative eyebrow at the demand. The room became deadly quiet. He continued to stare at me while I waited to see what would happen. Never had I felt so picked apart. I swallowed involuntarily. At last, he spoke, and I could have sagged with relief.

"Have a seat. I can answer your questions."

I eyed the chair he indicated, my relief vanishing. I'd come here for Vera, not him.

"Do you want to know or not?" he asked, taking a seat across from the one meant for me. This felt like a bad idea, but I needed to know. Reluctantly, I joined him.

"Why are you helping me?" I asked, not trusting this.

"You mean, aside from the fact that you just broke into my wife's house?" I could feel my embarrassment creeping up my face. It hadn't even occurred to me what this would look like. "Aside from that, I am also a teacher. Helping is kind of what I do."

"You don't exactly strike me as the helpful-type." Or the teacher-type, I mentally added.

"I helped you, did I not?" He had a point there. "You're welcome, by the way." My flush deepened, and he chuckled. It was a rich sound that started low and got louder. "You and Vera are remarkably similar. I can't help but wonder if it is a generational thing or perhaps it is the unprecedented way you two have become so strong. Of course, it's entirely possible I've just had enough time to mellow."

"Just how old are you, anyway?" I blurted, instantly wishing I could take back the impertinent question. Something told me that the way I interacted would Vera would not fly with this demon. I held my breath, waiting for the rebuke.

He sat back, giving up his speculation. "I'm not sure how well you are in history, but, to be brief, I was born in Mesopotamia." For a fraction of a second, my mind completely stalled out. He wasn't serious. History was by far not my best subject before or after Arminius, but even *I* knew that was an unbelievably long time ago.

My mouth fell open. "But wasn't that... I mean... didn't they..."

"Yes, you are thinking of the right civilization. It really is a shame they never finished the Tower of Babel," he mused to himself.

There was just no way. He didn't look a day over forty. And Vera taught *him* tricks? I didn't believe that for a second.

"I can clearly see that you're not handling this very well. What do you say we move on to why you came here? Uninvited, I might add."

"Um... I want to know what's going on?"

"So you said. Understandable really. After all, they did kidnap and torture your lover. I can certainly empathize with the desire to seek retribution." I looked up at him, surprised. "What part got your attention? The lover comment or that I'm capable of empathy?"

"Did something happen to Vera?" It was a stupid question. Obviously, something *had* given her reaction that night.

He nodded his head. "They stole her from the group in the middle of a mission. It took me months to find her."

I blanched. No wonder she'd freaked when she saw the marks.

"I am pleased, however, to see that you have gotten over referring to Alexi as your lover. I told you he would be fine." Was he really pulling an "I told you so"? "Back to what is going on. Admittedly, we aren't having much success. Of course, now we have a better idea of what likely happened to the other recruits that vanished before we could get to them." I vaguely recalled Vera mentioning something along those lines eons ago.

"Are you suggesting that the Order of Light was abducting people before class even started?" This whole thing was so much bigger than I had imagined.

"You know the Warde mission statement." He gave me a strange look. I didn't like to think I fell in that category. Yes, I'd always wanted to know who I was, but not this, not them. "However, I doubt that those poor souls were nearly as fortunate as Alexi."

Rage swept through me. "There was nothing *lucky* about what happened to Alex."

He failed to acknowledge my outcry. "Strange that you still insist on calling him Alex. I wonder why that is," he mused.

I bristled. "Alex—Alexi," I corrected myself, "endured unspeakable horrors. Tell me, what's lucky about that?"

"He's alive."

That gave me pause. "Just how many recruits went missing?"

His face darkened. "Too many. If we had known that Thomas and Douglas were involved, we would not have assumed it was cold feet. I should have listened to her when she said it didn't feel right. Knowing what we know now, it is a good thing she picked you up early. You were relatively safe in the human system, but the moment you set foot in Superno House, red flags would have popped up. Most people, even in the supernatural community, can't recognize a manifesting Shadow Demon. But the Order of Light would have recognized the signs right away. Is it true that you took on all four by yourself?"

My head spun with the horrific information. I nodded numbly, noting the impressed glint in his eye. Never in all my years would I have viewed those houses as anything other than hell-holes. To think they were keeping me safe was mind-boggling.

Without warning, he shifted the conversation back to its original track. "Regrettably, the pair seem to have vanished once again. Now, before you accuse us of not looking hard enough, know that I am *particularly* motivated to find them. The last time I was this close, I had to choose between saving my other half or exacting vengeance. Much like your own decision, it was an easy one to make." The hardness in his eyes suggested that when he finally got his hands on them, they would wish they were already dead.

"What about the others? His lackeys," I added for clarity. I already knew what he thought had happened to the demons Vera hadn't found. It was awful. Though having been a person more often forgotten than not, I couldn't help but think someone should still look. Just in case.

"Gone without a trace. Though I do not believe they have fled the school. Not yet anyway. They are here somewhere and we will find them. I also believe Thomas is still lurking about. There is something here he still wants very much."

I squirmed in my seat beneath his hard, penetrating stare. It was difficult to determine if he was sizing me up to put me on a battlefield or to use me as bait. Suddenly, Vera's voice cut through the mounting tension.

"What the hell is going on?" I looked up to see her marching towards us. She stopped at the end of the table with her hands on her hips, her eyes filled with fire as she waited impatiently for an explanation.

"Young Matthew here was simply stopping by to see you. He had some questions, though I think I have answered most of them," Gabriel supplied more calmly than I felt.

"Is that so? And what sorts of questions did you have, Matt?" she asked, turning her fiery gaze on me. The nerve to be mad at me when she was the one intentionally keeping me in the dark. She should know better than anyone how wrong that was. I was a breath away from giving her a piece of my mind when Gabriel once again interjected.

"He was inquiring about some abilities he used the other day. You were right, my love, he is quite the natural, much like yourself." She narrowed her eyes at him. My gaze darted between the two of them. Could she tell he was lying? Despite the obvious animosity she was sporting, Gabriel remained the essence of calm.

"I think it's time you went back to the campus, Matt. Don't you?" Her gaze swiveled around and I quickly found my feet. If Gabriel didn't want her to know what we'd been talking about, that was his business, and I had no desire to stick around to see it blow up in his face.

"Alex is probably back by now anyway," I said, although I didn't know how long had passed since I'd left. She let me leave without another word and I could bet good money that the door got sealed behind me. I stared back at the portal once I reemerged in her office, tempted to test my theory, then caught sight of a clock. Shit, Alex had likely been back for hours. Without further ado, I shadowed back to the dorm. Sure enough, he was sitting on the couch organizing supplies.

"There you are," he said from where he was sitting on the couch, organizing supplies.

"Sorry, I lost track of time." That was an understatement. I was still struggling to make sense of half of what Gabriel had told me.

"What did you get up to?" The question was innocent enough, but it held a definitive undercurrent.

"I went to go talk to Vera. She wasn't in her office, though."

"And you got lost on the way back?" he teased.

"No, I took the portal to the manor to look for her there," I said, putting the slip on the table. His mouth fell open as shock exploded across his face. "She wasn't there either, or at least, not when I got there. So, I ended up talking with Gabriel."

"You what!"

I blanched in the face of his fury. "W-what?" It had been a while since I'd heard him shout.

"You mean to tell me you simply let yourself into one of the most heavily guarded houses *in the world* and then casually sat around sipping tea with Gabriel Xiander the entire afternoon?" There were a few parts of that question that should have given me pause, but they didn't seem to be the actual issue.

"Well, yeah. I had questions, and he was willing to answer them. Insisted on it, in fact. And we didn't have tea." This latest information didn't seem to help my case.

"What sorts of questions would you have for him that you couldn't ask me?" His eyes took on a dark cast and suddenly his anger made more sense.

"I don't know what you think went on, but all we did was sit at a table and talk."

"For an entire afternoon?" he pressed, his disbelief palpable.

"Again, I wanted to talk to Vera. She wasn't there. *He* was." This didn't seem to be getting me anywhere. It was almost as if...

"That's not an excuse."

"Alex, are you jealous?"

"What? No," he replied a little too quickly.

"Nothing happened. Besides, Vera eventually showed up and sent me home anyway, otherwise I'd probably still be there." Too late, I realized that was the wrong thing to say. Anger flashed through his eyes and he turned away to march into his room. "Alex, wait, that's not... Come on, don't be like this," I called as I chased after him. I eventually caught him in the middle of his room, but he refused to look at me. I didn't understand what this was about. There was no reason for him to feel threatened like this. Gabriel may look a bit like him, but past that, they were nothing alike. "Alex, please," I said, shaking him.

He intentionally kept his gaze averted.

"I love you."

He finally glanced at me out of the corner of his eye. Success.

"I love you, Alex."

He blinked.

"What do you say you tell me about your adventures in town? Were you able to find everything you were looking for?" It was clear he recognized the obvious attempt at distraction, but he allowed it and walked back into the living room. I let out a relieved breath and followed him, sending up a silent prayer that this would not become "a thing". Unfortunately, I feared it was too late for that.

CHAPTER 23

FUTURE PLANS

A

I wasn't sure if our meeting with Vera and Gabriel accomplished anything beyond getting us all on the same page. Aside from Matt gallivanting off on his own to get answers, there'd been no communication at all. Part of me hoped the reason they hadn't reached out was because they were going to handle it themselves; we were just students after all.

I looked over at Matt sketching on the couch. Life should never have been this complicated, and he deserved some peace after what he'd been through the last few months. He wouldn't see it that way of course. He'd want to be involved right until the end, especially after what they'd done to me. I still couldn't believe he hadn't killed any of them when he'd gone to confront them. But I worried now he knew who was mostly responsible for my injuries he wouldn't stop until Douglas was dead. If I wanted to make sure he didn't, I'd have to go with him. He wasn't going to like that.

"You're thinking very loudly over there," his voice drifted back.

I shook my head and walked over to join him and his weird sixth sense for whenever I was thinking about him. "What are you working on?" I asked, taking a seat beside him.

He shrugged.

"Fine, don't tell me." He laughed under his breath and tilted the page so I could see. To my surprise, it was little Lelana.

There were three images in total on the page. One was her sitting on my lap trying to look very behaved, another was her looking up at Matt waiting for him to give her permission to crawl into his, while the last was just of me looking at him. She'd been quite the adorable surprise. I hadn't expected Matt to pick her up or let her sit on his lap. Actually, I had no idea how he felt about kids at all.

"You're doing it again," he said as he added texture to Lelana's hair with soft scratches of his pencil. "I didn't know Vera had a kid. Did you?" He spared me a quick glance.

"I feel like I did, but confess I was still a little surprised. She's sweet."

He looked at me out of the corner of his eye. "What gives with volunteering us for babysitting duty, by the way?"

"What? I like kids."

"I could tell," he replied with a smirk.

"Shut up." I playfully shoved him. He gave me a scandalized look when the pencil almost made several extra marks across the page. "It really is amazing how you can do all of that from memory."

He shrugged. "It's not as much fun as a living model." He closed the book and gave me a pensive expression. "You should let me draw you sometime." he leaned forward to place the book safely on the table with the assortment of pencils, then caught me with an unexpected kiss.

I chuckled. "Don't you draw me enough?" He deepened the kiss and his hands slid beneath my shirt. I didn't resist as he pulled it up.

"That isn't the kind of drawing I had in mind." The low, sultry statement sent heat flooding through me.

My face burned. "Matt."

"You really do have beautiful skin, Alex." He trailed his fingers down my back as if to emphasize his point. "One of these days I'm going to trace every last inch of you," he whispered between kisses along my neck and shoulder. I shivered, and he returned to my mouth, where the heat of the kiss effectively banished any thought of cold. "Alexi." My breath caught. His fire was all-consuming, and I so loved how it burned. There was a brief sensation of him touching me everywhere, then we rematerialized on the bed. He fell back into the pillows, taking me with him.

I laughed, working to remove his clothes. "You're such a devil."

"I've been called worse." He raised his hips to aid in my endeavor. The moment he was free, he pulled me back down. A moan escaped as he pressed hard against me. I slid an arm under him and rolled us. He instantly set to work liberating me as well, then made to roll us back. I resisted, and he looked down at me curiously.

"Oh no, you started this, you can finish it."

He gave me that devil's grin of his, then slid his hand up my leg to grip my thigh and pulled me closer. "What do you want, Alex?"

"Whatever you'll give me," I replied, breathless with anticipation.

"Don't I always give you everything?"

I had a sneaking suspicion my eyes were black, judging by the heated look he was giving me. I wanted to respond with an equally quippy remark, but the snap of the lid on the bottle of lube distracted me. By the time I got my wits back about me, he'd shimmied between my legs. I groaned as he took his sweet time, slowly sucking me down until he'd buried his nose in my groin. I had just enough time to register his pleased hum before he popped back off to do it all over again. He nuzzled my bent legs farther apart. A hiss escaped between my teeth as a lubed finger tapped at my entrance and electricity shot up my spine. "I shouldn't need to remind you it's been a little while since I bottomed," I said through panted breaths.

He released my cock after a firm suck on the head and angled up to face me. "No, you don't," he said before snaring me in a kiss. Then his finger breached the tight ring of muscle.

I gasped at the simultaneous burn and buzz of pleasure. "Just... you know, take it easy."

"I would never hurt you, Alexi." He stared into my eyes, the crystalline blue holding me captive as he gently thrust his finger in and out. I held his gaze until he added more lube and another finger, then squeezed my eyes shut as he curled them, rubbing my prostate and stealing my breath.

"Night, Matt, I don't know how long I'll actually last at this rate." Already I could feel the imminent release building at the base of my spine and tightening my balls.

Abruptly, his fingers vanished, as did my pending orgasm. "Turn over. I want to try something."

Curious where this was going and hoping it involved at least his fingers returning if not his cock, I quickly shifted so I was on my hands and knees. At his soft sigh, I glanced over my shoulder. "What?"

"I ever tell you you have a beautiful ass?" He softly caressed the globes as he looked at them with a reverence that had my face heating.

"Can't say you have."

He snorted. "Well, you do. Eventually I'll sketch it properly, but right now..." He trailed off, and I released a long moan as his fingers glided back inside. Sadly, they didn't stay long. In short order, they were gone and the blunt head of his cock pressed against my hole.

The familiar burn of being stretched melded into waves of pleasure pulsing up my spine. I squirmed with impatience, desperate for him to move, but he continued his agonizingly unhurried pace. "Matt," I groaned. "You're killing me, love."

"So impatient," he teased, though his voice was strained. "I told you, I have an idea."

I was a breath away from telling him I'd die by the time he got around to it when he wrapped an arm around my torso and pulled me up so that my back was flush against his chest. I'd only thought he'd been fully seated before. The change of angle helped him slide even deeper. I moaned, sinking onto him, and reached for my aching cock, though I wasn't sure whether it was to stave off the pending explosion or encourage it. Centimeters from my destination, Matt grabbed my wrist and pulled it away. I let out an undignified whine.

"That can go right here." He placed the captive hand on the back of his neck, then took my other one and set it on his thigh. Once he had me positioned the way he wanted, he lightly ran his hands down my torso while he lavished open-mouthed kisses along my neck and shoulders. I reflexively dug my fingers into his thigh, pulling him even deeper, and gasped at the overwhelming fullness. His hands continued their leisurely exploration, noticeably ignoring my throbbing cock, until they eventually settled on my hips. "I love you so much," he whispered in my ear as he shifted his hips back and thrust back inside me in one smooth motion.

I moaned and dropped my head onto his shoulder. My one hand shifted higher to tangle in his hair while I used my other to encourage him. Pleasure bordered on pain with each roll of his hips, bringing me that much closer to release. But despite my needy moans, he continued to lazily thrust in and out as if we had all the time in the world. I moved my hips in counterpoint to his thrusts, driving down on him until he was groaning every bit as loudly as I was, but my orgasm still hovered just out of reach. "Matt, *please...*"

He finally took mercy and wrapped a hand around my neglected cock. The sudden stimulus had me arching into him so hard I nearly fell forward. Matt's firm grip on my hip kept me in place. He quickened his pace, matching his strokes with the rhythm. My movements faltered, and I used my hold on his hair to bring him in for an awkward kiss. We panted into each other, our breath mingling, as he continued to drive in and out with increasing speed. He adjusted his grip on my leaking cock and twisted his wrist.

My release ripped through me. I jerked against him while he milked me dry and kept pounding my ass. After several more thrusts, his grip on my hip tightened, and he stiffened as warmth pulsed inside of me. I dug my nails into his ass as wave after wave of spine-tingling pleasure washed over me. Whatever coherency I laid claim to slid into addled ecstasy. I scarcely even noticed when he pulled out beyond the slight sting and sudden emptiness. Nor could I muster more than contented happy sounds as he cleaned us up.

When I could finally think straight again, our legs were tangled, and I was at a loss for what had happened to the sheets. "What are you thinking?" he asked as he traced a finger along my arm.

I rolled my head to face him, and warmth filled my chest. "You should do that more often."

"And why is that?" he asked with a crooked grin.

"Because you're *very* good at it." He turned a light shade of pink. I chuckled, then scooted closer and stole a kiss. Almost immediately, his arm went around me, pulling me tight against him. "And apparently insatiable."

A wicked smile replaced his blush. "It's a demon's life."

"That it is," I responded, returning for a deeper kiss. His lips met mine with equal enthusiasm, and his grip tightened. This is everything, I thought as we got lost once more to the fiery whirlwind.

By the time the storm died down, I felt thoroughly spent, and he looked it. Also, the sheets had made a reappearance. In the quiet, my mind wandered back to our meeting at the manor. I prayed Vera wouldn't reach back out. If Matt didn't know, then he couldn't insist on joining. Of course, there was no telling how long he'd be willing to put with radio silence.

"Your thoughts look noisy again." I turned to face him and his serene smile. He lightly tapped my forehead. "What's going on up here?"

I couldn't very well tell him my concerns about the possible pending mission or tell him I didn't want him to go. In lieu of that, I chose a different tract. "Would babysitting Lelana really bother you?"

He laughed. "That's what all that noise is about? No, it wouldn't bother me. I just wasn't expecting to be volunteered."

"Have you ever thought about kids? I mean, like kids of your own?" I wasn't sure where the question came from, it just popped out.

He raised an eyebrow and seemed to really consider the query. "Honestly? I never really thought about it. I doubt I'd make a very good father, though. Not with my issues." He rolled his eyes to play it off, but his casual dismissal of his own life experiences made me sad. In truth, I suspected Matt would make an exceptional father *because* of his history.

I rolled to look up at the ceiling. "I've always wanted a family of my own and I know my mom certainly wants grandchildren." His chuckle shook the bed. "I'm serious. She can be very pushy when she wants something." The bed shook again, and I smiled. "For the record, I think you'd make a great dad." His hand slid across my stomach as he snuggled closer.

"I'm not opposed to having kids, if that's what you're driving at." I wrapped an arm around him and he kissed my collar. "It just depends, I guess."

"On what?"

"I've told you, Alex—whatever you want, I'm yours."

My heart stopped beating and my hand froze. "I love you."

"I love you too," he mumbled, burrowing deeper.

Thoughts raced through my head to the point I was sure he'd accuse me of having loud thoughts again. But it couldn't be helped. I couldn't wrap my mind around what he'd so casually put out there. He'd give me kids if I wanted them. All I had to do was ask. I tightened my arm tightened around him and he sighed in his sleep. How he could sleep so easily after dropping that was beyond me.

By the time morning came around, I was still just as flabbergasted and trying to get my thoughts in order when a loud curse came from the kitchen. In a flash, I grabbed some pants off of the floor and shadowed into the other room. "What is it? What's the matter?" I asked as I materialized. He did a double take at seeing my state of dress. Now that I could clearly see that there was no immediate danger, I took the opportunity to put on the pants I was still holding.

"We got a letter." He waved a piece of paper. Unlike the previous missive, this one didn't appear to be spelled. "From the devil-woman herself," he added with extra acidity. I frowned. Despite his supposed continued grudge for her initial treatment of him, I suspected he actually liked Vera quite a bit.

"Well, what's it say? Are they calling us for another meeting?" I mentally crossed my fingers.

"No," he said bitterly, and I let out the breath I was holding. "Plenty else though. Apparently, Thomas has fled the coop—not that I'm surprised—but they don't want me getting involved anymore. And not so much as a mention of the rest of them. Can you fucking believe that?" He shook his head. I could believe it and was glad that she was being an adult about this and choosing to keep Matt out of that world. "But get this, to 'sweeten' the news, she says that I can enroll in spring classes. Apparently, between our research and what Gabriel saw at the house, I have sufficient knowledge to have passed both finals."

"What about your other classes?"

He waved a dismissive hand. "I didn't miss as many of those." I frowned, and he looked up as if realizing what he had said. "Alex, I..."

"Don't, it's done now," I said, trying to shake off the pain. Knowing why he'd avoided me didn't make it hurt any less. I walked closer to him. The guilt was still plainly written on his face. I took a deep breath and let it out, trying to let the traces of resentment go as well. "What else does she say?"

He looked back down at the letter. "That's it. She doesn't say anything else. But there was this as well." He passed me a second piece of paper written in a different hand. "I won't do it if you don't want me to."

Curious, I began reading, but each line was more unbelievable than the last. "Gabriel wants to teach you. Private lessons. And something about a job after school?" I asked incredulously.

"Apparently, I bear a striking resemblance to his last pupil."

"He married his last pupil," I snapped, and he flushed beat red up to his ears. I struggled to reign in the unexpected ire, but it kept slipping through my grip.

"Like I said, I won't do it if you don't want me to."

I closed my eyes. It wasn't fair to punish Matt because Gabriel made me anxious. But still....

"He reminds me of you, you know. That's why. But he's different. He's *not* you and he never will be. I'm yours, Alex, and only yours. Just tell me what you want me to do."

"No." Guilt wriggled uncomfortably in my chest.

He nodded, calmly accepting the verdict, and my guilt increased.

"No, I won't tell you not to do it. You would probably benefit from one-on-one training. Vera obviously has her hands full with the class and whatever she's doing when she's not actually teaching. And... I agree with him," I finished with a resigned huff. "I think you and Vera have a lot in common. If he can handle her, then he can probably handle you, too." I had expected some sort of enthusiasm at hearing that I wouldn't stand in his way. Instead, he searched my face as if doubting my sincerity. To be fair, I did a little as well.

Then he surprised me by saying, "He was very concerned that I hadn't told you I loved you before I left. He's also the reason I didn't kill George. It would have been easy. He was already down and I'd taken the shadow light that he'd used to stab me. I was ready to return the favor when Gabriel stopped me. He said that you wouldn't want that."

My lingering animosity toward Gabriel softened somewhat. I hadn't realized how close he'd come. I stretched my arms out and Matt willingly stepped into the embrace. I tightened my hold around him and he melted against me.

"I love you, Alex." I doubted my heart would ever not skip when he said that.

CHAPTER 24

BLACK RINGS

M

I was less than thrilled at being left out of plans to track down Thomas. That son of a bitch needed to face the consequences of what he'd done to Alex. The thought that he might get away scot-free made my blood boil. Alex, on the other hand, didn't even try to hide his relief that I wouldn't be involved. I could understand where he was coming from, but that didn't make it any easier. Knowing at least would be better than nothing. Maybe if I talked to Vera, she'd be willing to tell me something.

"Did you finish registering for classes yet?" Alex asked, interrupting my thoughts.

"Um, yeah," I replied absently.

"How does it work with the added lessons? Do you still have to take Battle Tactics like the rest of us, or what?" He wouldn't admit it, but I could tell he was bothered at the prospect of me spending time with Gabriel regularly. I didn't know what to do to make him feel better about it, though.

"He said that we'd train while I'd typically be in class, so to register for it, anyway. Apparently, the private training may not be a hundred percent consistent and I'll be expected to go to class like normal otherwise."

"That's thought out. How will you know if the lesson is canceled? More mysteriously appearing letters?" he asked jokingly.

"Actually..." I held up a phone similar to his. "Vera thought it would be a good idea." Probably to prevent me from showing up at her house again, I mentally added.

"That's awesome! How many times would that have come in handy last semester?" he mused aloud while reaching for his own phone.

"I've already put your number in it as well as your mom's. I hope that's okay."

"Of course, that's okay," he said, finally pulling out the device. "What's the number?"

I smiled, "It's in there already, under Matt."

He rolled his eyes. "You've been busy this morning. Wait. You went through my phone?"

I shuffled my feet. I'd done a bit more than that. I cleared my throat. Time to come clean. "I might have also deleted Daniel's number."

For a second, Alex looked really confused, then he flapped a hand. "Good riddance."

I sighed in relief. He wasn't mad. When the name had popped up, I hadn't been able to stop myself. Before I knew it, I was confirming the deletion. By then, it was too late.

"I hope his nose healed crooked," he sneered.

"Alex," I said in disbelief.

"What? Just because I'm not naturally violent doesn't mean I can't hope that your meeting left a lasting impression."

"You're ridiculous." I laughed and turned to go to my room. I really did just need to move the rest of my things over. It was basically just an over-sized closet at this point, anyway.

"Are you sure you can put up with me? Forever is a long time," he teased.

"Yes." I laughed again and stuck out my tongue. Forever wasn't nearly long enough in my book.

"Hey, wait a sec," he said, sounding unusually animated for only one cup of coffee. I turned in time to see him vault effortlessly over the couch. Damn, he was graceful. "I have an idea."

I turned to fully face him. "Oh? And what would that be?"

"Marry me."

Unsure if he was joking or perfectly serious, I chose an ambiguous response. "What, no knee?" I quirked an eyebrow, and he smiled.

"Matt, I will gladly get down on one knee if it means you will say yes."

Sweet Mother of Night, he was serious. I tried to remain calm, but my heart was racing so fast it was a wonder it didn't speed off without me. "Do you even have a ring?" I stalled.

His face fell.

"Didn't think that far did you?"

"I mean, do we really need rings? I can always get one later."

"This kind of thing calls for a ring." He looked at a loss, then I had a thought. "Hold on." I spun to go back into my room.

"But, Matt..." he called after me.

"I'll be right back. Just give me a minute." I ran in and glanced around. Now where did I put that thing? For a split second, I was afraid I'd left it in the house I'd been squatting in, then I spied it beneath several other school books. "There you are," I said, pulling out the shadow grimoire. There was a spell in here somewhere that I'd been wanting to play with more. I found the page and my notes stuck to it. I quickly scanned through the fundamentals of the spell. At its heart, it was fairly basic, but what I wanted to do with it was far from it. *Hopefully, this works.*

I took a deep breath and began pulling apart some of my essence. It was a strange sensation, but not painful, even when it officially separated from me. The small sphere of shadow—of me—easily took the shape of a ring. Now for the hard part. I examined the spell and my scribbles as I considered how to modify the spell. I didn't want to confine the essence, just make it keep its shape and not try to return to me. In a stroke of genius, I switched some notes around and the result was the perfect spell. I cast the spell and instantly the shadow in my hand stop trying to reunite with my body.

"Matt?" Alex called, the slight waver in his voice betraying his nerves.

I shook my head at his impatience and raced back into the living room with the book and my prize. "I've got it."

"Got what?" he asked, taking in the open book I was balancing in one hand.

I quickly set it down on the table. "Give me your hand." He hesitated a moment, then raised his right hand. "No, your other one."

His eyes widened. "In Europe, we wear bands on the right."

"Oh, well, in that case." I snagged his hand before he could drop it.

"Matt, what are you doing?"

I slid the ring on, unable to contain my grin. As I expected, it naturally adjusted to a perfect fit.

"What is this? It feels... different."

"It's me, Alex. Now you'll always be able to find me."

He looked from me to the ring, then held up his hand to inspect it closer. "This is incredible. But what? I mean how? This is really *you*?"

"Yep." Pride surged in my chest. "I used my essence to make it and I found a spell to keep it just like that... forever."

"Forever," he echoed. Then his gaze snapped back to mine, intensity shining from the depths of green. "How do I do it?" I picked the book back up and held it open for him. He immediately began scanning the page. "You made the spell?"

I shrugged, though it was pretty hard not to preen at the sound of his awe. "Adjusted really. It's not hard, and it doesn't hurt."

"What made you think of using your own essence?"

I blinked at him. Wasn't it obvious? "So I can always be with you."

He paused, staring at me, then returned his attention to the makeshift spell. "Okay, I think I've got it. Does it matter where the essence comes from?" I shook my head. "Of course not. Essence is essence." I watched as he repeated the same steps I had. His eyes lit with wonder as he finished the spell. "Incredible. Put the book down."

I closed it and set it safely aside. A more serious expression replaced his look of awe. He caught my eye and my heart skipped. Night, I loved him. I stood there motionless, unsure if I was even breathing.

"Matt, I love you with all that I am. I don't want to spend another minute of any day without you. You truly are my forever. Will you marry me?" I was grinning from ear to ear long before he ever finished.

"One condition." I brought up my right hand, and anxiety flashed across his face. "I get to take your name." He laughed and slid the ring on my finger. It fit perfectly and I suddenly understood his reaction. Having someone else's essence so close was strange and a little exhilarating.

"Done. You can have whatever name you want."

"I want yours."

He smiled harder. "So... is that a yes?"

"That's a hell yes." I pulled him close for a kiss. I couldn't believe it. I'd just agreed to marry Alex. "This calls for a celebration."

"In a minute. I'm kissing my fiancé." He tightened his arms around me and stole another kiss that I felt all the way to my toes and left me breathless. I could *definitely* do this forever. "My mother is going to freak."

An unwelcome punch of anxiety hit me in the gut. "You lied about her liking me?"

"No! She absolutely *adores* you. I just don't think she ever thought I'd settle down." He chuckled and leaned down to touch his lips to mine again. I gladly gave in. A forever of getting lost in Alex sounded just fine to me. "I love you, Matt."

"I love you, Alex."

He smiled against my lips. "Say my name, Matt. My *real* name."

"Alexi," I sighed into another captivating kiss.

"You know, when you say my name, it sounds a lot like when you say you love me."

I thought about that. Funny, it felt a bit like it, too.

"Now what did you have in mind for celebrating?" he asked, loosening his hold.

I'd almost forgotten. I whirled back to the freezer. "What else? Ice cream, of course." His laughter was warm as he wrapped his arms around my middle and propped his head to look over my shoulder. My enthusiasm died a bit at seeing the barren space. How was it possible for us to have run out?

"Looks like we're making a trip. Go get dressed and we'll head out." He smacked my ass, and I moved to comply. "Oh, and Matt," I turned back to look at him, "I expect the rest of your things in our room by the end of the week."

I flashed him a smile and shadowed the rest of the way. *Our room*, I liked the sound of that. Once changed, I met him in the living room, no doubt still smiling like a fool. At least I wasn't the only one. He extended a hand, and I laced our fingers. The door closed silently behind us and we were off. We walked close together to ward off the intense chill that had settled over the campus. But even with the blinding snow crunching underfoot, it was a beautiful day. We laughed as we sank into unseen pitfalls and kicked the powder up to float down in crystal flurries. Everything about it was perfect. I couldn't have asked for a better day.

"The golden boy lives." The hissing statement sliced through my wonderful bubble of happiness.

One day. Why couldn't I have just one day be good from start to finish? I looked up to see the last person I'd ever thought to see again and shoved Alex behind me.

"Who is that?" Alex whispered in my ear.

"What do you want, Neese?" I asked, not bothering to keep the sharpness from my voice. He shrugged his shoulders in that weird, snake-like way. My resulting shiver had nothing to do with the cold that fogged our breath.

"Neese?" Alex hissed behind me. Suddenly, he was pushing to get around me. "You son of a bitch. You want a fight, I'll give you one. Get your scaly ass over here so I can rearrange your fucking face!" The level of animosity shocked and alarmed me.

I grabbed Alex's arms and struggled to hold him back.

"Damn it, Matt, let me go," he demanded, fighting against the hold.

"I don't think your boyfriend likes me very much."

"Fiancé," I corrected him.

Neese's eyebrows climbed up his forehead.

Meanwhile, I was having a hell of a time preventing Alex from launching himself at Neese's face. "He's not worth it," I repeated, and he finally let me pull him back until he ran into me. I wrapped my arms around his chest, effectively pinning both arms. He'd yet to relax, though, and I was pretty sure he was still staring daggers at Neese. I let out an irritated huff. "What do you want, Neese? I'm not coming back. I'll never go back to that place."

He laughed in that awful hissing way of his. "Never is a long time. Don't worry though, you're off the hook. Seems you've got friends in high places. We got shut down." He flipped a dismissive hand, and I suddenly realized that almost none of his scaly exterior was exposed to the elements. "It's no matter. We'll find another place. Look us up if you ever change your mind. In the meantime, enjoy married life. I never would have guessed. He's cute," he added, shaking his head as he walked past us. When it was clear that he was truly gone, the tension finally left Alex.

"Why did he call you the golden boy?" he asked, almost too low to hear as he turned to face me.

I looked into his eyes, so filled with sadness, and told him the truth. "Because I was the prizefighter." He nodded like the news didn't surprise him. I felt a tug on my arm and we resumed our walk to the dining hall, albeit far more somber than it had started.

"He's the one that made you throw the fight?"

"Yes."

"How many fights?"

"A lot. Too many to count." The information clearly upset him, but I suspected there was more to it than what he was asking. "You want to know if I ever stopped going in the first place."

He glanced at me. Yep, that was it.

"Of course I did, Alex. You are far more important than some stupid bruiser club," I said, but he didn't appear reassured. I stopped in the middle of the walkway, pulling us up short. "I'm serious. Look at me." When he did, it almost broke my heart. What had happened to our beautiful day? "I know things got rocky the last couple months, but I need you to believe me when I say I never wanted to see that place again. You told me to stop fighting, and I did. The only reason I ended back there was because of fucking George and his need for bloodsport. Even then, I'm positive that Neese and Eric manipulated him into it. I love you, Alex. You are the most important thing in my life, and I will always choose you over anyone or anything else."

He gave me a half smile. "Will you still say that when we have kids?" Well, that confirmed that suspicion.

"I'll just have to save everyone."

"Like a knight?" He laughed.

"Yes, like a knight." I chuckled and pulled him in for a lingering kiss. "Whatever you want, Alex. I'll find a way to give it to you."

"How about we start with ice cream?"

"I can do that," I said, re-lacing our fingers.

We'd gone several paces when Alex suddenly missed a step. I quickly turned to him. "What? What's wrong?"

"Neese."

"Yeah..." Fear circled in my belly.

He smacked his head. "I *knew* I recognized that name. Neese is Rubio's roommate. You know, Rubio actually propositioned me to have a threesome with them."

"Rubio's roommate? Really? I knew I didn't like that guy for a reason," I said, then the back half of Alex's statement registered. "He did what!"

Alex laughed and tugged me further along the sidewalk. "I didn't *agree*. And why do you dislike Rubio?"

I glowered at him. "Besides the fact that he hit you up for a threesome with his psychotic roommate?"

"To be fair, I'm fairly confident Rubio doesn't know Neese runs a fight club. Or, at least, I hope he doesn't." Alex paled.

"Look, you don't like Gabriel and I don't like Rubio. Fair's fair."

He squinted at me, but kept walking. "Yeah... I don't think that's how it works."

CHAPTER 25

BAIT

A

"Have you told your mom yet?" Matt asked, and I grimaced. "I'll take that as a no." His following chuckle was warm and relaxed. It was so good to have the real Matt back, *my* Matt. I felt his hand slide over mine and he squeezed my fingers. The extra bits were nice too.

"I figured we could tell her together," I offered, sparing him a hopeful glance.

He gave me a look, no doubt recognizing the stalling tactic for what it was. "She's *your* mom."

"She'll be yours too," I fired back.

His eyes widened as if I'd goosed him. "Mine?" he echoed.

"Of course. My family will be your family. It may just be the two of us, but it'll still be yours," I said, shifting on the couch to face him. Getting nervous when he didn't respond, I asked, "Is that okay?"

"I... I've never had a...." he trailed off, still looking like he couldn't quite wrap his head around this latest tidbit.

Great, I broke him. "Hey, talk to me." I jostled him. "What are you thinking?"

Suddenly, his face erupted into a dazzling smile. "I'm thinking marrying you comes with a lot of perks."

"Oh really? And what are some of these perks?" I asked dubiously. He simply chuckled and leaned forward to place a slow, lingering kiss on my lips that made them tingle. "Yeah,

I'd qualify that as a perk. What else?" I felt him smile against my mouth and kiss me deep enough to steal my breath all over again. I was about to reach up and tangle my fingers in his hair when he suddenly pulled back. "What?"

"Shh." He held up a hand to stall further questions. I was about to ask again anyway, when all the playfulness left his face and he got super serious.

"Matt, you're freaking me out. What is it?"

His eyes were sharp and focused as he turned his gaze to me. "Do you feel that?"

Fear trickled through my veins. Then I felt something. A kind of... pull at my very essence, not unlike when Vera had her little freak out and unceremoniously yanked at every shadow in the vicinity. This, however, was nowhere near as intense. It was faint, like it was coming from far away, and almost like...

"Someone's calling for help," Matt said, finishing my thought aloud. He surged to his feet, nearly toppling me off the couch.

"What are you doing?"

"We have to help them."

"We don't even know where they are," I argued. Not that I didn't want to help, but we were students, not warriors. This wasn't our job.

"I do."

A horrible sinking sensation started in my stomach and worked its way up to my throat. "Matt, no."

"I can't just leave them there. You know what that place is like."

"Exactly, which is why you shouldn't go. Besides, Vera told you to stay out of it. Let her handle it."

He shook his head. "She doesn't know the place like I do."

"But Matt. Things are finally getting back to normal. It's likely a trap anyway," I floundered. This wasn't happening.

"You're probably right. And knowing Thomas, it'll be just as deadly for the bait as for the intended targets."

"At least *call* Vera first." It was a last ditch effort, and we both knew it, but he didn't fight me. He quickly removed his new device and placed the call.

"Voicemail," he mouthed, then left a somewhat detailed message before hanging up.

The look of determination in his eye left little doubt in my mind how this was going to play out, but I had to try. "We should really wait for Vera." Though at this point, I'd be willing to settle for Gabriel if it meant Matt wouldn't set foot in that awful place again.

"We don't know how long they have. I won't sit here and wait Nyx knows how long for her to decide to check her phone."

As expected. I gave a resigned sigh and stood up. "Fine, then I'm going with you."

"I can't let you do that."

I arched an eyebrow. "*Let* me? What are you going to do to *stop* me?" For a fraction of a second, I saw him actually consider it and my heart sank. Matt was stronger than me and if he wanted to, he could absolutely make sure I didn't follow him.

"But, Alex... what they did to you."

"Is nothing compared to what they'll do to you if they catch you. If you go, I go. You're not the only one who almost lost someone," I added.

"Alex, please," he begged.

I understood the pain, but there was no way I was going to sit idly by while he raced into the jaws of death, no matter how scared I was. "I won't lose you, Matt, not again," I said with enough force to take him aback. Still, he hesitated.

"O-okay. We'll do this together."

"Like we'll do everything." I held out my hand.

He took it, and we blinked into the shadow world. Normally, Matt shadowing both of us would have its usual extreme reaction, but I was far too distracted by my worry to be consumed by desire. Even then, I was still breathing hard by the time we emerged on the old fraternity row. To my credit, so was he. The horrid place was a lot farther than I'd thought.

I glanced around at where he'd brought us. We were immediately outside the last house in the row and the gloom overhead promised rain. Fitting, as how the place looked like an abandoned graveyard. Unlike the rest of the campus, here, evidence of the epic battle that had taken place at the university had not been wiped clean. Columns decorated the scorched earth in broken, jagged pieces much like the Regency that had once made this their base of operations. I shuddered. It was said that the spell used to cover their retreat had tainted the masonry so bad the not even Kyra Hallow with a team of fifty of the strongest witches at the time could purify it. Only time could do that. Until then, an undeniable atmosphere of evil permeated the area. The kind that felt like slime oozing over your skin.

"Its coming from in there," Matt said, snapping me out of my dark thoughts.

"I feel it." Now that we were so close, there was no denying it was absolutely a call for help or that we were in the right place. Something was still off. I frowned at the desolate entrance, unable to shake how much it looked like a cavernous maw ready to swallow us whole. "Why is it so faint? It's almost like it's muffled somehow."

He shrugged and walked towards the skeletal remains of the massive house.

"Why didn't you shadow us inside?" I asked, scrambling to catch up.

He paused at the threshold, looking up at the crumbling façade. "Because this place is likely booby trapped down to the studs." Trepidation rolled off of him, reaffirming my decision to come. I couldn't let him face this alone. "Whatever you do, *don't* shadow," he cautioned.

After my last experience here, that was kind of a given. I scanned the ground, toeing aside bits of rubble as I searched.

"What are you doing?"

"Looking for a weapon. If we can't shadow, I feel like it would be prudent. Don't you?" At last I found a piece of loose ironwork. I worked it free and gave it a couple of practice swipes. "This should do. Of course, I'd feel more confident if we'd actually had any training with actual weapons rather than just hand to hand."

Matt squinted at me and I looked over my shoulder, not sure what had caught his attention.

"What?" I dropped the hand holding the iron to my side, suddenly self conscious.

"Night, you're smart," he said before scanning the immediate area himself. Eventually, something caught his eye, and he walked over to tear off an exposed piece of structure, resulting in something that vaguely resembled a quarter staff. He brandished the makeshift weapon. "You ready?"

"Wait." I stepped close, then pulled him in tight, ignoring his squeak of surprise, and kissed him for all I was worth. "I love you, Matt." I didn't want to die without telling him at least one more time.

He squeezed me hard enough my ribs creaked. "I love you too, Alex." He let me go and swallowed hard, as if bracing himself for what was to come. The phantom SOS we'd followed here was still fading in and out. I doubted that bode well for whoever was broadcasting it. After another deep breath, his bright blues captured me. "Stay close. Don't wander. And for

Nyx's sake, don't touch anything." I nodded, and we crossed the threshold of the main entrance.

The house was darker than I remembered. Of course, my memory was a tad skewed, having been unconscious for most of the traveling parts. Then I realized the glow spheres were gone. Between the gray light drifting through the entrance and the boarded-up windows, the creepy levels were off the charts. It felt like an abandoned crypt or some kind of tomb and it *definitely* felt like a trap. The darkness was undoubtedly intentional to encourage a sense of safety for any Shadow demon dumb enough to be there. Sadly, that list included us. I fought the urge to reach out with my essence. At least then, I'd have a better idea of what might lurk beyond our limited field of vision. The temptation was unusually strong, almost like we were being baited by the darkness itself.

I pulled up short. "Do you feel that?"

"Feel what?" he whispered back.

I wasn't sure how to explain the paranoia, so I focused on finding a solution. "We need light. Any chance this place still has running electricity or candles lying around?" I couldn't really make out his frown in the gloom, but then, I didn't need to see it to know it was there.

Abruptly, he spun on his heel and ventured to an unfamiliar part of the house. The room we ventured into was noticeably smaller than the main foyer. A distinction made more pro-nounced by the odd assortment of chairs and tables cluttering the space, including what appeared to be the dilapidated remains of what I hoped was a couch.

"What is that?" I asked, unable to hide my revulsion.

He glanced at the furniture without me having to clarify. His lip curled in disgust. "One guess who brought that trash in here." My money was on Kyle. Guy had no sense of personal hygiene. But then, Travis was vile in his own right. However, I couldn't imagine George deigning to dirty his hands by touching it.

"Is this where you were all that time?"

He stiffened. "Sometimes, but mostly I was out stalking our class mates like some deranged sociopath or at the bruiser club being taught a lesson." The level of hatred in his response was like a knife in my heart. The physical pains I'd suffered during those few days were nothing compared to the torture he'd endured for months. I doubted he saw it that way, though.

I took in the overturned tables and eerie sense of abandonment. While I wasn't prone to paranoia, the place felt haunted. The rest of my life might not be as long as I'd hoped. I looked over at Matt and tried not to be consumed by sadness. He needed me focused. "You think there are candles in here?" I asked, trying to sound confident.

He stopped at chest and leaned down to inspect it. "Fucking great."

"What?"

"This is going to hurt," he said and gently pushed me a couple of paces away. Before I could ask, he shadowed his quarter staff and brought it down with enough force to smash the flimsy chest. The moment the shadow touched the wood, an eerie purple lightning sprung to life. In the lurid light I saw Matt strain not to shout and then, just like that, it went out.

I rushed to his side to find him breathing hard and no longer holding onto the shadow world. "Are you okay? What was that?"

His only answer was to pass me the staff so he could lean down and retrieve a couple of torches. He flicked the switch on each, but alas, only one produced a wavering pool of dim yellow light. "That's what I was afraid of. Virtually everything in here is hard-wired to zap."

I clutched my iron bar tighter. "This is impossible. How are we supposed to get someone out when we can't touch anything?"

"We've got bigger problems."

"What could possibly be a bigger problem?" I asked, rounding on him. This was a ridiculous suicide mission and I should have tried harder to get a hold of someone more qualified to handle this than us.

"For starters, them." He angled the flashlight towards the far wall.

"Oh shit," I whispered at finding several faces leering back at us.

Matt hiked his quarter staff up while I white-knuckled my makeshift sword. I had just enough time to wonder if the iron was rusted through when the nameless faces surged towards us en masse. "Try not to shadow as much as you can," Matt said as we stepped closer to each other. I didn't need the reminder, but then I had no idea how we could hope to escape so many without it.

A loud crack echoed through the space and I glanced behind me to see that Matt had slammed his staff into the side of a snarling face. My stomach heaved. I'd never been in an actual fight before. What was I doing here? This was insane. I didn't know how to fight one person, let alone half a dozen. My panic threatened to strangle me. Suddenly, the hairs on the back of my neck stood on end. Out of pure reflex, I reached into the shadows and threw the person sneaking up on me across the room. Shadow lights filled my vision, drowning everything in that lurid, crackling purple glow. I screamed. Douglas's face hovered before me, his characteristic snarl twisting his face as he plunged first one and then another light into me. My continued screams swallowed up all the other sounds, including Douglas's maniacal cackle. I was going to die strapped to a chair, unable to defend myself or see the love of my life ever again. But I wouldn't give them Matt. More lights, more pain. Searing agony dominated every inch of my world. There was no escape. I'd be trapped here, burning into eternity.

"Alex!" Matt's desperate cry dragged me out of my personal hell and I realized I wasn't still in the chair. There was no evil torturer, and none of the lights were actually touching me, at least not yet.

CHAPTER 26

THE TRAP

M

Alex's scream rang in my ears. I never should have let him come. And now we were surrounded by several of Thomas's non-demon minions who were completely immune to the deadliest weapon in the room. I spun my weapon around and punched it in the gut of the latest attacker. They crumpled to the ground, only to be replaced by another. I grunted as I blocked an assault, then sent them staggering back several steps with almost no effort. If it wasn't for the overwhelming odds and presence of Shadow lights, this would have been a cakewalk on my own. A terrifying thought occurred to me—what if they were human? Suddenly, I was very grateful I'd opted for a blunt weapon. I checked my strength as I sent another assailant soaring across the room and shifted closer towards the main entrance to the room.

"Work your way towards the source of the call! Maybe if we can break through whatever is holding them, then they can help," I shouted over the melee. It was a desperate hope that they'd be in any condition to help or that someone was even here to save. Everything about this place was one big trap tailor-made for Shadow Demons. If I hadn't believed the Warde mission statement before, I certainly did now. No Shadow was meant to leave here alive.

"We need to get out of here," Alex gritted through clenched teeth as he fought off a faceless figure freely waving a Shadow light. Whatever panic he'd had at initially seeing the lights was gone now. He fought with everything he had to make sure the purple glow never so much as grazed him. And I'd brought him here. Would I ever stop doing reckless shit that put his life in danger? I quickly refocused my attention to parry an assault that almost crushed my skull. The force of the defense sent my attacker staggering back, but it didn't deter him. Already, he was running full tilt back into the fray.

"I know, but there are too many." My latest assailant went down, only to be replaced by two more. I snarled in frustration. They were multiplying.

"Then we'll have to use the dark, Matt."

That sounded like a terrible idea, but we were out of options. "I have a feeling this will not go well," I said as he turned to shadow before my very eyes. I followed suit and met him in a larger room. Outraged cries drifted from the room we had just vacated. Thankfully, I still had hold of the flashlight, a minor miracle after the chaos we'd stumbled into. I kept it off for the time being, reluctant to give away our new location.

"That went better than expected," Alex said, sounding as surprised as I felt. "Now what?"

"Now we get out of here, before those things find us again." I struggled to get my bearings, having never shadowed in here before and uncertain of our location without the usual paraphernalia decorating the space. "This way," I said with all the confidence I could muster, leading us deeper into the house. If I got Alex killed, I'd never forgive myself.

Alex walked close enough to touch me as we crept down the hallway. My skin itched with a sense of anticipation and imminent danger. I very intentionally did not touch the walls and noticed Alex being equally cautious. The hallway ended, and we stumbled completely exposed into the open. The abrupt expansion put me off balance and it took a second longer than it should have for me to recognize where we were. This space I was intimately familiar with. I didn't need to see to know that not 20 feet to my right was a wall of pictures, most adorned with garish red X's and a picture of Vera herself atop it all.

Without thinking, I shadowed to the wall, briefly leaving Alex's side. I reached for the dagger stabbed through Vera's face and regretted it the second my hand closed around the hilt. Pain ripped through my arm and I bit down on my tongue to keep from crying out. In the light of the purple flames, I could just make out Alex's expression of abject horror. I fought to relinquish my hold on the Shadow world, but kept trying to pull me deeper, intensifying the pain from the Shadow light trap. Finally, it relented, and I sagged against the wall. Still shaking, I ripped the dagger free of the wall, sending Vera's mutilated picture floating to the ground.

"Are you out of your mind?" Alex hissed, striding up to me. He snatched the flashlight from my grasp and turned it on, keeping it pointed to the ground to limit its field of light. Howls of rage drifted down the hallway.

"Come on. We need to move." Before I stepped away, I tore his picture off of the wall. Damn thing was the whole reason I'd gotten into this mess. He didn't argue or comment, just shook his head and eyed the exceptionally sharp tip of the long dagger. In retrospect, grabbing the blade hadn't been the best idea, but I'd be damned if I let those *things* have it. As quietly as I could, I led the way down a corridor that I hoped would bring us closer to the source of the SOS. "I don't understand how it can't still feel so distant," I whispered. "The house isn't *that* big. We have to be practically on top of them by now."

"Assuming it *is* an actual person, they're probably in a warded room."

I glanced at him out of the corner of my eye. "You're a damn genius."

He rolled his eyes and walked toward the same entrance I'd seen Thomas use a hundred times. As we stepped into the space, my anxiety increased tenfold. We were officially in uncharted territory. The adjoining pathways and doors struck me as unnecessarily complicated, and I couldn't help but wonder if that was real or a spell designed to confuse trespassers. Knowing Thomas' proclivity for creating confusion, I was inclined to believe the latter.

How had Gabriel found me through all of this? Hell, how did he even get in?

"Why haven't they caught up with us yet?" Alex asked.

I glanced over at him and the flashlight shaking in his hand. I didn't know, and it had me equally worried. But I wasn't about to tell him that. "Maybe Vera finally checked her phone." Even in the half light, his relief was evident. If only that were the case. I didn't expect help to come. We'd either find it inside or never leave here at all. I swallowed and once again questioned my life choices that had gotten us here. "Come on, we're getting closer. I feel like we're practically standing on the source."

He nodded and continued down the latest hall. A loud screech came from the far end and we froze. Liquid adrenaline poured like ice through my veins. It had been stupid to think that all the people in this place were behind us. On cue, two bodies rushed toward us. The narrow space wouldn't have been so bad if we could shadow, but that wasn't an option. Alex grunted as one of them made impact. There was nothing I could do to help, though. I already had my hands full with the one clawing to get at my throat. The light of the flashlight swung wildly against the walls until it landed with an ominous crack against the ancient wooden floors. Light poured down the hall to reveal several more pairs of beady eyes.

"Shit. There's more!" The thing attacking me took advantage of my distraction and outrageously sharp teeth pierced my shoulder. I shouted in surprise, dropping the dagger. Alex spun to see what had happened while his opponent was busy picking itself off of the ground. The mediocre glow of the flashlight revealed a face twisted into a savage snarl and and two perfectly spaced porcelain teeth. Dread swirled in my stomach. *Vampires.*

Ignoring the excruciating pain in my shoulder, I frantically searched the ground for the dagger. My fingers had scarcely closed on the hilt before I sent it flying. Alex's eyes widened as it whizzed past him to land with a thunk in the chest of the one sneaking up behind him. His alarm became palpable when he realized what had almost happened. I reached behind me and yanked at the creature clinging to my back. Teeth dug in deeper, and I let out a hiss. We didn't have time for this. Those eyes were getting closer, and the call was fainter. If we took much longer, we might lose the signal altogether and this whole thing would have been for nothing. I slammed into the wall, shadowing partway. The second I contacted the paneling, shadow light burned my skin far worse than the electric barricade at the fight club ever had. It wasn't nearly as potent as the free standing lights though and I could still shadow the vampire on my back into the wall, which is exactly where I left him.

"*Matt*, more are coming..." Alex's worry was palpable. We'd barely managed two. I didn't like our odds against a horde, especially without the ability to Shadow. Why they weren't charging headlong at us was a mystery though.

I grabbed his hand and veered us back the way we'd come. We had to dismiss two routes due to one being cluttered with pieces of broken furniture and rubble and the other holding yet more eyes and matching screeches. Fear clutched at my heart as I realized we were running out of places to run.

"In here!" Alex yelled and pulled me through an unlocked door.

A distinct sense of wrongness prickled my skin. "This doesn't feel right," I said as we stepped into what appeared to be a sitting room similar to the one George and his goons had commandeered. Except, the SOS was closer than ever. In fact, it felt like it was...

"They're in there," Alex finished my thought, gesturing with the light to a door that had an unholy amount of locks on it.

As he walked closer to inspect the overly-guarded door, I examined the room. Unbelievably, the sounds of angry screeches had vanished the moment the door closed behind us. While something still felt decidedly off about the space, maybe it wasn't such a bad hiding spot after all. I used the reprieve to take stock. The presence of the locks, which were undoubtedly spelled, could have been the source of my unease, but I doubted was it. Something else was in here. I just had to figure out what.

The room seemed ordinary enough. Several winged back chairs were set far back from the center, as were any other pieces of furniture, almost as if they'd been moved. Confused why anyone would need to shift furniture like that, I scanned the ground. Scratches on the floor caught the shifting light, and I squinted to make them out. They weren't just scratches; they were marks, designs. I stepped further back to put together the complete picture. It seemed familiar somehow. I stepped a few feet over to get a different vantage and realized what I was seeing. The symbol for the Order of Light was carved into the ground with additional symbols surrounding it. They'd led us into a trap.

"Alex, no!" I shouted as he stepped onto perfect likeness of the sigil.

Instantly, he went completely black and Shadow light erupted from the floor. His scream of agony reverberated through me until I thought I'd go deaf with it. Gritting my teeth, I charged the circle, aiming for where he was standing. By some miracle, I made it through and knocked him out of the sphere of deadly light. I barely registered him crumpling to the ground before the searing pain saturated every cell in my body. Pain unlike anything I'd ever known consumed me, forcing me deeper into the shadow world, all the while seeking to burn out the essence of my soul. But it still couldn't compare to the pain in my chest. Alex was dead, and it was my fault. I deserved this and so much more. I couldn't tell if I was shouting or not. There was only Alex's scream trapped inside my skull.

The world became an empty void defined by light and never-ending pain. My very being continued to reach out despite the agony, desperate for an escape from something that there was no way to escape.

I'm going to die here.

The thought was insubstantial beside my heartache. Alex was gone. Forever.

Distantly, I heard another shout and Alex swam into my field of vision.

Oh good, the hallucinations were back. Except he looked so scared. I didn't want him to be afraid. I wanted to see him smile before I finally gave into the darkness that had been trying to consume me my whole life.

"Don't look sad." My voice sounded weird, like it wasn't coming from the right place. Did I even have a body anymore? Horror flashed in his eyes, but he quickly regained his composure. Even then, he looked like he was in pain and fighting it.

"Matt, you have to fight! Focus on me."

Except you're not real. You never are. I'm still in that damn house, all alone, trying to keep you safe. Except you died anyway. You died because of me.

I crumpled in on myself. There was nothing to live for anymore. Why was I fighting it? Giving up would be so much easier, then the pain would be gone. Did demons have an afterlife? Would Alex be there?

"Damn it, Matt. I won't let you go! You want to be a Roman? Well, Romans don't give up."

That sparked something. But it was distant, and I had to chase it down amidst the tide of agony. How was I even conscious? All I wanted was to slip into the night and let all feeling go. The blinding purple light cast a lurid shadow across the face of the greatest love I'd ever known. Even as a hallucination covered in burns, he was beautiful. I very much wanted to be a Roman, but that would never happen now. Alex was dead, and I was going to die here as well. At least we were together.

"Matt," his voice cracked as he hovered just outside the bubble of pure pain that had become my world. "You promised me children. We're going to have a family. You're going to be a great dad. We're going to watch the times pass together. Forever isn't long enough. Remember? This is *not* where we end." Tears flowed down his face. He clenched his shaking hand and a thin band of black winked back. He followed where my gaze had landed and inspiration seemed to glow in his eyes. "Focus on me, Matt. Focus on the ring."

I didn't have a ring, though. I didn't even have hands.

"Quit being such a stubborn ass and do as you're told," he barked.

Clarity snapped back and suddenly I could see my hand in front of my face, complete with its own black band. That was Alex. That was why he was hurting, because he was in here with me.

He eyed my hand like it was the answer to everything. "Give me your hand, Matt," he ordered calmly, though his own still shook.

I reached for him, struggling against the current of pain until my fingers stopped inches from the outer rim. But I couldn't force my hand any further. I was trapped in this sphere of torture, a breath away from salvation. It would have been nice to touch him one more time. Abruptly, his hand closed over my wrist and the pain intensified, as if every molecule of my body had been doused in oil and set alight. Then there was only darkness.

The floor shaking and the sound of smashing brought me back to consciousness. I blinked, feeling wearier than seemed physically possible. Everything was fuzzy around me and nothing looked familiar. Where was I? Even my bones were tired and every part of me still ached from the memory of the shadow light. Could your soul hurt? There was a solid thunk, followed by the sound of splintering wood. What the hell was that? I groaned as I forced my head up and was rewarded with a vision of Alex holding an iron poker. Beneath him were the shattered remains of the sigil for the Order of Light.

Alex.

The world came into sharp focus and I surged to my feet, ignoring the immense pain it caused. He turned at the scrapping sound. The relief in his eyes made me want to sob. The metal in his hand clattered to the floor, and the ringing echoed off of the walls. In two steps, he walked over to where I was barely standing. As he got closer, I realized there were tracks in the dirt covering his face. When had he been crying? He wrapped his arms tightly around me. The embrace hurt, but touching him was worth the pain.

"You're alive," I said in disbelief.

"I thought I lost you," he whispered into my shoulder, clinging tighter. "No more Shadow lights, okay?"

"Agreed," I said, pushing him back and glancing toward the locked door. "What do you say we finish this?"

He nodded, then reached down to retrieve the poker and tossed me a splinter of wood that resembled my shadow club. I hefted it in my hand and looked at him. We walked over to the warded door and aimed for a spot just to the right of all the locks. There was no way the wall itself could hold up to demonic strength.

"Together?"

"Together."

We swung in unison as hard as we could, where the bolted locks would do no good. The frame cracked beneath our combined assault and wisps of purple Shadow light leaked out. We swung again, and the crack grew. Again. Wood splintered off, flying into the room and decorating us with tiny cuts. Again. The space beside the door imploded, leaving behind a sizable hole.

Alex quickly dropped his weapon and retrieved the flashlight. In the yellow glow, we both appeared covered in layers of shadow burns. He angled the beam of light into the room and a figure took shape. All I could do was hope that it was harmless or too injured to be dangerous. As the form shuffled closer, I noticed they were using their arm to shield their eyes. They also looked terrible, covered head to toe in their own gruesome wounds.

"Lower the light," I whispered. Alex quickly adjusted the angle of the flashlight. The arm fell, and we saw the haggard face of a girl who had clearly been through hell.

"Ellie?" Alex asked in disbelief.

She glanced from him to me, taking in our own state of disaster. "Matt? Alex? Oh, thank goodness! I thought no one would ever come," she sobbed, then promptly collapsed. We caught her together, and another voice rang out behind us.

"Dorian is going to be *pissed*," Vera said, looking every bit as roughed up as we were.

I looked back at Alex over Ellie's practically lifeless form. He seemed just as surprised as I was at her appearance. "Guess she checked her phone after all."

CHAPTER 27

RETRIBUTION

A

A s Vera surmised, Dorian looked less than pleased to be seeing us a second time. We were back in the manor, only this time we hadn't been taken to the library. I was fairly sure we were on the second level, but couldn't recall going up any stairs. In fact, how we'd gotten here at all was fuzzy. Had we used a portal? Had we shadow walked? I shook my head. Right now, my only concern was making sure Matt got healed and there was no telling what I looked like. I knew logically that I had shadow burns all over my body, but Matt's appearance was worse. He looked like he'd been left in a broiler and forgotten. I had no idea how he was standing or how he'd even survived.

Dorian and Vera's voices drifted into the hall despite the closed door separating us. Matt and I shared a look as their volume increased. Thankfully, Dorian wasn't shouting at Ellie, but at Vera.

"Just once, could you *not* to end up a shredded mess?"

"I already told you, Dorian, I don't need healing. Besides, it's nothing I haven't healed naturally from before," Vera added dismissively.

"Over my dead body are you walking out there without even a minor healing. For Christ's sake, look at you!"

"That's not funny."

"You're right. It's not. Neither is getting called up repeatedly to heal children. Children, Vera. What were they doing there in the first place? I thought you said you were going to leave them out of this?"

"I don't need a lecture and I can't control other people's actions. As for them being children, they're older than we were that first summer."

"And how wrong was what we went through?" Dorian paused in his tirade. "You know what? Forget I said anything. Let's get this over with. On the upside, none of them seem so bad that I should need to borrow energy."

"You should take some anyway," Vera insisted.

"I told you I don't need it."

"Stop arguing and just fucking take it. I know what this does to you. I'll deal with Gabriel."

"Where is he, anyway?"

"Still trying to track down Thomas and his cohort."

"He told you that?"

"No," Vera deadpanned. Silence fell.

I glanced at Matt. "He'll find them," I whispered, reaching out to him.

He clenched his charred fists in his lap, causing them to crack and reveal raw, bleeding skin beneath. "No he won't. Thomas is long gone."

"In that case, I hope we never see either of them again."

Matt shook his head. "They won't give up hunting us so easily."

"But for now, at least, we're safe. *You're* safe," I emphasized.

He opened his mouth, no doubt to argue, when Dorian stepped out. We turned to face the irate healer, who looked like he'd been sucking lemons for the last hour.

"Right, who's first?" he grumbled.

"Matt." "Alex." We said at the same time.

I glanced at my stubborn angel. "You need more than I do. You're going first."

"I'm fine. You're going," he insisted.

"Look, I don't have all day. Either one of you gets in that room right now, or neither of you is getting healed." Dorian crossed his arms and stared us down.

I suspected he was bluffing, but Matt clearly wasn't taking chances. He glowered at me and I caved. He'd absolutely refuse healing until I was seen to. We needed to have a serious talk about how little he seemed to value his own life. I took a step forward and Dorian grabbed me in order to haul me the rest of the way. We passed Vera on her way out, looking pale and exhausted. She'd obviously won the argument to give up energy after all. The door closed behind her, leaving me alone with Dorian. I glanced around the pristine room, which was set up as a minimalist doctor's office, and wondered where they'd taken Ellie. She hadn't come out with Vera and I didn't see any other exists. At a curt gesture from Dorian, I took a seat on the metal table.

"I'm sorry you had to be dragged out here again. Why do you keep coming if it's so difficult for you?" I asked to take my mind off the unpleasantness of sitting.

"I'm here because I'm a healer and it's what I do. As for the other, I keep coming because I can't seem to tell the damn woman no. This was so much easier when she thought I was dead," he mumbled under his breath.

"I can understand not being able to deny someone. It sucks. If it's any consolation, I have no intention of repeating any of this," I offered.

He frowned. "That's what they all say. Now, care to explain exactly what happened? Your friend—"

"Fiancé," I corrected.

Dorian blinked. "My apologies. Your fiancé looks absolutely terrible."

"We tripped a spell. I'm not really sure what it was. It felt like it was forcing me into my Shadow state amidst a ring of Shadow light. Matt knocked me out of it and got himself stuck. He was in it much longer." I looked at the ground, ashamed. If I hadn't just blindly walked into the room, we could have avoided it all together. "It was horrible, I thought... I thought he was gone. All of his essence was spread out. He didn't even have a body anymore. And... and he couldn't recognize me." I hiccupped as the fear I'd felt welled up inside of me.

A warm hand covered my shoulder, and the familiar rush of ice swept through me. As the tide receded, it took all the physical pain but left the heartache. I didn't think I could live without Matt and he was so determined to sacrifice himself. "He's alive. What ever you did, saved him," Dorian said gently.

I lifted my head to look at him. I hadn't said I'd done anything.

"What? You think I don't know how self-sacrificing demons can be? You guys may be reckless and a tad suicidal, but you're also loyal and honorable to a fault."

I snorted. "I'm pretty sure that no one has ever referred to a Shadow demon as honorable in the history of ever. That's not really a word you associate with the Chaos Class."

"Maybe you've been misclassified. Every Shadow demon I've ever met has behaved much the same. Now, in all fairness, I also am a firm believer that each one of you is also certifiably insane."

"You really have the strangest bedside manner."

"Yeah, yeah. Everybody's a critic. Now, send in your fiancé, so I can get on with the rest of my patients." Patients? How many did he have?

"Thank you, Dr. Valens," I said, making my way out. He simply nodded and retrieved Matt before he had the chance to stall again. Matt shot him a downright sinister look at being denied the chance to confirm the thoroughness of my healing. Dorian remained completely unaffected and dragged him off anyway. To my surprise, Matt actually didn't fight him, nor did I hear any telltale arguing. Now I was even more convinced that Matt was experiencing more pain than he was showing. That was the problem with Matt. There was never any telling just how much he was hurting, because he kept it all bottled up. But I knew the truth.

I glanced down at the thin black band encircling my ring finger. He couldn't hide the hurt from me anymore. I'd felt it. The moment he'd pushed me out of the circle, acute agony had radiated from the small connection. The force of it had been crippling, far surpassing my experience in the ring. I whole-heartedly believed that while the spell had been Shadow Demon specific, it had been *designed* for Matt. He was a Warde that shouldn't exist. The entire house was an elaborate trap designed by someone to eradicate the last of Matthias' line once and for all. I was a collateral bonus. That either of us had escaped still breathing was a miracle in and of itself.

The door opened again, and Matt walked out. My heart swelled at seeing that the garish burns and charred flesh were gone, replaced with perfectly healthy, albeit filthy, skin. "That doesn't get any better with repetition," Matt said, looking back into the room where Dorian was still standing.

I tentatively reached up to touch his face. "It really is incredible," I whispered in awe. Before he could say anything, I pulled him into a tight embrace. He gave an "oof" then wrapped his arms around me. "I thought I lost you." He squeezed tighter, and I pulled back to look at him. The perfect crystal of his eyes shone back with their own level of concern.

"Are you okay? What that spell did to you. I don't even know..."
I trailed off.

"I'm fine, Alex. I'm more worried about you."

Anger sprung up unexpectedly. "I'm going to need you to stop treating my life like it's more valuable than yours."

"But it is."

"Only to you." I snared him, and he met the fierce kiss with one of his own. That fire I craved swept through us, a blinding inferno binding us together. "I need you to live, Matt. Forever will be very short if you keep up with these suicide missions."

"Okay, Alex," he sighed before recapturing me. "I really do love kissing you," he whispered, deepening the kiss. It felt like he was seriously trying to steal every breath I'd ever had and I was perfectly alright with that.

There was a faint squeak of surprise somewhere far outside our bubble of bliss. We stopped kissing long enough to see who had joined us.

"Hi, Ellie," Matt said breathlessly.

"Well, that explains a lot," she said calmly, in direct contrast to the pink flush spreading across her cheeks.

I tried to step away from Matt, but he wasn't letting go. I rolled my eyes and removed his hands from my waist. He rewarded me with a look like someone had just stolen his candy right out of his mouth. Chuckling to myself, I walked over to Ellie. "I can't believe you're awake." I said.

She blinked, dragging her gaze away from Matt, who undoubtedly still looked like a petulant child.

"Um, yeah," she replied absently, then the rest of her wits returned. "Though I wouldn't be if it weren't for you two. I don't know how much longer I had. That room was lined with... That room was awful." She shuddered.

"I know." Matt placed a comforting hand on her arm. "You're okay now, though. They won't hurt you anymore. They're gone."

Her eyes lit up. "Oh, right. Ms. Scry wants you in the library."

"You should probably call her Vera," Matt offered helpfully as he took my hand. Ellie looked at him like he'd grown a second head.

I cleared my throat. "If you'll lead the way. I'm not really sure where we are."

"Of course, follow me." She spun on her heel and we dutifully trailed after her. She was in surprising spirits given her ordeal. But then again, I glanced at Matt, so was I.

The journey didn't take near as long as I expected. Turned out the library was closer than I realized. We walked in just in time to see Vera end a call. She turned to us and gave an appreciative nod.

"Thank you, Miss Thornton. If y'all will have a seat, there are a few things we should cover." We did as we were told, clustering around a smaller version of the table we'd sat at the last time.

"Where is Thomas? Has Gabriel caught him yet?" Matt asked without preamble. He clearly assumed that Gabriel had been on the other end of the line. I squeezed his hand, but he remained hyper-focused on Vera and it didn't look like she had good news.

"Thomas is in the wind, as is the rest of his operation. None of those he coerced into waiting in that house have any inkling of where he might be. No matter the persuasion," she added darkly. I swallowed at what sort of "persuasion" had been used.

"He can't just be gone. He has to answer for what he did," Matt said emphatically, releasing my hand to gesture wildly. "What he did to Alex, to Ellie, and who knows who else." I noticed he hadn't included himself in the list of injured parties. I sighed to myself. It seemed ensuring Matt had self-worth was going to be a lifelong struggle.

"I understand your frustration, Matt—believe me, I do—but just because they've slipped away doesn't mean they'll elude us forever. I want retribution every bit as much as you do. The things I've seen and endured... There's not a question in my mind that this cruel order needs to be eliminated." Vera held up a hand to forestall the argument brewing on Matt's face. "*However*, we can only work with what we have. Is there nothing else you can remember from your time spying for him? Even the tiniest detail could be of use."

"I already told you everything I remember. It's not like he was passing out his darkest secrets. Don't you think if I knew more, I would have already done something?" He waved wildly in my general direction.

Of that, I had no doubt. It was the main reason I'd been keeping such a close eye on him. I simply couldn't trust that he wouldn't run off on some hair-brained scheme, today's adventure not withstanding. She glared back at him, clearly ready to yell herself. The both of them made quite a pair of hot heads. Meanwhile, Ellie glanced from Vera to Matt like she was watching a tennis match. Poor thing probably had no idea what was going on.

I sat back in my chair expecting a rather long evening, mostly composed of the two of them shouting at each other. Unexpectedly, a door on the far side open and a familiar TA walked into the room with three people trailing behind her. Upon closer inspection, I realized manacles connected the three. Then recognition dawned. I let out an involuntary gasp.

"What's the matter?" Matt asked. He turned to me, then followed my line of sight. Before I could react, he blinked out to reappear across the room.

"Matt, no!" I shouted as he crashed into George, near-ly sending the whole grisly caravan to the ground. His fist slammed into George's face repeatedly. He struggled to de-fend himself against the brutal assault of rage while Travis and Kyle cowered as far away as their chains would allow. I was paralyzed with shock as I watched Matt wail on George and he'd only broken my cheek. What would Matt do when he finally found Douglas?

"Get off of me!" Matt howled as Vera pulled him off of his victim. George remained huddled on the ground. "Where the fuck did these assholes crawl out of? Why are they even still alive? Where is your master, you son of a bitch?" Matt asked furiously, spitting on George and fighting Vera's grip. Despite her higher power level, she seemed to struggle to constrain him. I'd never seen so much anger, and it terrified me.

"Are you serious!" Dorian shouted upon entering the mad-house. "Damn it, Vera, I'm not healing these people just so they can rip each other apart all over again. That's it. Do you hear? I'm done. His nose can stay broken. I'm taking the portal home."

"Dorian, wait," Vera tried to call him back, but she was still fighting Matt, who was determined to finish what he'd started. "Damn it Matt, cut it out. He's done. It's over."

Matt snarled. "It's not over until he's in a lead-lined box six feet underground." He was going to kill him, anyway. I couldn't let him do that. He may not regret it now, but one day he would.

I shadowed over and laid a hand on Matt's shoulder. "Matt, stop. We talked about this." The fight instantly left him, but the rage stayed plastered on his face. There was nothing I could do about that, but I wasn't worried he would continue the attack. George, however, did not seem so confident. "I've got him," I said to Vera. She looked amazed and dubious. After all,

I wasn't even holding him. Nonetheless, she relinquished him to me.

"Get them out of here," she ordered the TA. "And get him cleaned up." She watched as the troop left the library. "Good grief, Matt. What the hell is wrong with you?" she asked, rubbing her temples.

"Why are they here?" he demanded.

"Because I had the same questions as you." Her mouth twisted to the side as she gave him a withering look. "They're clueless. Thomas kept them every bit as much in the dark as you. That idiot didn't even know that he was working for the Order of Light. There's no telling what he thought he was actually hunting. But that doesn't absolve him. He'll pay for his crimes. He didn't just hurt you two." Her subtle glance back towards the table suggested Ellie had not been spared the wrath of George.

"And the others?" I asked before Matt could launch into a fresh tirade.

"The other two are fools. Blind sheep following a wolf."

"They're just as culpable," Matt hissed angrily.

"I'm not disputing that. They have their own crimes to atone for, but the severity is far less."

"What will happen to them?" I asked.

"George is going to prison. Maybe after a century we can visit the idea of parole. The others? I'm still working on that."

"He doesn't deserve to live after what he did." Matt's words dripped with acid and I wrapped an arm around him, surprised to find him shaking. Would my beautiful angel ever be able to move beyond this rage?

Vera shook her head. "I know how you feel, Matt, I really do, but there just aren't enough of us left in the world to go around executing other Shadow Demons with impunity. Incarceration will have to suffice for now."

Matt sagged, defeated, and leaned against me. "I'm sorry," he whispered, barely loud enough for me to hear.

"It's okay," I reassured him, placing a small kiss on his forehead. "All that matters is that they've been stopped and we're all okay."

CHAPTER 28

LESSON ONE

M

S pring semester was officially in session. Being in a class-room felt surreal after the absolute chaos of the last few months. Personally, I was over the constant brushes with death, though that didn't seem to prevent them. I made sure that this semester Alex and I would have more classes together and intentionally signed up for as many of the same as I could. Regretfully, that list only comprised two. My over-achiever fiancé had either already taken or tested out of most of the core curriculum, which only left Demonic History III and Advanced Battle Tactics. However, despite all of my efforts, I ended up in the same class at a different time. Apparently, more shadow demons appeared out of nowhere and enrolled, forcing Vera to have more than one class. That I did take up with Vera. I'd be damned if I was going to be in a different time slot than Alex.

She conceded without much of a fight, which should have given me pause. Talking to her was never that easy. Sure enough, I got Alex *and* two parolees. Apparently, I'd be keeping an eye on Travis and Kyle, while Alex kept an eye on me. I was less than pleased about the arrangement, but wasn't willing to argue in case it meant my schedule got shifted again. Consequently, my first couple of lessons with Gabriel didn't happen. Now that I was taking Advanced Tactics in the afternoon instead of the morning, everything was out of whack. We were drawing to the close of our third week by the time I finally got the call that I'd be having a lesson.

"And you're sure it's today?" Alex asked for the fifth time.

"Yes, Alex. You saw the message yourself." I knew he didn't like the private lessons, but I couldn't seem to make him understand that there was no reason to dislike Gabriel. He was a teacher, that was all.

"And it's in the manor?" He definitely didn't like that part. Logically, though, where else would it be?

"Yes."

"And you have everything you need?"

"Alex, enough. Stop mothering me."

"I'm not mothering you," he responded with a scowl.

"Yes, you are. Speaking of which, have you told yours yet?" He frowned. I didn't know what was taking him so long and was beginning to fear he just didn't want her to know. Was it because it was me? Was that why?

"Not yet. But seriously, are you sure you don't need to bring anything?" He would not be diverted.

I rolled my eyes. "He's not exactly giving me a history lesson." The moment the words were out, I regretted them. The look on Alex's face said he was very aware I was not going for history. Without warning, he pulled me into an empty room and conquered me with a kiss that was entirely inappropriate for campus. "Damn, Alex," I finally managed, totally out of breath. He wasn't done, though. I let out a moan as I his teeth grazed my neck. Okay, there *might* have been some upsides to this inexplicable jealousy his. "I really have to get going. You do too, otherwise you'll be late." That did it.

"Fine. Go to your damnable lesson." He stepped away, releasing me from where he'd pinned me against the wall. There wasn't a doubt in my mind that I was now sporting an impressive hickey. He paused before leaving and turned back to look at me. "And, Matt, behave." There was a lot more in the quiet command than simply an order to keep my temper. I gave him a crooked smile and stepped up to him to steal one last kiss, albeit a more chaste one.

"Of course," I said before shadowing out.

When I finally stepped through the portal created specifically for these lessons, I was definitely late. I let out a sigh. Already off on the wrong foot. After stepping through the portal, I surveyed my surroundings. I appeared to be in a training room, but it didn't resemble any of those on campus.

"You're late," Gabriel's voice came from the shadows across the room. In what was proving to be his signature style, he followed his voice into the room. One of these days, I was going to figure out why they looked so similar. It could just be the area they were from, random genetics, or maybe they shared a common ancestor.

"Yeah, I got held up."

"I can see that," he replied, casually tipping my collar. I fought back the burn of embarrassment. "Is that going to be a common occurrence?" That was an excellent question and one I didn't have an answer for.

"Are we going to train or what?" I asked, to refocus the conversation.

"Yes, but we need to cover a few items of business first." That didn't sound good. I tensed. He shook his head and commented, "I swear you and Vera have to be related somewhere down the line. Obviously, not through the Warde side, but perhaps through Teala's."

"Who?"

"Sopteală. She had other partners before Matthias, you know. I would like to say that I thought their union was preposterous, but I have a better understanding of it now," he finished, glancing at the ceiling. Vera must be in the house, and we were definitely not on the top floor.

I did a double-take. "Wait, you *knew* her?"

"Naturally. There may have been more Shadow Demons back then, but we have never been a numerous species. We are not quite the rabbits our cousins are," he said, with no small amount of scorn.

"Did you?"

"Did I what?"

"Did you have other lovers before...?" One of these days I'd stop indulging my curiosity like this.

He gave me a deadpan expression. "I *am* several hundreds of years old. If you are trying to ask if I am Alexi's father, then you should just ask."

My face went cold as all the blood drained from it. I hadn't even thought of that, though it would certainly explain why they looked so similar. "The answer is no. I intentionally had no progeny. My relationship with my father was not exactly conducive to cultivating any desire to carry on the family line."

"Your father is an original." The regurgitated information fell out of my mouth.

"He is. But back to what I was talking about. Sopteală was more than just a rebel who fell for a mortal. She was also the head of the Knights of Nyx, which I plan to reconstitute. Starting with you."

I stared at him. I didn't even have enough wits to make some noncommittal noise.

"Well, you haven't said no yet, so this is already going better than Vera expected."

"Is this where you trained her?" It was a stupid question, but I was still struggling to wrap my head around the other. I'd never heard anything even resembling the Knights of Nyx.

There had been no mention of them in any of the texts we'd found.

"Yes, although most of her initial training began in the library." He rolled his eyes at seeing my confused expression and elaborated. "Being raised mortal, she was seriously lacking in history. Before I could teach her how to use her powers, she needed to understand what she was, where she came from. Not so unlike yourself. Besides, it was the first time someone had ever summoned me to be a teacher, and I wasn't really sure where to begin. I was—am—a history professor, so I started there."

"You teach history?" This conversation was getting more unbelievable by the second. He nodded. "But I thought..." I trailed off.

"I am still one of the oldest Shadow Demons left, thus making me the most qualified."

"One of? There are more?"

"Of course there are more. Alright, enough stalling. Let's see what you've got."

I snorted. "You already know what I've got. You were there."

"That was different." He created a long stick out of shadow. "This is a quarter staff. You'll be training with one of these."

"Why not swords? Why a weapon at all?" I was on a roll with the inane questions.

"First, I've seen you in hand to hand as you so eloquently pointed out, and second, I have also seen that temper—you do not need anything with a sharp edge to it."

I scowled. I was here to learn how to use my powers, not get some sporadic history lesson and a beating. Which is exactly what it would be, given how severely he outclassed me. However, before I could argue, he bore down on me. I quickly summoned a quarterstaff and barely blocked him in time from sweeping my legs out from under me. My speed meant nothing in the face of Gabriel's assault. For every attack I countered, two more landed. I rubbed my rump, where the latest smack still stung like a bitch.

"Come on, Matthew, you can do better than this. If you are going to be a knight in the order, I need to know you can do more than defend. Attack me."

I parried the latest strike and danced back, narrowly evading his backswing. "Why do you want me to be part of this, anyway? Is that why you offered to teach me?" My body ached from the countless raps I'd received, and I was definitely winded from trying—unsuccessfully—to avoid his relentless assault.

"In part. Demons are over due for representation. The disaster with the Order of Light just proves that we need our own driving force to stand up for those who cannot stand up for themselves." He spun around and disappeared, only to materialize behind me. The butt of his quarter staff smacked into my back, not hard enough to bruise, but enough to knock me off balance.

I shadowed out of reach to buy time to regain my footing.

"Attack me. Attack me or I will find someone else to take your place. Perhaps Alexi would be more suited for this work." Rage swept through me. "He certainly doesn't have any qualms about fighting for what he believes in or dying, for that matter."

I rushed him and our shadowed weapons met with jarring force. "You don't touch him. Alex isn't a fighter."

"Neither are you, apparently. Perhaps if you had spent less time skulking around, you would have been able to prevent him from being taken."

I black. Our movements became a total blur as I completely unleashed. The frenzied attack came to a sudden halt in a perfect stalemate.

"Much better," he said with an evil glint in his eye. Where I was panting from exertion, he wasn't even breathing hard. "Next time, we will work on your control. Interesting that you do not use the shadows when you fight. Don't worry, I will break you of that." I bristled at the low key threat and the belated realization that he'd been playing with me. The only person in this world allowed to toy with me was Alex.

I dropped my hold on the staff, and it vanished. "I'm done."

"You are done when I say you are done." He swung his quarterstaff at me and I used shadows to halt the movement.

"Alex taught me that little trick. And just to be clear, you don't go anywhere near him." I narrowed my eyes at him. "Does Vera know about the Knights of Nyx?"

He stopped maintaining his staff and straightened. "No."

"I won't keep this from Alex."

"I would expect nothing less." His casual assumption only pissed me off more. I spun on my heel to return to the portal. "And Matthew, I will see you here again on Friday. Unless, of course, you would prefer I reach out to your friend." My steps faltered, but I kept moving.

"Fiancé," I corrected. His congratulations hardly even registered before I walked through the door.

No sooner did I emerge than I shadowed directly to the dorm. Even with anger still ricocheting inside me, I could have sighed with relief to see Alex already there. I was furious with Gabriel and myself. Once again, I'd willingly signed myself up to fight. That brought me up short. I didn't recall having agreed, but I knew I would, that I already had. Alex was going to be pissed. I doubted he'd be comforted that this time it wasn't for sport.

"You're back sooner than I expected." He stood, abandoning the mountain of papers on the breakfast table.

In two shadow steps, I was on top of him and pulling him in close. I needed an outlet for the fire inside of me. I needed Alex. I always needed Alex.

"Whoa, bad day? Did the training not go well?" he tried to ask between my relentless kisses.

I grabbed his hand and dragged him to our room, still not answering. There, I slipped my hands beneath his shirt to feel the perfectly smooth skin beneath. I couldn't believe I'd let Gabriel get to me. He was infuriating. The nerve, using Alex to get me worked up. That was cheap.

"Matt, talk to me."

"I need you."

His gaze searched mine. "I'm always here for you."

"No, Alex. I want... I *need* what you do." I didn't know how else to say it. Alex had a way, and right now, I needed that more than anything. He stared down at me and I saw the moment it registered what I was really asking for. I let out a breath of relief because I really didn't know how to say it. He captured me in a demanding kiss I felt in my core. When he released me, I was entirely out of breath. *That*, I needed that. I needed his fire to burn as hot as mine.

"Okay, Matt, but after, you *will* tell me what happened," he said with a fierce look.

I nodded, then swallowed nervously as he continued to just look at me. "Alex, please." I felt so adrift in the world. If he didn't anchor me, there was no telling where I'd end up.

He took his time with the next, teasing my lips apart and lightly sucking on my lip before gliding his tongue in. I moaned and completely melted as our tongues danced together. Then he removed my hands from his hips and pulled them over my head. My breath hitched as he left them suspended in order to slide my shirt over my head. Once it was free, he tugged them down to rest on his shoulders. I tangled my fingers in his hair as he deepened the kiss and guided me backwards. My arms fell back over me as he laid me out before him. He removed my pants and returned to claim my mouth.

"What do you want?" The sultry question sent electricity coursing through me.

"This," I groaned and kissed him harder for emphasis. It was so easy to get lost in Alex and I was quickly becoming completely addled.

"My mouth, huh?"

What? No. That didn't make any sense. But as he worked his way across my shoulders and torso, I didn't argue. His kisses really were wonderful, especially when he paired them with those light nips. I buried my hand in his hair again and arched into him, then let out a gasp when his lips wrapped around my dick. That wasn't what I'd meant at all, but that didn't stop my eyes from rolling back or my moan. He took me down to the root and I nearly passed out from the incredible constriction of his throat when he swallowed. Per usual, he took his time playing with me, slowly dragging his tongue up the shaft before lightly sucking on the swollen crown. I was afraid I'd pull his hair out when he mouthed and sucked my balls. Alex needed to not be so good at blowjobs. Already I was tiptoeing the edge and struggling to decide if it would be better to let go or keep holding on to enjoy more of the mind-blowing sensations. He returned his attention to my dick, and I got that much closer to falling over. Then he pulled off, leaving me shaking and the wrong side of completely wrecked.

I immediately sat up to capture him with a kiss, but only got the briefest one before he pushed me back down and pinned my arms up above me. "Alex," I moaned into the following kiss. Distantly, I felt shadow encircle my wrists and tighten. Trepidation shot through me.

"Don't break it again." The husky command liquefied my insides.

My heart beat uncontrollably and I squirmed in tortured ecstasy as he used his mouth and fingers to explore my body and eventually open me up. I struggled against the bond, very conscious not to snap it. Then, all sensation vanished and I could have cried with denied want, but I kept the strip of shadow intact. I lifted my head and watched Alex slowly and deliberately remove his clothing with what I was positive were black eyes. When he finally stepped closer, I desperately wanted to reach out and feel him, but dutifully remained as he'd left me. His palms tickled the hair on my legs as he caressed their full length. Then he grabbed my thighs, and he pulled me to the edge of the mattress, forcing my arms to stretch out above me. My breath came in stuttered pants as he positioned my legs so that my calves rested on his shoulders.

I heard the pop of a cap, though I hadn't seen him grab the lube. His fingers returned to my clenching hole and my toes curled as he stretched me more, taking time to rub that special bundle of nerves that drove me wild. When he was satisfied I was ready, he positioned the swollen head of his dick at my entrance. I clenched in anticipation, then remembered to relax. In one powerful thrust, he breached the outer rim of tight muscle and buried himself to the hilt. I let out a strangled cry, barely maintaining the thin band of darkness. He rolled his hips, driving me into the mattress again and again until I felt spilt in two. All thought fled as I dissolved into him. There was only Alex and his touch. I was his to do with whatever he wanted. Now, later, forever.

Eventually, I floated back down to Earth and lay there lost in contended bliss. I had no idea how he did that, but he did it every time and it was wonderful.

"Tell me what you're thinking about." The soft command felt like a caress on my already sensitive skin.

"That I rather like being your plaything." My eyes widened as the unfiltered honesty left my tongue. Instantly, my face burned. If the damn thing got any hotter, you could fry an egg on it. Meanwhile, Alex's laughter rolled out to envelop me like a blanket.

"Is that how you think of it?" he asked, laughter still playing at the edges.

I didn't even try to manage words. Was it possible to die of mortification? He shifted so he could look down at me. Judging by the heat in my face, I was likely still the color of a beet. Night, this was awful.

He slid his hand across my abdomen as he nuzzled my neck. "If it's any consolation, I've never had a plaything before. And, for the record, I rather enjoy it as well." The low, whispered words sent a corresponding heat rushing through me. I was all set to dissolve back into ecstasy when he unexpectedly changed the topic. "Now, about this day of yours. What made it so bad?"

It would have been easy to override the question and focus more on his touch, except it had been part of his terms. I took a heavy breath and released it a put-upon sigh. He starred down at me expectantly and unfazed. This wasn't exactly a conversation I wanted to have in bed, but I'd agreed. He raised his eyebrow, no doubt wondering what was taking me so longer to answer. Here goes nothing.

"I had my first private lesson today," I began awkwardly.

"I know." Something flashed in his eyes, but he said nothing past the scary monotone words.

I swallowed anxiously and searched his face. Stalling was making this so much worse. But I wouldn't lie to him, not anymore. "Gabriel knew Sopteală." Shock exploded across his face. "There's more." He sat back and waited. I shifted to a sitting position and looked back. He wasn't going to like this. "Remember that job the note mentioned? Well, it's a task force. Kind of like..."

"The Shadows," he finished for me. If I'd thought he sounded scary before, I was wrong. Dead wrong. Every hair on my body stood on end and I shuddered at the sheer malevolence in which he uttered those two words. His lip curled in a snarl as his eyes turned to green fire. "I can't believe this. He wants to fucking resurrect the Shadows."

"Not quite."

The look he speared me with made me really wish there wasn't more. Fury and disbelief warred for dominance in his emerald eyes.

"He wants to revive an ancient order. They've been disbanded for centuries. Apparently Sopteală was actually running the whole thing before she died. Have you ever heard of the Knights of Nyx?" I desperately hoped that the play on history would help soften the blow. It didn't.

"Are you fucking serious? And before you ask again, no, I haven't heard of the Knights of Nyx. But it doesn't make a difference what you call it, the result is still the same. You'd be an enforcer, a fighter, a bloody fucking peacekeeper! Your job would *literally* be to hurt other people. You just got away from all of that and he wants you to—What? Dive right back in?" His disbelief was as palpable as his anger. He threw the covers off and got up. This was already going way worse than I'd feared.

I quickly scrambled after him. "Alex, please. It's not like that. I'd—"

Suddenly, he spun around to face me. "You want to do it, don't you?" He didn't even wait for me to respond. "Of course you do," he said, throwing up his hands and turning away from me. "That's why you haven't even asked how *I* feel about it. You're not asking for permission or even a blessing, you're simply telling me. You've already decided. I knew it wouldn't end at just the lessons. Any excuse, right?" he scoffed. Already he was halfway to the door. He wouldn't listen to anything I said if it related to Gabriel.

"Alexi Roman."

He froze at the use of his full name, anger clearly etched in every line of his body.

"What are you more upset about? The job or that it's Gabriel?"

He stiffened at the name which answered that question.

"This isn't some arbitrary militant squad. This is for demons, for us, *our* kind. They are out there, Alex, and too afraid to come out." His shoulders slumped and I could tell I was getting through to him. I reached out and turned him around, but he refused to meet my eye. "On top of which, this is in my blood, my legacy."

"I always knew you were a knight in shining armor," he commented snidely.

"You've always been mine." That got his attention. I took another step toward him, effectively invading his bubble. At least he was looking at me again. "I don't want us to fight about this," I said, cupping his face so he couldn't turn away again.

Uncertainty swam in his eyes. "I just don't understand why you'd agree to this. You don't even *like* fighting. You told me so yourself."

"That's not why I'm doing this. Plus, it's a far cry from that night-forsaken bruiser club. I'll be protecting people that can't fend for themselves."

"Bloody knight," he mumbled under his breath.

"I thought you wanted a knight?" I asked quietly, with just a hint of teasing. The question earned me the hint of a smile. "I love you, Alex."

He blinked back at me. My heart hammered against my ribs like it always did when he looked at me. I leaned forward and placed my lips against his. Time seemed to stand still while I waited for him to kiss me back. When he did, it was like the black and white of the world became awash with color. I wrapped my other arm around him and pulled him close as I deepened the kiss. His return was equally impassioned, and tendrils of desire curled through me.

"It'll only ever be you," I said breathlessly. His arms tangled around me, crushing my body against his. I let out a gasp, and he claimed my mouth with a fierce, unforgiving kiss that reverberated through my very being. Alex was possessive, overbearing, and demanding... and he was mine.

EPILOGUE

A

I t was surreal being back home after everything that had
happened. The world barely even made sense anymore.
Yet, amidst all the chaos, there was one thing I knew with
perfect clarity: I loved Matt. That Matt loved me back, however, hardly felt real. Selfishly, I wanted to keep him all to
myself, but as much as I was willing to wait, there was only
so long I could put off telling my mom about us. Not the least
of which because he kept asking if I had, to which the answer
was always a vague I'll get to it.

I worried he was taking my reluctance as a sign that I didn't
think this would go over very well. The truth was quite the
opposite. I was wary of my mother's enthusiasm when she
found out about our recent status change. Trepidation aside,
I couldn't put it off forever. Today, we'd tell my mother we
were engaged. However, we'd unanimously decided to omit
anything related to the Order of Light. I fully expected that
at some point the truth would come out, but until then, I
believed we'd earned ourselves a reprieve. Besides, it'd be
nice to enjoy the moment before seasoning it with all the
tragedy that had led to it.

I'd opted to walk to the house from the portal in order to
give us a chance to talk things through again. It seemed safest
to have a plan regarding breaking the news to my mother. I
had zero doubts that Matt believed it was to soften the blow

of what he viewed as bad news, whereas I simply wanted to minimize the potential and inevitable chaos that would erupt. The side door appeared with its welcoming glow amidst the bronze afternoon light.

I took a deep breath. This was it. "So again, we're not saying anything to my mom about what happened last month," I repeated anxiously.

"Or the last few months," Matt added. "Having to explain it to you several times over was bad enough." The eye roll was a bit much, but I couldn't really blame him. He promised to be an open book, but I still wasn't completely satisfied with some of his explanations. But it wasn't fair to hold the decisions of yesterday against him today; that was no way to live life. At least in his own mind, he'd thought he was doing the right thing.

"Maybe next time, don't keep secrets," I said, shifting my bag and opening the door. Unsurprisingly, the handle turned without resistance. I was barely across the threshold when I was forcibly dragged the rest of the way inside by an over-eager hug. "Hi mom," I said as I attempted to disentangle myself and failed.

"Don't give me that. It's been ages since I've seen you. You don't call. You don't write. What am I supposed to think? A mother is entitled to be happy to see her child," she said, fussing with my hair and collar.

"Come on, mom, at least let me put my things down so I can hug you properly," I griped. Matt snickered behind me, capturing her attention.

"I see you two have worked things out." She gave me another once over.

"You could say that." I gave him a sidelong look. His eyes glinted with a promise of heat, and I gave him a sidelong look, wondering if the no fooling around business still applied now that we were betrothed.

"Its good to see you again too, Matthew." I gave an inward groan at her use of his full name. "Though I confess," she went on oblivious, "I'm a little surprised y'all would choose this weekend of all weekends to visit."

"I have my reasons," I said, now finally at liberty to set my bag down. Matt closed the door and raised his hand in greeting as my mom advanced towards him for his own crushing hug.

"Hi Ms. Roman."

She immediately zeroed in on his waving hand. "What's that?"

"What's what?" he asked.

"On your hand."

He looked at the appendage in question and immediately snapped it back down to his side, guilt clearly stamped on his face. Then he looked at me, which only intensified the appearance of guilt.

I let out a sigh and walked towards him.

"Alexi Roman, what is going on?" my mother demanded, with her hands on her hips.

"I didn't even think," Matt whispered apologetically when I reached his side.

"It's okay," I whispered back and slid an arm around his waist. This was as good a way as any to break the news. "So, mom... we have something we'd like to tell you."

Her foot tapped impatiently on the tile as she waited.

"Matt and I are engaged." I raised my hand so she could see the matching band. There was no denying the grin that spread across my face. I loved saying that.

Her eyes went wide and she let out an ear piercing squeal. We both flinched. Then, she clutched her chest, and for a moment, I thought the news was too much for her and she'd simply keel over right there in the kitchen. She took an exaggerated breath and her words came out in an almost unintelligible tide. "This is wonderful! I couldn't ask for better news. Oh, and here I thought... Well, never mind what I thought. I get a son-in-law and grandbabies and I'll get to use my book after all. This is amazing! There's so much that'll need to be done. And I'm so happy for both of you." She rushed us and squeezed the life out of our frozen forms, then spun on her heel, her curly hair flaring around her head, and practically raced out of the room, still rambling to herself. I had no idea what book she was referring to, but the moment she was out of sight, words bubbled out of Matt as well.

"I'm so sorry. I didn't mean to. You just wave. That's what you do. In my defense, it's typically on the other hand where I come from. How was I supposed to know it would be the first thing she saw?"

I laughed and ebbed the tide of defenses with a kiss. At last he stopped trying to talk around it and gave in. "Its okay. Now, it's done," I tried to reassure him. "Plans are great, but the only real goal was to tell her, and we did that."

"But," he tried to protest.

I shook my head and stole another kiss. He sighed and let it go. His wonderfully blue eyes searched my face, and I reached up to stroke his cheek. "I told you she'd freak out."

He gave a low laugh, and my mom made a reappearance.

"What's so funny?" she asked, struggling with her burden. She was clutching an extremely bulky scrapbook, with bits of fabric, ribbons, and paper peeking out.

"Nothing," I said, stroking Matt's side while trying to figure out where she'd been hiding such a massive book.

She gave a flippant wave of her hand, dismissing my non-committal response. "I thought this thing would never get used. This is going to be so much fun. And the planning!" she exclaimed, opening the book. At last, it dawned on me what it was—a wedding planner.

"Mom," I groaned, releasing Matt.

"I will not be denied, Alexi. Though now I'm even more surprised that you'd wait until the day before Valentine's to tell me," she remarked positively in a tizzy.

I gave Matt a dubious smile. Astoundingly, he still hadn't put it together. "Because, mum, today is Matt's birthday." I shifted my gaze back to Matt. "I thought he might like to celebrate with his family."

Matt's jaw literally fell, while my mother's face melted into a tender expression. She clasped her hands over her heart and I prayed she wouldn't make too much of a to-do about it. Matt could be oversensitive about his past, and I really didn't want to spoil the weekend by upsetting him.

"How... how did you know?" he asked, disbelief coloring the inquiry.

"You told me. Remember? I even have a gift for you... from Vera." That bit certainly took him off guard. I reached into my bag and fished out the thick folder, then passed it to him.

He looked down at the tenuous stack of papers as if unsure what to do next.

"Go ahead, look." The words *Happy Birthday Matt* were elegantly written on the cover, but it was what was at the end that made it truly special.

"What is it?" he asked.

"It's your file, Matt."

For a second, I thought he was going to close it without flipping through at all. Then, with hesitant hands, he turned the pages. Page after page detailed the horrible life Matt had endured while living in a world that could never hope to understand. It had been difficult, but I'd forced myself to read every last incident where he'd been in fights. The earliest records were by far the worst, no doubt because he wasn't defending himself. Yet, as the years progressed, the tables shifted, and the violence increased. It broke my heart, but this was part of who he was and I wouldn't ignore it just because it wasn't pretty. His eyes glazed over as he looked at his history, and I waited somewhat impatiently for him to reach the last page. It would all be worth it once he got to that. At last, he was there. I watched his face go from puzzled curiosity to baffled amazement.

He looked up from Vera's note and I thought my heart would burst with love for him. "I don't understand."

"Congratulations, Matt. You are no longer a ward of the state *or* Vera. You are perfectly free in all fifty states and in every other country, too, for that matter," I said with a smile.

He barked a disbelieving laugh. The folder fell to the ground with a smack, sending papers and pictures sliding in every direction. Ignoring them, he stepped across the small space and grabbed me. The resulting kiss was full of all the fire and passion that defined him. And love, so much love.

I pulled him in close, not caring that my mother was watching. Matt was everything and loving him felt like the most important thing I'd ever done in my life.

"I'm not a Warde anymore," he said, his eyes sparkling with unshed tears.

I smiled, my heart on the verge of bursting. "No, you're a Roman now."

About the Author

Sam Bolanos (she/they) is a genderqueer author and founder of Chaotic Neutral Press LLC. They believe in love, equality, and the Oxford comma. When not playing with her three dogs, who you can follow on Instagram @austendogs, or spending time with her incredible husband, she's probably agonizing over edits or escaping into her latest fantasy.

Welcome to the adventure!

Newsletter: subscribe
Website: Booksbysbolanos.com
Facebook: @Booksbysbolanos
Twitter: @Booksbysbolanos
Instagram: @Sbolanosbooks

SERIES

<u>Paranormal Stories</u>

War on Darkness
Darkness Defined (MM)
Order of Light (MM)
Knights of Nyx (MM)

Moons of Mystery
Sara's Moon (MF)
Charline's Solstice (MF)
Diana's Eclipse (MF)

<u>Contemporary Romances</u>

Ulwich Preparatory Academy
Our Last Fall (MM)
Our Secret Winter (MM)
Our Epic Spring (MM)

Oak Haven Romance
One Brave Thing (Enby/M)
All the Hype (MM)

www.ingramcontent.com/pod-product-compliance
Lightning Source LLC
Chambersburg PA
CBHW061521210726
48287CB00006B/1766

9 781956 128383